CHRISTIAN WALLIS

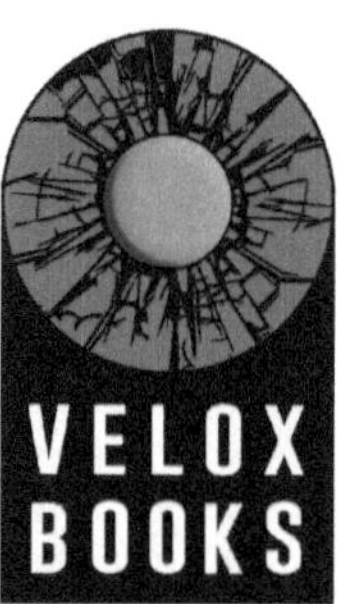

Published by arrangement with the author.

**FOLLOW VELOX TO KEEP
THE NIGHTMARES COMING:**

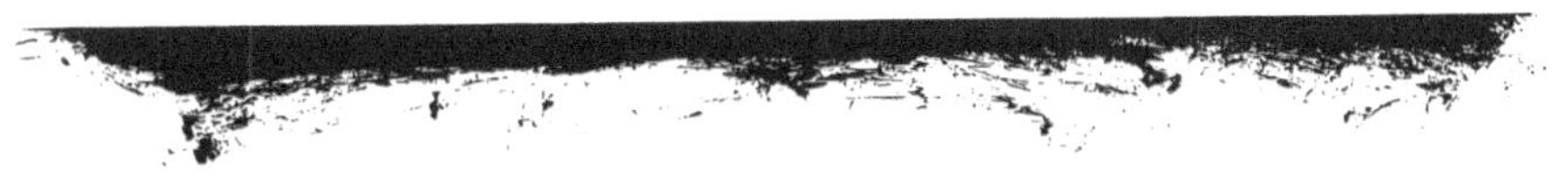

CONTENTS

FORECLOSURE

I get shot at.

A lot.

But it isn't what scares me about this job. When I arrive at a home and see someone burst out of the front door clutching a rifle, I know what to expect. They have something to lose. They're scared and they don't know what to do. So I tell them. I give them resources on fighting back. I refer them to law firms who do pro bono work. Government bodies and charities that can help them get back on their feet. I speak calmly and with empathy. And people listen. Some even thank me as they pack their things up and drive away.

The suicides are harder to deal with. I get at least three or four a year. And people who kill themselves out of spite really go all out on the spectacle. The harder it is for the bank to clean up, the better. And people assume the bank puts their house on the market the second it's seized, but a house can sit forgotten for years before I'm sent to look it over. Lone bodies swinging in empty living rooms, flesh like melted candle wax from all that time left in open air. I find it profoundly sad. These people lay themselves out like a spiteful diorama and then no one turns up. They slit their throats while clutching eviction notices; and by the time I arrive, the blood has dried and the ink has faded. The worst ones don't just hurt themselves, but their loved ones too. Suicide pacts are more common with the elderly, but it isn't always octogenarians. Families too. It's rare, but it does happen. A sun-baked house with drawn curtains, so much time passed in the dry Autumn heat that their skin turned paper-thin. Receding lips. Black toothless gums borne in a rictus grin.

Hell of a thing to see staring out of a crib.

Each house is its own apocalypse. Its own ruined city for me to wander. Whiskey in the toilet's cistern. Fentanyl under the bed. Bills passed due. And it doesn't just end with the people we kick out. These places are empty so long you'll often get squatters. Usually harmless. Not always. Some have the potential to be thoroughly lethal. Stringy men and women with flinty eyes and missing teeth who come bursting out of mouldy old blankets and indoor tents, slashing box cutters wildly at the air. You could play tic-tac-toe on my forearms from all the defensive wounds.

Even when they've moved on, the things they leave behind aren't exactly safe. Fumes from homemade labs can rot your lungs, and HIV positive needles stuffed down the sides of old sofa cushions wait to prick curious fingers. And the cooks get real paranoid about being robbed, so they like to rig their homes with traps. They get inventive with whatever's lying around. Shards of glass on spring loaded broom handles. Trick floorboards over boxes of razor blades. Shit smeared knives hidden beneath false windowsills. Every now and again, I find a trap that's been set off. A baseball bat rigged to lash out at anyone entering the kitchen, blood and hair dripping from the bent nails hammered into the wood. No sign of the poor fucker who set it off, just a grizzly trail of gore leading outta the house and into the nearby woods. Most likely candidate is the guy who set the trap. These addicts stay up for days and pass out, then when they wake up the first thing they do is head for their stash, not remembering what they left behind.

One time, I found the guy lying a few feet away from his own trap. He kept his money in this old metal lunch box at the back of a cupboard and he'd rigged it so anyone reaching in would get a hell of a surprise. The blade went in at his elbow and left just below the knuckle on his thumb. No helping him after that. He died bleeding out on his late grandmother's cold linoleum. What a God-awful way to go. And his little lunchbox? On the ground and empty of everything worth taking. Police reckon someone was with him when it happened. Must've gotten scared, so they took the cash and left him to die. It'd take a full month before I found him, and no one even reported him missing in the interim. You'd think the kid would be angry, but he wasn't. He just looked like he was scared. Nineteen, going through withdrawal and dying slowly. Curled up like a baby, one hand gripping his opened wrist. You can't trap the ocean in your fist. It leaks through your fingers. That kid knew what was coming. I could see it in his eyes. Terrified. *Fucking terrified.*

Meth is a hell of a drug. These poor guys fry their brains out in the middle of nowhere. I can't even begin to imagine what they think they see out there. What visits them in the dark. Found this trailer once that'd been rigged with damn near a hundred traps. They weren't particularly sophisticated, but they were numerous and vicious and desperate, and they circled the lone motorhome out in the middle of the desert like an invading army made of knives and bear traps and stolen guns and even a few hastily made IEDs. Took me and a bomb squad a week just to get to the front door and by the time we opened it we were all fairly certain of one simple fact—this place hadn't been rigged to keep thieves out. Whoever had set the traps had been scared of something leaving. Probably just drug fuelled paranoia on behalf of whoever set them, but I think the idea that something was in there waiting for us got under our skin, anyway. During the operation, we'd sometimes get shouted reports of someone moving around in the trailer and the whole site would go to hell. Armed men and women lying on their bellies, iron sights lined up on the front door, hands shaking. I guess we kept asking ourselves over and over *what's in there that had someone so scared they set all these traps?*

When we finally got our answer, the first thing we found was a meth lab, pretty par for the course. Less normal was a body that had been torn to fucking pieces. Halfway to dust after all that time in the heat had passed, but it was strewn all over the interior. Walls. Floors. Ceiling. Couldn't argue it was a natural death or a product of scavengers, not unless coyotes can work a lock and key. What was left of his head and torso looked like he'd gone through hell. I'm hardly a forensic expert, but it looked to me like he'd died slowly and painfully. Missing fingers. Teeth. One eye plucked out. Torture is what it made me think of. Even stranger than all that, though, was what we found sat on the kitchen counter next to all those broken beakers and stained chemistry equipment. A doll. Not like a kid's doll. Porcelain, like a collector's item that had seen better days. Scared the shit out of me, given the circumstances and all. Couldn't shake the feeling whoever had made all those traps had done so with that thing in mind. Which begged the question: who was the poor guy stuck inside the trailer? And what had happened to him?

Cops wrote it off. Meth is a hell of a drug, so they say. We all knew that. Only I wasn't so sure. I've seen a lot of weird shit. Who knows what visited that poor guy out in the wild, so far from civilization. A lot of life gets lived out in the world, out on the plains or in forests and amongst hills, far from prying eyes. You get a sense of it in my job. The sheer quantity of untold stories. Failed dreams, great triumphs. Abandoned canvases. Well-worn guitars. Haydays that came and went, or simply never came at all. Most stories follow a rhythm. *Most.* Some, like that doll, raise profound questions. Others aren't really stories at all, so much as nightmares just waiting for the next victim.

This world is full of hidden needles waiting for probing hands.

There are rare occasions where I'll advise the bank to not sell a property. They become part of a kinda no-go zone the government has set up around the country. I only see bits of this machinery at work. Whatever bureaucracy manages it is way over my paygrade. But there is a system in place for managing the worst of the worst. I'm not talking ghosts either. None of the examples I've given so far would be candidates. Sounds fucked up, I know. Scrub the blood. Scrape the brains. Pick the shotgun pellets out of the plaster. If the next family who moves in has to contend with the ghosts of a few clumsy methheads or disgruntled former owners, well, so be it. No, for a place to be deemed a no-go, it has to be beyond recovery and an active threat to life. I'm talking factories with bottomless holes that pump out enough radiation that the government has to build a nuclear dump site just to make a convincing cover.

Although that is a bit of an extreme example. Most of the time, we just blame it on radon or meth fumes and condemn it. Had this one place. A farmhouse where a family of five had lived for nearly sixty years. By the time I got there, the kids were adults and the parents had been dead for a while. The children had resisted selling the family home, tried to keep up with the payments. But they had their own debts and in the end the bank got its pound of flesh. At a glance, the house didn't look too bad. Bit rundown, sure. But my standards are low. Crack den low. Windows were intact. No graffiti. Roof hadn't been stripped. Satellite dish was still up. From where I sat in my car, gulping down a lukewarm bottle of water that had spent the drive tumbling around the passenger footwell, the house was relatively untouched by anything except nature and time.

Something about that gave me pause. Shame I didn't listen to the gut feeling telling me it was all sorts of weird that an isolated house had gone unmolested for so long. I grabbed the keys the Sheriff had given me and went inside, hoping for an easy gig. Three hours later and I was crawling out a kitchen window I'd smashed, the shirt and skin on my back cut to ribbons. I stumbled to my car, chest near bursting from the pounding of my heart, and my eyes fixed on the empty window frame I'd just escaped. A lone figure, barely visible with the bright sun in my eyes, but still too substantial to be a mere ghost. My wounds were a testament to that.

Once the doctor had finished patching me up, I sat in the waiting room and tried calling the former owners. The siblings. One after the other. I wanted to know what had attacked me, if anyone knew what I was walking into. There'd be hell to pay if so. The oldest son was the first to answer. I didn't go all in straight away. I asked probing questions, took my time before I mentioned the basement. The guy laughed when I brought it up. Told me he hated going down there as a kid because he'd hear the weirdest noises, like someone moaning. They all thought a ghost lived down there in the dark, and to keep them from hurting themselves or playing around with stuff they shouldn't, their father had embellished this ghost. Given it a name. Marion, he called her.

Marion lived in the basement, hiding amongst the crates of old photos and clothes. She lurked behind the half-disassembled lawnmower, scuttling always to the dark places at the very edge of your eyesight. Marion had long fingernails and a haggard flour sack dress. She had black lips and a pointed nose and a wart the size of your thumb. Marion ate children, their dad had told them with glee. And if Marion knew there were three bite sized kids living just above her, she'd come out of the basement and come crawling up the stairs with arms as long as her body, and she'd slink her way into their bedrooms using the shadows as cover, and she'd start by taking tiny little bites out of any bare feet that lay dangling in the cold.

"What about that freezer? Did you ever use it?" I asked.

"Oh God no," he said. "Even now, that basement gives me the creeps, and that freezer was where Marion lived, or so we figured as kids, so we stayed the hell away from it. It was just always there in the back, looking old and forgotten. I think Dad used to go hunting when we were little and that's where he'd keep the meat, but he phased all that out before I'd turned five."

He seemed sincere, so I didn't tell him what I'd found in the house at the end of my inspection. He didn't know that behind that freezer was a false wall, and behind that wall, *basement number two.* Homemade. God knows how the father managed it with no one noticing, but he'd dug it out and made a private, sound-proofed space. Hollowed out a room about the size of your typical jail cell. The furniture was threadbare, deliberately so. A single mattress propped up against one wall. An iron shackle bolted into the foundation.

A dentist's chair modified with restraints.

And a stain. A vague Rorschach blob of ancient browns and almost-greens that pooled outwards from a patch in the corner. It had texture. I knew that stain. I'd seen it before. *Residue* left behind after the professionals have finished peeling a desiccated corpse off a hard surface. At first, I assumed someone had moved the source of that stain. There were even footprints. But they didn't look right. Something about them made me queasy. They had not been left *in* the residue. They were made of it. Something or someone covered in that stuff had been stomping around down there. Until that moment, the inspection had been mundane and boring, but it isn't every day you stumble across a hidden dungeon. Now I was suddenly presented with a hell of a family secret, and one that didn't quite make sense. I stood there for a good minute, trying to make the pieces of that puzzle fit. Had someone moved a corpse and gotten covered in rotten flesh, then walked around leaving a trail? Why the fuck had they done it barefoot? And why not clean it up afterwards? And how had they been so clumsy, yet so clean as well? There were no drag marks...

I took another look at those prints, and something inside my gut soured. Small feet. A woman's. We all know this story. Don't make me go over it. Basement out in the middle of nowhere. Restraints. A family man that no one suspects. He'd hunted alright. Sick fuck. So, who had died in that basement? And who had left those prints?

Not all of them were on the floor, either. With an increasingly shaky hand, I tracked a few to the wall where they mounted the vertical surface and continued upwards and onto the ceiling. Just like that a cold sweat gathered on the back of my neck, and a powerful sense of the uncanny ran over me like ice water. Somewhere overhead, the wind blew, and the boughs of trees groaned in the yard. Sounds of another world. I could see it in my mind, up there, not far away. My car sitting in the shade. Those images felt like they belonged to another world. I desperately wanted to rejoin it, to leave this squalid little hole behind. All I had to do was walk out of that basement and make for my car. Only I wasn't so sure I wanted to move at all. Felt like I might break something brittle, the notion that the creeping dread I felt was all in my head. A product of an overactive imagination, nothing more. And yet I got this feeling that if I tried to run, the nightmare would spill out into the real world and give chase. I even tried telling myself I didn't know what happened in that room. Not for sure. It could've been a game, one played between him and the wife... But then I looked at the chair again. At the cracked and frayed leather of ancient straps.

There were teeth marks on some of them.

I took a deep breath and regained control of my legs. Unless I saw something alive down there, I had to assume I really was alone down there, so I turned and began to walk. Eyes forward. Mind steeled against the myriad of little groans and creaks that felt as if they followed me, going from shadow to shadow. I couldn't stop myself from filling in the blanks of that basement's history, even as I told myself to stop.

Maybe she died first. Maybe he did. Maybe he got bored and left her to starve, or maybe he nearly got caught and decided to put it all to an end. Maybe she snuck something sharp and killed herself. But she died for sure, and she stayed dead a long time. At least a couple months for that kind of liquefaction. She lost cohesion. Skin. Muscle. Blood like the plug of mould that forms on top of forgotten coffee. I could see it in my head, her collapse. A claymation timelapse. A riot of colours. Only somehow the natural cycle broke. She didn't go away completely. And no one came to take her away. Those were her prints on the floor and walls and ceiling, weren't they?

She laid down.

She died.

And then, somehow, she got back up.

By the time I reached the top of the basement steps, I'd scared myself so bad that sweat was pouring off me. So far, the only things I'd seen on my way were just old boxes and crates and ancient bits of crap, weed wackers and leaf blowers with cobwebs and defunct logos fading away. But that didn't mean I was alone. There was something wrong with that place. I could feel it. A radiant heat. A palpable aura of hatred, even in the absence of anything seemingly real. It was so bad that as I opened the door, I actually felt a moment of childlike relief, a little like how you might feel racing back to bed after going to the toilet in the middle of the night, convinced some ghost was just inches behind you.

I laughed.

And something cold and hard wrapped around my ankle. A hand had reached up between the slats of the stairs, like it was reaching straight out of the world of make believe and into this one where things are real. I stared down, heartbeat like thunder in my ears, and slowly began to process what I was seeing in bits and pieces. First was the hand. Gnarled. Black. Like a badly sketched shadow visible only because it caught the light coming through the open door. And then beneath it, in the shadow, a face like a skull wrapped in a garbage bag, the plastic pulled tight so you could see the suffocating outline of empty eyes and a gaping mouth. I'd expected something *wetter,* something straight out of a bad horror movie. In reality, whatever was in that basement had undergone a strange transformation. I only ever saw it in parts, so I can't say for sure what all of it was like. But it sure as shit didn't look like a ghost or a corpse or anything else I'd ever seen or thought I'd seen in life or movies.

Looked like a monster, the real deal, and I reacted like a child seeing the bogeyman. I made some weird half-muffled groan of fear and ripped my leg away so quickly that I surprised myself and got free. But whatever was hiding under those stairs was quick. Before I had time to take another step, it had left its hiding place, climbed the stairs, and was already driving me to the ground. The last thing I saw before my chin smashed into the kitchen floor was that Marion really did wear a flour sack dress. At the time, this strange detail passed over me without notice. But in hindsight, the fact that the son would later recount that particular item of clothing convinced me his father had been the man responsible for that hidden basement. It wasn't like it had been waiting undiscovered when the family moved in. And on top of that, the father must have been a real piece of shit to inject that sort of sickening detail into a story he told his kids. He'd likely done it so if his prisoner ever escaped and his kids saw her, their first instinct would be to scream for their lives and run.

I didn't know any of this at the time, of course. I had only vague notions of what had attacked me. Something hateful, for sure. Something that had died in that awful room and come back to life. God, she was so fucking angry. She pinned me, knelt on my back, and howled like a banshee that'd been hit by a car. I pissed myself at the sound, at the feeling of helplessness. At the realisation this was a nightmare I couldn't wake up from.

She went to work on my back with fingers I couldn't see but could feel as white-hot tattoo-needle pain. It lasted only a few seconds. The agony was enough to send me into spasms that knocked her off and onto the floor. That tiny moment of freedom was all I needed. I crawled to my feet and jumped headfirst out of the nearest window. I didn't give a fuck about any cuts I might acquire. If you could've felt what I felt, you wouldn't have either. These weren't scratches. Doctors compared my wounds to those left by a box jellyfish, the kind of thing that causes the muscle beneath to wilt and wither after a million hypodermic needles have turned the flesh to a porous sponge. I had to get skin grafts. I had to get rid of my car because they couldn't scrub what I'd left of my skin from the leather seats. Even now my back looks like I got run over by a mower. Still hurts when I put my top on each morning.

Somehow, they're not even the worst of my wounds. Just the biggest. The most visible. At least those scars made it easy to convince the bank not to sell. Normally it takes a lot of effort, but they took one look at the doctor's reports and agreed to condemn it thoroughly, pass the land onto whatever strange governmental department handles this kinda thing. That particular house has been left to crumble. No piece of paper or deed or mortgage payment is taking it back from Marion. We can only shut it off. The land is fenced, and every window has been slapped with so many toxic gas signs that I can only hope no one else is stupid enough to ever go back inside.

Looking back, I really should've listened to my instincts. Squatters don't leave a place alone without good reason.

INHERITANCE

"Do we need another girl?"

I was used to him asking me questions, sometimes ones that didn't even make sense. But this one surprised me. He'd looked at me with an odd glint in his eye that I'd never seen before, not even as a kid. He'd always been a quiet withdrawn man, disinterested in anyone who wasn't my mother. But something about the sly tone of voice made me feel like I'd glimpsed some part of him I shouldn't have, and I struggled to think of anything to say in response. In the end, all I managed was,

"What do you mean?"

He briefly looked angry, but some kind of realisation dawned on him, and his features softened to sullen disappointment.

"You Nettie's boy?" he asked.

"Yeah," I said. "I've been looking after you for the last few months."

He turned his eyes to his frail legs before eyeing the beeping machine and the oxygen tank that sat next to the recliner. After a long pause, he sighed, and his shoulders slumped.

"Do you want a cup of tea?" I asked.

He took a deep breath and leaned back in his chair.

"Why not?" he grunted before blowing his nose.

"It was only meant to be two," he said from his chair, and something in his voice made me look up from the dishes and give him my full attention. He sat dull eyed and staring at the muted TV.

"Three girls," he carried on. "A trade with that thing in the basement. You know books'll say these things like rules, but that's just a waste of everybody's time. If these things followed rules, they'd be working like the rest of us." Something about that image made him laugh, and I realised it was probably the first time I'd seen him smile since moving in. "What is it with people, eh? Acting like you can make rules up for a world that we all know damn well will do what it wants when it wants. I remember thinking to myself, *why two? Why does it have to be two girls?*"

He laughed, and this time it wasn't so playful.

"What were we gonna do once it gave us what we wanted, eh? Give it back? No. It had us on the hook and it knew it! It asked for a third, a fourth, a fifth, and a sixth."

He turned in his chair and looked at me and I realised he wasn't really rambling or trapped in some long-forgotten memory. If anything, he looked more lucid than he had in the entire three months I'd been caring for him.

"None of them were easy. No one follows anyone into a basement without getting spooked. None of them knew *why*, exactly. But they knew *enough*. Hardest thing I ever had to do…"

With that, he turned back around and unmuted the TV, and I was left struggling to make sense of what he'd just said. If any part of it stood out, it was the mention of the basement, and without meaning to, I found my gaze slowly drifting towards a quiet little corridor that I knew led to the house's only cellar.

The basement door had always frightened me as a child. The whole house had been a cobweb haunted labyrinth of ancestral figures looming down at me from ancient oil paintings. Everything was too old to touch. Every door led to a new a room. Every action I took had my grandmother or mother shuffling after me and crying reproaches, eyeing me like I was about to step out into oncoming traffic. The greenhouse was full of broken glass that I could cut myself on. One room belonged to my grandfather's sister, who died at a young age of a penicillin allergy. Another room belonged to his father's first wife, who'd spent her life going mad while writing children's fiction. A vase on one shelf might be older than America, another might be worth more than our family car. Everything was to be looked at, but never touched. And with every new visit, I was left with the impression that the whole damn house was a mausoleum filled with disapproving ghosts. You never had to ask if the house was haunted. It was an inevitability, and on the nights when my mother made me stay over, I couldn't escape the feeling I was one wrong door away from stumbling into some Victorian spectre's clutches.

But the basement... I never got a lecture on the basement. No child wanted to go near that thing. No stories surrounded it. It only existed, the door standing alone at the end of a long and dark hallway with a single bare bulb that looked like it had been smashed on purpose. And for some reason—and I'll admit I never got the courage to ask—someone had sketched an enormous X across the ancient door in red duct tape, like some kind of modern-day plague warning.

I had deliberately stayed away during my time as a carer, secretly thankful I hadn't been given a reason to go down there. But after my grandfather had mentioned some girls and the basement, well... it wasn't a huge leap of imagination, right? My grandfather wasn't a loving man, and our family had been rife with black sheep for generations. Scandal followed us like a bad smell. Hadn't my grandfather's own aunt once abducted him and his sister for a whole afternoon, only to be found at a pier filling their coat pockets with rocks? I couldn't help but wonder what a lifetime of trauma had done to him. The family graveyard was full of dates that spoke of tragically short lives. Could anyone be raised amidst all that and still be normal?

I had to know. Not just because it was my family, but because I was stuck there ferrying tea and food to this man and washing him down day after day. If he really had done something, if there was something down there that people should know about, then I might be the only person willing or able to do something about it.

So, with much trepidation, I went to the door and spent a few hesitant seconds tracing the duct-taped X with my hands. It did not escape my attention that the tape was brand new, but without knowing how to interpret that knowledge, I pushed it aside and forced myself to turn the handle.

The seal broke with an audible hiss, and the air that rushed out stank of ethanol and compost. Using my light, I took in the first few steps and saw that they were made out of solid stone and had grooves worn in from a thousand feet. I hadn't seen anything like that since a holiday in Rome, and I immediately knew that this part of the house must somehow be even older than the rest. Heading further down, I found a surprisingly mundane looking cellar filled with old moving boxes and spiders as big as my fist, many of which hung dead and petrified in their webs. I did, however, notice one archway made of the same stone as the stairs, and went through to find yet another room filled with the same junk as before, if only slightly older.

It turned out the cellar was every bit as big as the manor above, housing dozens of large chambers, each separated by vaulted archways made of ancient stone. The whole place was organised in a haphazard fashion that made it all too easy to get lost, and I marvelled at the way it seemed to never end. Not all the rooms were for storage, either. One was an old workshop for a carpenter where the tools had rusted to the hooks they hung on, and the machines I saw lacked motors and wires. Another room was filled with glass vials and distillation equipment for brewing some kind of alcohol. Dark bottles plugged with corks sat in crates and I was surprised to find that they were full of sloshing fluid.

Another was a dark room for photo development, only the cameras were so old they had cloaks for the photographer to hide behind and metal plates as big as my head. Looking through some old picture books piled up in the corner, I found a well-preserved picture of a young girl standing next to a grave. It was dated 1968 and to my surprise I recognised the young girl and the name on the tombstone. It was Michael, the name of my mother's brother, and the po-faced child must be my own mother, the photo taken at a funeral as some kind of remembrance, perhaps? I had vague memories of a dead uncle somewhere. The only problem was I'd met an Uncle Michael at more than a few birthday parties, so it made little sense that it was his tomb she stood over. I waved the discrepancy off and moved on. Maybe I was just misremembering my uncle's name? After all, I'd only met him three or four times.

One after another the rooms came on, and after a good hour I was no closer to having explored them all. This became especially clear after I found an old stairway descending to another level. These steps were as worn down as the others and looked every bit as old, and when I shone my light down them, I damn nearly had a heart attack as a young girl became visible in the beam. For a moment, she was a featureless child, slumped against the wall half-way down the stairs, until my eyes adjusted, and I realised I was only looking at a doll.

I breathed a sigh of relief and nearly went down there to pick her up, but I faltered at the last moment. The darkness lurking at the foot of the tunnel was as thick as water, and I had the strange notion it wasn't empty. The silence around me seemed unusually heavy as well, and I couldn't escape the feeling my eyes and ears were sensing something and my brain hadn't caught up. Any boyish curiosity I'd felt while exploring was gone in an instant, and I was painfully aware of the vast subterranean space that surrounded me. Looking behind me, the flashlight picked out a thousand wiry shadows painted by box after box of long-forgotten nick-nacks. Could I be sure I was alone down there? I tried to laugh the idea off. *What could be lurking in those shadows?* I asked myself. But the fact I didn't have an answer only unsettled me further, and before my mind could begin filling in the blanks, I decided to leave.

I took one last look down the stairs and froze when I saw it empty of everything but dust and stone. The doll was gone.

I ran to the exit.

When the doorbell rang, I jumped, and my grandfather let out a little chuckle. I had an inclination he knew I'd been rummaging down in the basement, but I couldn't be sure. Maybe he just found my newfound nerves amusing. Ever since coming back from that damn basement, I'd struggled to shake off an insipid paranoia.

"That'll be Elizabeth from the village," he said. "Brings me food now and again. Cakes, that sort of thing. They're good. Go let her in."

I did as he asked and went to the door and found a young woman standing on the other side.

"Hello Alex," she said with a beaming smile, sliding past me and into the kitchen without another word.

"Oh hello," I said, and in trying to clear my thoughts, I found myself going to the usual polite refrain in this kind of situation. "Would you like a cup of tea?"

"Yes please!" she said.

I made her a drink while we both filled the silence with small talk. She awkwardly unpacked several brown boxes from a plain brown bag, dropping more than half of them and picking them up with stiff fingers. Opening one that had fallen, she laughed and offered me a battered custard tart that I gratefully took and ate.

"Sorry," she said. "I've always been quite clumsy."

But as I ate, and we continued to speak, I couldn't help but notice that something was off with the young woman. It wasn't just that she dropped the odd box, or even that the tea in her hands shook so badly that half of it ended up in the saucer. It was the way she began to grimace with every small motion, tightening her lips and exhaling squeaky breaths like she was in tremendous pain and doing everything in her power to ignore it. And the longer we talked, the worse it became. She began to sway from side to side, and her movements became stiff and rigid. When she'd finished spilling her tea, I offered to take the cup from her pale and shaking hands, but she waved me off, and tottered over to a nearby counter with all the difficulty of someone walking on ice-skates. Once there, she turned to face me with a girlish grin and went to speak, but instead slumped suddenly to the side, her ankle twisting unnaturally beneath the skin. I couldn't keep the expression of shock from my face, and it only grew worse when she caught me staring and gave a flirtish wink from where she lay bent over the counter at an impossible angle.

Like a click of the fingers, she snapped back upright, and I winced at the sound of creaking bones.

"Sorry," she giggled. "I'm just a little nervous. He talks a lot about you. The third..."

Taking a deep breath, she pushed herself upright and leaned against the counter in what I think was supposed to be a friendly pose. She even pressed her ear to her shoulder coquettishly before going to say something, but the pose lasted barely a second as her elbow bent inwards like a piece of straw and she hit her head against the marble top. I rushed towards her, instinctively trying to help, but I stopped when I realised the hysterical squeals she let out weren't cries of pain, but rather laughter.

"Sorry," she said, putting her hand to her mouth as she cackled. "I'm such a mess today! I've waited so long to meet you."

"That looked painful," I stuttered. "Are you okay?"

"Ohhhh it's fine," she cooed as she tried once more to balance on her feet. "Just a… just a condition. Your grandfather, angel that he is, oversaw my treatment when I was just a girl."

"Is that right?" I asked.

"He's a generous man, don't you think?"

She looked like a drunk person trying sincerely not to laugh, and I had the distinct feeling that she thought this was some kind of joke. As if to confirm this, she raised one arm and pointed at me with finger guns while pulling the trigger and winking.

Snap! Without any warning, her arm broke in two, dangling half-way between her wrist and elbow. Looking down, the girl muffled a chuckle that slowly turned into whinnying and hysterical laughter. With a flick of her elbow, the arm reset, and she appeared suddenly sober. "Hey," she said. "Wanna see something *really* funny?"

She collapsed screaming, eyes wide open, mouth agape, her whole body turning into a mess of crumpled bones. She lay on the floor looking like someone had draped a rubber sheet over a model village, and the sight turned me sick to my stomach. Then, without any warning, she snapped up into a crawling position and came howling at me like a moth to firelight.

I'd barely taken a few steps back when her hand latched around my ankle and squeezed unnaturally hard. I was still trying to figure out where one part of her started and the other ended when she was already using her other hand to claw deep gouges in my leg. The pain, at least, helped me get my priorities straight, and I lashed out, kicking her so hard I heard teeth clack. But it didn't slow her, not in the least. She just spat a few out and grinned at me with a bloody mouth.

I switched tactics and tried using my hands to pry her grip away, but only succeeded in letting her tear the back of my right hand to ribbons. The scratches hurt so badly I snatched a nearby kitchen knife from the counter. I had this notion I'd cut her hand right off with one clean swipe, but the blade hit bone immediately and flew out my hand. I still hoped that maybe the deep cut would hurt her, but if anything, her expression told me she considered it a funny little joke.

That hand has to come off, I thought as she continued to shred my calf and ankle. I threw myself after the knife, but she had my one leg pinned so well that I fell over. With cat-like ease, she twisted her broken body upwards and over me as I dragged myself backwards. She was visibly delighted in my revulsion, but whatever her play was, she didn't seem impatient and she sat upright, savouring my attempts to reach the knife. I kept expecting her to stop me, but after only a few short lunges, I managed to wriggle within reach of the knife.

By the time I twisted back around and drove the knife into her face, I realised she'd been expecting the attack. She looked positively delighted and thrust her head onto the knife, the blade entering vertically into her open mouth. She held her jaw rigid as it ground between her central incisors, letting out a delighted squeal as she stalled my jab with her clenched jaw. She could have easily stopped me—her hands were free—but she just kept leaning into it. I tried to reverse direction, but she was having none of it. With one short sharp effort, she gave a final thrust and plunged the knife into the back of her throat, where I felt it tear through thick muscle and cartilage.

Her arms went slack with the final blow, but she continued to convulse and lean further backwards. Carefully I slid out from under her, grimacing at the way her seizures caused her broken bones to rub together like broken shards of glass. She remained kneeling in a half up-right position, blood pooling in her mouth as she twitched and groaned as if in awe of the kitchen ceiling and its cracked plasterwork.

"She always was an odd one."

My grandfather was stood in the doorway, looking at the scene with a tilted head.

"What the fuck just happened?" I gasped, already shaking at the first signs of shock.

"Just an early draft," he said, kicking the heel of her foot. "Come on, we need to drag this back where it came from."

"Took a while to make them come back right," he said as he watched me roll the brown sack down the basement stairs. By this point, I was hardly surprised he had a waterproof body-sized bag on hand. If anything, I was secretly thankful. "But out of the two, Lizzy here was the best of a bad lot. First one came out with the wrong soul. Lizzy... well, she was put together in a funny way. But, for the most part, she had all the right pieces."

At that moment, the bag slipped from my fingers and both my grandfather and I were left to grimace and wince at the sound of Lizzy's mishmash skeleton tumbling down the last few unforgiving steps. It sounded eerily similar to someone dropping a stack of plates.

"She was one of the girls you brought down here, wasn't she?" I asked when the bag finally came to a stop.

"The second," he answered.

"How many were there?"

"In the end it got nine, but the bargain began with two," he replied. "When it was over and we got what we wanted, we used it to bring back the first two as a kind of practice. When you're able to have kids, you might understand one day. I woulda done anything for mine. Anything. And, well... I did."

He gestured to the broken bag that lay at my feet.

"Just leave it there," he said. "She'll make it the rest of the way on her own."

He turned and went back upstairs, and I followed.

"Don't forget the X," he said as he handed me the duct tape at the top.

"Won't anyone come looking for her?" I asked.

"Lizzy!?" He cried. "She's only resting. You come back once and after that it doesn't stick. You just… you just get worse. If anything, we've just given the village a chance to rest easy for a few nights. Lizzy is well known in the area for not being kind to children and pets."

"Came back from what?" I asked as I stretched the roll out and applied the first bit of tape.

He didn't reply, instead he looked at me like I was an idiot.

"What about the other girl?" I asked. "Where is she?"

"They're all still down there, rotting away," he said. "We only brought two back. Well, three counting…" he stopped like he'd just let slip a terrible secret. For a moment, I thought he'd try to steer the conversation back around, but instead he went quiet for a little while before speaking up in an almost broken whisper.

"It didn't *eat* the kids," he said, idly playing with some loose wool on his jumper. "You can't trade a soul, but you *can* ruin it so badly its creator won't take it back.

"That's what it wanted. We flat out refused torturing them, but in the end, we compromised on starvation. That meant we had to live our lives upstairs while knowing they were down there, going hungry. Cold and alone. That was exactly the kind of stain it wanted to see growing on our souls. So, we starved 'em. And after it gave us the knowledge we wanted, we went back and brought a few back. I thought we could have our cake and eat it too, see? Only it didn't really work out. Lizzy was the best of a bad lot, but even then, I'm not sure we ever should've let her out."

"Jesus! Are you saying there's another one like her?" I asked, realising the import of what he was saying.

"Oh no," he sighed. "No one was like her. The other one was much, much worse."

The following night passed anxiously for me, and I was convinced we'd soon see a visit of the police or possibly even a distraught family member. For my part, I kept expecting to feel some guilt, but the memory of those broken bones writhing over me was hard to shake, so if anything, I felt fear and nervousness, but no real guilt. I'd acted in self defence, that I was sure of.

My grandfather, on the other hand, insisted all would be well, and he guffawed loudly a few days later when the doorbell went. I stood up, ready to get the door (and convinced it would be the police), when the old man held his hand out and told me to stay where I was.

"Best stay out of sight," he said. "Don't want to excite her."

A few moments later, he returned with a plain brown bag that he plopped onto the table with some effort. One by one, he unpacked box after box of pastry until he came to the very last. Grimacing, he reached in and pulled out a greasy-looking container that dripped something foul all over the floor.

"Oh boy," he grumbled. "This is for you." He handed it over and waited while I gingerly unfolded it. I was immediately struck by a pungent ammonia smell that wafted out.

"Are those teeth?" I asked.

Little ivory baubles sat in what looked like three or four inches of snail slime, albeit run through with bloody capillaries and a vague wash of rancid green.

"Even worse," my grandfather groaned. "I think she likes you."

"What happened to Michael?" I asked my mother over the phone, one hand clutching the photograph of her and the grave. It had been a nerve-wrecking journey to retrieve the photo, but outside of

Lizzy's body no longer being where I'd left it, nothing dangerous had happened.

"I think he's chasing some women around Thailand, probably to the theme of Benny Hill," my mother quipped, and she immediately laughed at her own joke.

"I thought he passed away when you were younger?" I asked.

"Why do you ask?" she said while her voice dropped several degrees in temperature.

"Mum, Grandad is... I mean... he's saying some pretty weird stuff, and this girl came to visit and—"

"You know he's sick," she said. "You shouldn't be taking what he says seriously."

"I don't think he's sick the way you first told me," I replied. "This isn't anything like the people I worked with in the care home. They had actual dementia, but Grandad, it's different. Mum, he keeps talking about people coming back. And the girl from the village she... I mean..."

"Lizzy is a very unwell young woman," she told me. "I've asked your grandfather to stop letting her visit, but he has a soft spot for those kinds of people. I mean, you've heard about his aunt."

"Mum, did Michael die?" I asked. "Grandad keeps talking about bringing someone back and doing anything for his kids and I just..."

"Oh, for goodness sake," she cried, her voice unusually shrill. "I wouldn't have let you take the job if I realised it was going to work you up like this. Please, just look after him, will you? He insisted you were the only one he'd let move in and every day that goes by, I regret it more and more. It isn't bloody hard, Alex! You looked after dozens in the old people's home. Surely this is easier, isn't it? Just the one!? I don't understand why you're acting like this!"

With that, she hung up, and I was left more convinced than ever that she was lying.

"So," I said, sitting opposite my grandfather, "you brought them back... presumably from the dead?"

He looked at me curiously, but didn't say anything.

"Does it really work?"

"You've seen Lizzy," he said. "You saw what you did to her, and you've seen her since. It's real. It works."

"What's in the basement?" I asked, but he stayed silent. "Fine," I said while standing. "I know where to look. I'll just go myself."

He reached out and grabbed my trousers, and this time he spoke up.

"Don't," he whimpered. "I don't remember what's down there, or even how it got there. I know it only has some of itself in this world. The rest of it is buried elsewhere. Getting too close, too often, well, it starts to poke holes in your mind. You can't remember it easy. Only one or two descriptions of it in the whole world, and people paid dearly to write those words down. All that really matters is it talks. And it can tell you things, for a price. But don't go down there without an offering."

"A little girl?" I asked.

"That was only cause I was so soft on your mother," he said. "It knew it'd tear me up inside to do it, to leave them down there to starve. The offering has to be different for each person. But it'll hurt. And your mother, she'll never forgive me. You'll understand if you can have children of your own."

"What does it give you in return?" I asked.

"Anything you want to know. There's nothing it can't teach you."

The doll was back, sitting slumped against a step half-way down the tunnel. I'd made my way down to the basement in oppressive silence, not even remotely sure of what it was I was looking for. But I had just enough of the mystery solved to leave the parts unknown glowing hot in my mind. I had stabbed Lizzy violently, and she'd come back from it like nothing. In fact, she was a regular visitor now, dropping off cakes and other assorted 'gifts' for me around twice a week. So long as I kept my grandfather in the room, she stayed relatively subdued, but that wasn't really the important bit, was it?

She was alive. And that fact set my whole damned brain on fire.

I'd be lying if I told you hanging around the elderly and dying doesn't start to weigh on you. I'd been doing it for nine years before I started working for my grandfather and I loved the work, I did, but there was an awful truth I'd learned while doing it.

The image we have of some octogenarian content with a long life and ready to face death? It's bullshit. Most people, especially people who still have their wits about them, are scared shitless. It doesn't matter if you're ten, or a hundred and ten, no one wants to die. And that knowledge has been weighing me down for a very long time. In fact, it had given me something of a complex. I'd spent years suffering nightmares of death, of being lowered slowly into the ground, trapped in a wooden box while I listened to the muffled sermon of a solemn priest. Often, the dream would leave me trapped in an eternity spent falling apart, forced to endure the dissolution of both my soul and body. Somehow, waking up was always worse, clawing my way out of the void and back into the light of day...

And my grandfather claimed he could beat it? *That he had already beaten it!?*

Would you walk away from something like that? The ability to beat death? Or even just delay it?

It was worth just about anything to me to escape that recurring nightmare. So I took the first step down, unsure of what I'd find...

The first basement level I'd explored weeks earlier had been a dusty tomb-like place filled with junk going back a century, but the second level down felt positively inhuman. The walls were bare stone that lacked any sort of finish and shone chalk-white in my torch. The ground was dust and soil stamped into dry paths that constantly diverted into curving tunnels that I lacked the bravery to explore. And the air was hot and fetid, so that at times I worried I wasn't walking along a dry tunnel at all, but rather had stumbled into the gullet of some grotesque monster buried in the hills. This was a place where people did secret things, that much I was sure of. Every now and again I'd find a little alcove filled with bizarre paper trinkets and pressed flowers, but no sign of who the tributes had been left for. In one empty room I found a plain robe. In another there was a scythe, and one wall was covered in what looked like cave paintings.

Throughout it all, I was terrified, but nothing I'd seen was remotely dangerous. The things I occasionally found tossed aside or hidden away were all ancient. Whoever had held them and used them, they'd come and gone a long time ago.

But then I found the room with hay on the floor and the dripping atmosphere immediately terrified me. The sight of it caused the breath to catch in my chest and my heart to stammer. Far from fresh, the soft padding on the floor reeked of piss and mould, and the walls were smeared with tar-like shit. The jamb on the stone entrance was also smeared with long finger trails of blood, and the floor by the entrance was disturbed by dozens of strange drag marks. Sheepishly flicking the light from side-to-side,

I glimpsed a bundle of old toys in the corner. I say toys... they were sticks and stones and garishly painted bundles of old cloth. But something about them made me think of toys, anyway. Maybe it was the chains that lay broken on the floor, and the unmistakeable realisation that it was here my grandfather must have left at least one poor victim to starve to death. And of course, there was that all-too-familiar doll sitting right beside them, both tragic and terrifying.

I felt shame looking in there. That was my family's legacy staring back at me, and for the first time since descending, I began to wonder if I had it in me to see this through. I had to wonder, what would this thing want from me?

That was when I heard a giggle, and it felt like the world was going to fall out of my stomach. For a second I was paralysed with fear as the skin across my body tightened and blood rushed to my head so quickly I felt faint. For the first time since descending, I actually dared to think of how I was going to get out and a whole new type of panic took hold. Every tunnel looked the same!

Not that I had any choice in my route. There were only two doorways in the room, and something lurked in the tunnel I'd just come from. It tucked away out of sight when my torch came close, but I caught a fleeting glimpse of pale and leathery skin and an unnatural silhouette. Once again, a giggle rang out of the dark, and I was forced to back away towards the nearest exit in the hope of putting distance between myself and that thing.

To my relief, it did not chase me, at least not with speed. I began to walk quickly down one tunnel after another, picking branches at random, and it always stayed just out of sight behind me. I started to think it might be afraid of the light, but I didn't want to bet on that fact. I just wanted to get away from it, because every time I glanced back, my light caught a little more of it and I saw something straight out of a damned nightmare.

It might have looked like a child once, but something else had gotten into her. The head was too large, by far. Easily as wide as my chest, and God if I couldn't stop thinking that its mouth was large enough to make a serious go at swallowing me whole. At the very least, it might be able to work its jaws around me, given enough time. *Perhaps that's what she'd want to do,* I thought*. Perhaps she'd catch me and trap me and leave me there to whittle away some time before she came and began to choke me down like a snake swallowing its prey whole...*

When I turned back once more, the thing stood its ground against the light and chuckled, and I swore it had some insight into my panicked thoughts. Those beady black eyes were mocking me and my flight, but what else could I do except keep going?

I kept hoping to find a way out, some sign of my passage into the warren of tunnels, but my pursuer picked up its pace and I was no longer able to walk briskly from one to tunnel to another. Each time I looked behind me it lingered in the light for longer and longer until, at last, it no longer hid at all, but instead bore down towards me in full sight of the torch and I was forced to turn and sprint for my life. Those black eyes had fixed me with malevolent hunger, no longer playful or happy to bide its time... I got the strangest sense it was angry at me.

It was not a good thought to have. What I'd seen spoke of gangly but muscular limbs that clutched at the wall, ceiling, and floor as if there was no difference. And even though I counted no extra limbs, the way each arm and leg had grown and bent into new shapes left me feeling strangely arachnophobic. I thought then of what my grandfather had said.

"One came back with the wrong soul..." he'd told me, and I began to wonder perhaps if this was what he'd meant.

I didn't have long to mull this idea over. I came at last to another tunnel and just as I went to lift one foot and spring past the threshold, my remaining leg was caught, and I was sent slamming into the floor with dizzying force. I got a good view of the tunnel ahead and was surprised to see steps leading even further downward. But time was not on my side, and I had to scramble forwards on my hands and knees even as that thing began to pluck and tear at my shirt. My hands managed to grip the first step just as the creature flipped me over and I was left staring into its eyes.

My grandfather was right. She was much, *much,* worse.

She... it... looked wrong, all wrong, and in an instant, I realised I was looking at the victim of a cosmic joke. A soul of a chittering thing put into the body of a human and tossed back into the world of the living. It was a bundle of pain that warped the very flesh it lived in, twisting it to a breaking point as it fought to act on instinct that simply couldn't function in that kind of body. Somehow it had already warped its host into something utterly inhuman, and all too quickly my sympathy was overridden with disgust. In the brief lull where it stopped its assault to look down at me, I kicked out and pushed myself past the arch and went tumbling, head-over-heels, down the stony steps.

The last thing I remember was it crying out after me.

I don't remember finding *it*. The thing that can teach you any-thing...

That doesn't surprise me, but I can't help but wonder how much time was lost wandering down there. All I know is that after I was thrown down to the next level, my experiences blurred and my mind's ability to stitch one event into another turned to mush. Some of the images feel like I lived them a decade ago. Wandering awe struck into a vaulted cavern that rivalled any theatre I'd ever been in, for example. While other memories are recent and clear, albeit disjointed. Did I spend a desperate few hours trapped in one dead end, sobbing hysterically? Or was it a few days instead? I have fleeting memories of scraping algae from rocks and licking condensation off my fingers. Just as I remember laying in an alcove, overcome with despair, shitting myself freely. But I couldn't have possibly been down there that long? Hours, perhaps. But not days?

At least, that's what I tell myself.

What is clear in my mind, at least, is finding the thing. I still struggle to see it whole, or even in pieces, but I'm left with the impression of a tree. Something that shimmered in the darkness, iridescent with the blue and purple sheen of exposed membranes and glistening organs. It was huge, filling the largest subterranean chamber I'd ever seen right to the very top and pushing veins into solid rock. But then there was the sense of space again behind it, of roots buried in unseen places that existed just beyond what was plainly visible. I have no real way to describe this aspect of it, except to say that it seemed like it had folded itself into a space too small to contain it.

Just thinking about it makes my eyes hurt.

When it spoke, my ears bled, and yet it wasn't a god. It wasn't interested in being worshipped. Oddly, I think it just wanted a chat. It asked me about things. Sometimes they were mundane, like how a clothes peg was used to fix items to a wash line. Sometimes it asked about technology, about the past, even about people who, it seemed, it once knew. When I finally worked up the courage to ask it for the gift I'd come down seeking, it emitted a sound that I guess can only be described as a laugh.

"Why would you want that?" It asked, its voice a burrowing worm in my head. "That door still remains open to you. Just as it does for all the others."

That's all I remember of the thing that lived down there. After that, there was Elizabeth, then light, and then my mother...

"I wish you would stop chasing this nonsense."

I awoke to the sound of my mother's voice, fresh from some feverish nightmare where I had been trapped in a wooden box. I found myself no longer in that dream and instead now lay in my bed while my mother sat at the foot of it. She looked down at me with both reproach and pity.

"Michael," I stuttered. "You brought him back."

"Oh you poor silly thing," she cooed. "Michael is alive and well and always has been."

"I saw the photo of you by his gravestone."

"Michael was the name of more than one brother," she said. "You know this. My father remarried, and his second wife had an existing son who later passed away. He'd been sickly his whole life, and died at the age of fifteen when I'd barely known him for more than a few years. But your uncle, my *brother*, is two years younger than me and has never seen an illness that couldn't be cured with antibiotics."

"I don't understand," I said. "Who did you bring back? Why did grandpa go through all that misery if not to bring back his dead son?"

"He did it for me," she said as she reached out once more and stroked my leg. "I never should have let you come here, but it was all but impossible to get you to stop. At least you have a kind of life here, I suppose, looking after your grandfather. He's supposed to keep you safe, but, well, I can't ask more of him than I already have. He promised me a miracle and to the man's credit, he delivered. And ultimately, he was right about letting you stay here. At first, I was terrified that you'd get too close to that *thing* and start to lose your memory, but now I see that might be a good thing.

"You might finally forget your own funeral."

VIVISECTION

It began with a black bag over my head. Six or seven men seizing me off the street on my way home from work, holding me at gunpoint in the back of a van. They explained in detail what would happen to my family if I didn't listen to them. Until that moment, torture was just a word. I had never given it much thought. I wasn't prepared to hear some of the things they told me. By the time they were loading me onto a helicopter, I would have done anything they asked.

I arrived at the black site, kicked out of the chopper, where my feet hit the hard-packed wet mud with a splash. Black hood torn off so hard it hurt the skin on the tip of my nose and then I got my first look at the place. Can't say if it met my expectations or not. I didn't have any idea where I was going, or what it was supposed to look like when I got there. Still, it managed to leave me feeling surprised. An abandoned village nestled in the jungle. Mostly one room hovels, lots of corrugated iron. Here and there lay burned allotments. Dying pepper plants left untended, their fruit stamped into the Earth by the passage of soldiers dressed in all black. Rotten fences and troughs to feed long-dead pigs and goats lay smashed to pieces. And then, lurking on a hill like some architectural jumpscare was a three-story hospital made of glass and steel. State-of-the art. Built in a place where tarmac was just a rumour. Officially it had been put there by a charitable non-profit wanting to research novel diseases and potential cures deep in the jungle. Unofficially, it had always belonged to the CIA. A useful place to test strange things with pox in the name. And, when the time came, a useful place to dissect the impossible.

Imagine my surprise when I was escorted by armed men to an office with my name on the door and discovered that I was to be in charge of its latest major project. *Head of Research* printed on the glass. Real official looking. Big black letters like I'd always worked there. First thing I thought was, *How long do they intend to keep me here!?* But that didn't last long. That hospital became my home and has been ever since. Less than 24 hours after my arrival and I had my feet up on the desk, barking orders at lab technicians. I slipped into the role easier than I'd like to admit. You see, where they got me was on scientific curiosity. That's how they ensured I was on board with the project. That's why they never pointed a gun at me after day one.

They didn't have to.

The second I saw that thing inside the messiah's chest cavity, I was a willing asset. No more *me*. Only the project. The discovery and the revelations. Lying on that slab, nestled in the flesh of an otherwise normal looking man, was a white-hot piece of divinity. A pin prick in the fabric of reality. I don't know how else to describe it. It was like I'd spent my whole life seeing two-dimensional shadows, and then I suddenly got a glimpse of the three-dimensional shapes casting them.

I haven't seen my children since they took me. Couldn't tell you their names. I was never the same after the first autopsy. No one in that place was sane after the scalpel first bit into His flesh. Attrition amongst the research staff was incredibly high. Every day another nurse seized by stigmata, or a once-faithless lab technician struck by the call to write the Third Testament. The guards dealt with the unwilling members of the team. Traumatised scientists and clinicians lined up, one by one, against an exposed brick wall in the jungle heat and shot. I remember smoking in the cafeteria in between surgeries, nervously shaking as I tried to ignore the *pop pop pop* of some of my more stubborn colleagues being executed. And then back to work, where I suppressed the feeling that I was the worst kind of traitor. Next day there'd be new faces scrubbing up and asking for orders, another pair of hands shipped in from God-knows-where.

Back to cataloguing divinity.

At times I imagined joining the objectors. The people who found religion in a sterile black ops lab. But that *thing* we pulled out of him, that baffling enigma that burned the eyes. It consumed the project. Everything we learned about it felt like a quantum leap in our understanding of microbiology. We tested everything we could get our hands on. Plants. Animals. Humans. I tried not to look any of them in the eye. Quiet people taken from some quiet part of the Earth where they wouldn't be missed. All of them scared. Did they know? I mean *really* know the suffering they were in for? Definitely not. They expected to be shot, I imagine. Not to wake up with the roof of their mouths lined with eyeballs. I'm ashamed to say, but those kinds of results invigorated me. Excited me, even. When it all fell apart and I missed the evacuation, I got to finally rifle through all those classified documents where I discovered I hadn't been selected because I was some genius of microbiology. But rather because my psychological profile made it clear I'd do anything if you dangled a big enough mystery in front of me.

That and the fact that I was actually quite good at managing projects. Geniuses usually aren't great at sending out memos or keeping track of performance numbers. Thankfully, I'm no genius. It was humbling at times, working with some of the guys down below, being senior to them even. I mean, Dr Coates was probably the smartest man I'd ever met. No real academic career because he had a habit of hyperfixating on things that either couldn't be solved, or which no one gave a shit about. But it was pretty clear this was a guy who could've turned his brain to just about anything and made a name for himself if he was just a little more on the ball. He was an odd'un, basically. Gave lectures barefoot. Would respond to last-minute marking deadlines by giving every student a B. Threw a stapler at the head of his department. That kind of thing. Intelligent but not particularly sensible.

The project broke him. Broke his worldview. Broke his mind and, towards the end, even his body. You might think the problem was asking a hyper-rational man to process the divine, but if anything, he processed it a little too well. He was the first person to read The Third Testament without going insane. Immediately insane, I should say. Or maybe he was always nuts to begin with. Either way, he managed to take all the random scribbles and bits of verse that we'd collected from the personal effects of the deceased and actually put it together into a single document. Then he read it and came out looking like nothing special had happened.

The next guy after him, not so lucky.

But Dr Coates, he carried on working for a few days after. Took measurements of this. Made recordings of that. Slipped into the background, out of my notice, while I focused on trying to figure out some way of getting The Third Testament scanned into a computer without it causing havoc. A lot like the people who read it, machines liked to commit suicide about half-way through reading the Third Testament. Not Coates though. He seemed just fine...

Should've known better.

First clue that something wasn't quite right was when I went to his office. A cramped space with metal walls and floors, no windows given it was below ground, and a countertop full of equipment. It was always a mess in there and usually a bit smelly too, but it was usually just that unwashed scientist smell. But one day, when I went to call on him, he opened the door and I got a whiff of something that was just... wrong. Smelled a little like death, only not quite. Just, *different*. Mouldy, almost. Course he was entitled to do some experiments on his own time, and that's what I figured it was. At the time, I wrote it off. Had other things on my mind.

Only the smell got worse with time. Turned up day after day and each time it stung my nose a little worse, hung around my sinuses a little longer. And Coates, he looked a little worse for wear each time, too. Again, nothing serious. The kind of thing that's actually quite normal for a man like him. I'm used to seeing scientists fixate on a problem, something quiet they won't share with anyone else until they know for sure what they've got. That's what he was like, and I figured when he was ready, he'd either show me something that would blow my socks off, or it'd be something stupid like he got his microwave to evenly heat up his lunch by taking it apart and rewiring its insides.

Sometimes I wonder if I'd caught it earlier, could I have done something about it? Someone smarter might've picked up the odd chemical mixtures on his shelf, or recognised the peculiar smells. Not me though.

All I can say in hindsight is thank fuck my office was above ground. By the time his little project had finished working its way through the floor he was on, he'd killed thirty-six people with his homemade nerve gas. Thankfully the facility was prepared for that kind of attack and the automated security systems had the entire level locked down very quickly, so the damage wasn't that bad. Could've been a lot worse. But what was weird was the venting system wasn't working. Should've cleared it all out in under a day, but four hours later and the gas levels were the same. The investigation, at least at first, had to happen remotely. CCTV from his lab was spotty. Something was corroding the cameras, but based on some of his material requests, we guessed he'd been culturing some unusual fungus to create the bioweapon.

Whatever it was, it was potent, and we were helpless to do anything about it. We had to wait and hope to God whatever awful thing he'd concocted would wear out on its own. What little the CCTV could capture made for a gruelling sight. Eight scientists dead at their desks. Slumped over, blood pouring out of their mouths. The fluid looked black on the grainy black-and-white monitor. But what upset me more were the assistants. Dozens of young men and women who didn't really belong in that place. Too much to live for, and all of them so scared of what was going to happen to them. And they were just lying there in the middle of whatever it was they were doing. In the labs themselves, smashed beakers and machines in disarray. In their rooms, some of them lay peacefully sleeping, others held each other in secret little trysts they thought no one knew about. All over the level, bodies lay on the floor in strange positions, and again that black fluid leaking from every orifice, staining the floor, their faces, and their clothes. Soaking their chests and groins.

I remember sitting there and just watching them twitch and foam at the mouths, waiting for death to finally come. Even then, the hours ticked on as we waited for the systems to purge the gas. Twelve. Twenty-four. Forty-eight. Nothing happened. It was like everything in there was frozen in time.

And then, somehow, the lights on that level went out. Emergency lighting came on, bathing everything in red, but combined with the low-quality cameras, it was like gazing at an old video game. Grainy. Fuzzy. Low resolution. We figured that Coates must've rigged up a remote timer on the electronics, which wasn't a good guess since his speciality was biochemistry and the security systems were of the highest tier.

But what else could it be? Wasn't like someone could've hit the circuit breaker.

We knew eventually we'd have to go in there. Sixty hours after shutdown, we just had to. There was too much high value material to leave behind, and there were reports of strange noises down there. Guards posted to the door heard faint sounds on the other side. Footsteps, they reckoned. Course I wrote that off. Utter nonsense, I told myself and them. And yet we still went in armed because, well, if Coates was smart enough to rig this whole nightmare, who's to say he didn't make himself a little gas mask to keep himself safe?

You think I'd be used to working in hazmat suits, and I sort of am, but going into that sealed off floor was something else. The visor felt restrictive. The squeak of the rubber suit was deafening. My breath was too loud. And everytime the in-suit radio came to life with one of the soldier's barks, I damn near jumped out of my skin.

And then the door actually opened. Nothing could've prepared me for that. The air was thick with mist, which lit up harshly with the emergency lighting's red hue. Old metal grates. Vents. Open doorways. All of it either blood-red or completely dark. There were far too many shadows for it to feel safe. Didn't help some of the bulbs were strobe lighting. Rotating sirens that lit the place up in periodic flashes of crimson light. God, even the four soldiers next to me looked nervous.

We passed more than a few bodies on our way to Coates' lab. All of them lay where they'd been on the CCTV, at least as far as I could tell. Sounds stupid, but I stared at a few of them closely just to make sure. All those reports of footsteps had started to worm their way into my brain. Couldn't shake the idea we weren't alone down there.

When we finally opened the door to Coates', what I saw left me frozen to the spot. The soldiers focused on the strange growth off to one corner of the room, which registered to me only as a dim sort of collection of thick fungal petals crawling up the wall. Veins pulsating like capillaries in the eye. But to me, what really hit home was the empty desk. Last time we had reliable footage of that room, Coates had been lying there dead as a dodo. Blood leaking from his still open eyes, pooling on the desk and dripping onto the floor. And that stain was still very much there. There was even the faint outline of where his head had been laying.

But the man himself was gone.

This, even more than the grotesque thing that took up one wall, terrified me. That quivering mass of fungus was pumping out enough toxic gas to kill half the base, but it was stationary at least. In another circumstance, I might've even found it fascinating. But Coates... he'd clearly gone off the deep end. Had he lain perfectly still for days on end to trick us? That didn't seem right. Again, I thought of the bodies we'd passed. The way they looked so still, but not lifeless. Like a porcelain doll, there was that slight suggestion of something working behind the eyes.

"What do we do with this?" one of the men asked.

"Take samples, burn the rest," I replied. "If gas levels don't go down in a week, we'll have to purge the whole floor with phosphorus." The whole time I had my eyes on the space around us. Under the desk. Up on top of the cupboards. If Coates wasn't at his desk, where was he?"

"Where the fuck did this thing come from?" the same soldier muttered as he laid a series of thermal charges on the fleshiest part of the mould. It seemed to flinch in response to his touch, but was otherwise benign.

"Uh, he probably took some of *the subject's* tissue samples. We know it propagates unusual levels of growth in plant and animal tissue. Explains why the gas levels don't go down."

"What's it metabolising?"

I gave the soldier an odd look.

"What?" he said. "You aren't the only ones with an education."

"Fair enough," I replied with a quick shake of the head. "It isn't metabolising anything except His tissue. It's uh, well, bluntly, I mean think of the fish and the bread, right? This is something we've known about His tissue samples for a while now. Spontaneous creation of matter and energy out of nothing. But to give Coates his credit, this is a pretty novel application. He's created an infinite bioweapon."

"Why?"

I was about to reply, *I haven't the slightest fucking clue,* when a loud bang drew our attention to the doorway. Outside lay a darkness broken only by the strobing of a red light. Flashing on and off, it revealed, for just a single instant, the outline of a man standing in the hallway.

The soldiers swore nervously as they raised their rifles. By the time the light came back, the figure was gone.

"Who the fuck was that?" one barked.

"Must be Coates!" another replied.

"Job's done," I cried while gesturing to the charges. "Let's get the fuck out of–"

"There are no miracles left for you. You have made your own miracles."

The words were growled so loud and deep they seemed to vibrate my very bones. The soldiers snapped to attention, but me... I took a little longer to turn back to the corner of the room. I knew what I was going to see, but God, I didn't want to see it.

"There are other gardens, but not for you. Do not spoil the other Edens."

Coates emerged from the thing on the wall, pulling himself free with a wet squelch. He stood not naked, but nearly naked, as his skin had begun to absorb his clothes. He looked like a burn victim coated in algae.

"He loves you. In spite of everything, He loves you. And there is a place in heaven for you all, but it is time to–"

I can't blame the soldier who pulled the trigger. It wasn't just the fact that Coates was speaking with a mouth that had grown grotesquely across his abdomen, but rather that the words were drilling straight into our heads like some pushing a hot needle straight into a dental nerve. It made my eyes cross, my ears ache, and my nose bleed. Two of the men had vomited, splattering the inside of their visors with thick fluid.

They were the first to go. They didn't see what hit them and I'm somewhat glad. Coates, angered by the gunshot, moved with the elegance of a dancer. I stumbled out into the corridor as he tore them apart, his arm seemingly flowing right through their biohazard suit. The remaining soldier, the triggerhappy one, was beside me as I fled. It wasn't far to the exit. I hoped we would make it the rest of the way without incident, that in just a few short hours I might be able to put the few images I had of Coates pulling flesh and fabric apart like it was tissue deep into some recess of my mind and just move on. But it was only a few short steps into the dark before the remaining soldier began to fire blindly at the corridor behind us.

It was a mistake for him to turn around. In the fraction of a second where his eyes had been turned away, he missed one of the bodies lying on the ground. I jumped. He didn't. I was dimly aware of there being no one beside me only when the gunshots grew fainter and fainter as I left him behind. One of the shots dinged off a panel by my head and to this day, I suspect it was not a ricochet, but a deliberate attempt to get revenge for me abandoning him.

Still, I didn't look back, not until I reached the secure door. I thumbed the keypad frantically, terrified as my ears registered the sound of approaching footsteps muffled by the biohazard suit. God, I couldn't stop myself. I looked. I had nothing else to do except wait for security to clear me and open the door, and there was no guarantee they'd even do that. I might be waiting forever, staring at nothing as Coates came closer and closer.

Without even realising what I was doing, I turned and saw.

The soldier with the gun... Jesus. Coates' office was out of sight, so I have no idea if he repeated this with the other two. But the man I saw, he was in pieces. Yellow and red in ragged strips that coated the ceiling as much as the floor. And barrelling towards me on all fours, legs and arms too long for a normal man, came Coates. Eyes wide. Jaw distended. Chunks of his head still missing. But his mouth, it silently spoke the same few words almost in time with his loping gallop. Over and over and over... it would take days for me to even realise what it was he was saying.

Thankfully, before he managed to reach me, the doors opened, and a hail of gunfire filled the corridor ahead. Coates, fast as lightning, disappeared into some dark crevice and I was dragged to safety before the worst might happen.

As soon as I was on the other side, I told security to flood the place with phosphorus and everything was purged. White hot fire on demand. By the time it was over, only metal remained and even then, a lot of it had melted and cooled in strange shapes on the floor. I also went out of my way to kill any attempts at reclaiming the lost workspace. Higher ups were pissed. All that square footage lost, but I said the risk of contamination was too great. Of course, I left out the part where I returned one quiet night a few days later and placed my ear against a thick steel wall that I knew ran close to one of the vents on that level.

It was faint, but I heard Coates whispering. Only then did I finally get the final clue to what Coates had been saying as he came towards me in the flashing red of that darkened corridor.

We love you we love you we love you we love you we love you...

Even now, the cameras show that level to be a sterile hollow space, but I cannot escape the feeling that if I were to open it, I would see Coates come slithering out of some long-forgotten vent. Perhaps worse for wear given all the time that has since passed, but Coates, nonetheless. Terrifying and misshapen, but desperate to spread the very Testament that twisted his mind and body, that caused him to try and breed something that might well have ended the entire world. And the worst thing of all? What he'd been saying to me in that corridor. What if it was true? What if he hadn't done it out of hate, but love?

At the time, I'd assumed the force we were dealing with was hostile, but what if it wasn't? Everyone who goes near the Third Testament kills themselves and, until Coates, I'd thought it some kind of twisted revenge. But what if that wasn't the case? What if He wasn't doing it out of spite or hostility. What would that mean for me? Forgiveness? If so, that terrified me, because after everything I'd been through, I doubted I'd have the strength to resist that kind of offer. For weeks I lay awake at night wondering just what the hell might be in those words that could compel people like Coates to do what they did. And yet, despite everything, I still haven't read The Third Testament. Coates was a genius, and he still gave in. I know that I did some pretty messed up stuff in the name of scientific curiosity, but, well, I guess I'm not ashamed to say I'm also a coward. I'm afraid of dying. Curiosity can only get you so far, and after seeing everything that happened to the people who read that thing, I couldn't bring myself to risk it.

Whatever the Third Testament is... hearing it seems pretty bad for your health.

I don't think I even deserve to be forgiven, if that's what He's offering. It was poetic justice that out of all the people who managed to make the evacuation, I wasn't one of them. Leaving on foot is hardly an option for me. I mean, even if I had the strength to hike through hundreds of miles of rainforest, I'd need to reach the outer fence first, and strange things have festered in the chemical pits where they disposed of the bodies. Soft mounds of ash and bone that sing from time to time, exciting the birds in the canopy to take off and make strange patterns in the sky. If they can sing, they must have mouths, right? And if they have mouths, what else? I think about Coates, about what kind of hands would reach out to drag me into those rotten pits of long-dead flesh and drown me in filth and I shudder. I could try and sneak past, but...

It really isn't safe outside the hospital.

It isn't safe inside, to be fair, but what choice do I have? At least there's still power. Internet. Food to last me over a century. And the security doors that keep everything below sub-level one firmly locked away. While out there, well... I see things, sometimes, moving quickly between the old buildings. The trees shake and stir. And where the jungle now grows thick and heavy against one of the glass walls of the hospital, the vines twist and turn and spell out odd messages. I shut my eyes firmly whenever I have to pass them, and yet even blind I can hear the tightening of fibrous coils as the cloying flora scratch against the glass. They want me. Hungering. All those corpses we buried out there. Rotting. Breaking down. Contaminated with divinity. What strange waters flow through the soil in this place. Nothing could make me risk opening the doors and try walking through that vegetation.

He might forgive, but I don't think my former test subjects have.

And as for down below...

You know I never met Him while he was alive. Don't know where they got him from, or even why. My bet? He pissed off the wrong people, got shot, and got back up. Maybe they shot him again and he got up again. Maybe they did it five times. Ten times. I don't know. Somewhere along the lines, someone worked out they had an anomaly on their hands. Maybe I wasn't the first person to even try cutting him open? It's just weird. No one ever told us who He was. We just *knew*. It'd be years before I wondered who mothered Him. Loved Him. Raised Him. I often wonder if this was the way it was meant to go? Or was it just an accident that He bumped into the wrong people at the wrong time?

The messiah came and the first thing we did was cut him up. No wonder we failed. Things in the project started to go really bad about six months after the first incision. High turnover amongst researchers was one thing, but, well, it turns out a lot of the soldiers had a religious inclination. Wasn't just us dealing with visions and voices. At some point, they worked out what they were part of. The agency likes compartmentalisation, but it can only go so far. After the religious element became clear to the guys on the ground, things started to break down. It was one thing to control the scientists, but the guards were armed. When they broke, they broke hard.

Most of His remains are stored on the lowest level, where it's easiest to keep things cool. Outside, there's this long corridor leading to the central chamber. Huge. Wide enough to drive four or five cars side by side. And that was where the first guard hanged himself. Simple enough. They dragged him away and cleaned it up. It wasn't long after Coates. In fact, it was one of the men who'd saved me at the door. But pretty soon, another two guys went down there and hanged themselves. And then five. And then eight. And then topside, some guys started blowing their brains out. In their barracks. In the canteens. Standing watch at the doors, looking out on the jungle, cigarette hanging loose on one lip. Seemed almost random, except there was a clear pattern of escalation. When those guys started killing their friends, that's when it reached the point where they couldn't ship new guys in fast enough to replace losses. Once that happened, orders started getting lost. Jobs started being left undone. One lab got written off because a test subject's body was left to fester over a weekend and by the time they got the door open, there was flesh growing up the walls. Not enough manpower to deal with it so they left it for another day and moved on. Only they forgot to tell the researcher who worked there, so come Monday he went in and had a hell of a surprise. Must've been like stepping into a wall of sourdough. I can only hope he suffocated, and it was quick, but who knows? Not like that stuff has hard and fast rules. For all I know, he's still in there, screaming for air.

Meanwhile, in that tunnel, people just kept going down there and hanging themselves. I mean, every day I'd wake up, and I'd be down a few researchers, and a couple more guards would be missing. Took a shockingly short amount of time for most of the six hundred people onsite to just disappear. God knows when security stopped taking the bodies down. Just another job that got lost in the growing panic. By the time evacuation orders came, we were down to a hundred people. I estimate that around four hundred killed themselves in that tunnel.

I've only visited Him once since the project shut down. Only had the guts to go looking once. Barely made it out alive. I felt compelled to try and face up to Him. To acknowledge the role I'd played. Only that meant actually getting to the door at the end of the tunnel, which was, by this point, pitch black except for my torch.

And blocked almost entirely with hanging bodies. So many pressed together so close that I had no hope of making my way through without bumping into one. Reminded me of the jungle, funnily enough. Of a thick claustrophobic forest made of dried skin and brittle ligaments. Different colours and shapes, and of course, different levels of decomposition. Some had lost their noses, lips, and eyes. Others were a little bloated, but still recognisable. Not friends, really. I don't think I ever actually made one solitary friend on that project. But colleagues. People who were under my charge.

They looked sad. All of them looked sad. They should have been buried at home with their families, but instead they were locked all the way in the ass-end of nowhere. Of course, you can bet your ass the agency will make sure no one ever knows the truth. You know I still have contact with them? Anything I post gets screened. Arrogant bastards know that no one's gonna take me seriously. No record of this project anywhere. All those people just ghosts in a system too big for any one person to keep track of it all. You know how many people go missing in the United States in a year? What about Europe? Or the whole fucking world?

God, this project was just a drop in the ocean.

I wanted to put it to bed. To see if I could get some kind of answer from Him. It was that idea, trying to get some resolution to this nightmare, that gave me the strength to push past the first dead body and go deeper into that tunnel. It reminded me of trying to make your way to the front of a gig, only deathly silent, and the people you barged past swung gently back and forth. The sound of makeshift nooses tightening in the dark. I think the worst part was the limited vision. My light was just a lone disk and God, it was pitch black in that place. Like caving, only the floor is slick, and you don't have to worry about a ravine. Made me think of being at the bottom of the ocean. With all the corpses, visibility was never more than just a foot ahead. I remember panicking at the realisation I could easily get turned around and, well, what if all those lost souls didn't let me go? What if I wound up going in circles for hours, days even, on end? Just round and round. The nearest wall could be right *there* and I wouldn't know it.

Just bones and teeth and ribs and hanging entrails. All of it, all of *them*, cold to the touch. Freezing. Obviously, that was why we'd put Him down there. The place was cold. My own breath visible in the air. But the bodies were like the meat you grab out of a fridge in a supermarket, and it was just fucking awful. I found the fresh ones the hardest to stomach. A really rotten body looks almost like a prop. *It isn't.* Don't get me wrong. You look at it and your brain tells you damn well it ain't a prop. But it's a hell of a lot easier to convince yourself it's just a *thing* when it hasn't got skin or eyes. But the fresh ones, sometimes they still had expressions like anger or sadness on their faces. They made me feel watched. And the fact they were cold and slick with condensation... every time I bumped into one, it took everything I had not to let out a whimper.

And they moved. They didn't *move*, not like that. But there were no drafts down there. It was perfectly still. They'd been perfectly still for months after the project shut down. And then I came along and disturbed them, and it was like a giant Newton's cradle. A static system that I put energy into. They began to sway and twist and bump. I'd knock one and fraction of a second later it would knock me back, jostling against my cheek or my arm as inertia rocked it back and forth.

Ten minutes in, too far to turn back. That was when the nightmare began. Started small. I lost my ability to track what body was where and which ones were sent swinging by my own clumsy movements. And then, fingers combed my hair. I cried out. Another set touched my beard. My face. I forced myself onwards and started making eye contact with one too many dead men for it to simply be an accident. Their expressions changed from sullen and listless to angry and cruel. Leering smiles and curled lips.

Then came the unmistakable sensation of someone deliberately grabbing for my arm. I had to shake it loose, too afraid to look back and face the possibility that I'd see one of them moving and scowling. I pushed on constantly, having to shake cold fingers off my elbow or my collar. They groped incessantly, looking for anything to hold onto. Firm grips pinched my belly fat. My shoulders. My chest. And then they started reaching for my eyes. At one point I made the mistake of crying out and a freezing cold finger with a slightly furry texture slid into my mouth. The only relief came when I dropped to my hands and knees and crawled. The entire time, my mind raced with the terrible possibility that I really was just being sent in circles, over and over and over.

And they were never going to let me leave.

I would die down there, in the dark, smothered by their rotting hands.

God damn... I came close to giving up. When my torch finally alighted upon an open space, I cried out. A heaving, wet sob made of relief and joy, and my muscles, given new life, worked over time to get me out of that horrible nightmare and into freedom. I didn't stop until I bumped my head against a steel wall with a dull *clang* and looked up to see the vault's door.

At last. The place we'd frozen Him. I got up with what little dignity I had left, brushed down my clothes, and risked only the briefest of glances back. The bodies looked inert now, just like they had before I entered. I could've tricked myself into thinking it was my imagination, only half my shirt was now in tatters on the floor, and I could see strips of it still clenched in a few of their hands.

I did my best to compose myself, and I entered the vault.

We hadn't left Him in a very nice state. The plan was to catalogue *everything*. Yes, we'd excised the most... *striking* biological anomalies, but the remaining flesh, I mean, we wanted to know everything. Every last capillary. Every last cell. We wanted it recorded. So, we had this special machine flown in. It works by taking a piece of flesh and slicing into a layer that's barely a micrometre thick and depositing it onto a slide. That slide is digitised and then stored in specialised cold refrigeration units. It's usually used on a sample not much bigger than a potato, but for Him, we had something specially made.

Frozen. Stood vertical. We put Him on the machine where it worked, creating about one slice every three hours. Only at the end, well, at first no one came to take the slides away, so they had gathered on the floor below in a terrible mess. And second, no one had bothered to check if He was still dead. Stupid of us, really.

Of course He came back to life. Only this time, He didn't get to leave the cave.

I often wonder if He had anything left to say.

But by then the machine had reached His nose. Just his eyes and the top of his head looking right at me... following me...

God, we made a fucking mess of things, didn't we? Made the Romans look gentle in comparison. I fell to my knees and begged for forgiveness and the worst part was He gave it. Obviously not verbally, but it shouldn't surprise you to know He had other ways of putting thoughts in my head. I was so angry at myself, I was positive I'd find some kind of punishment waiting for me. But I didn't. He forgave me, told me I was loved. After everything I'd done, I mean... God, that hurt the most. I didn't deserve it. Still don't.

And then He gave me the Third Testament, or rather the cliff notes. Not enough to drive me nuts but, the gist of it, so to speak. Did a number on me, anyway. By the time I was done sobbing on the floor, I looked up and He was gone. Nothing remained. Just broken glass and a machine cutting empty air.

Going back through the tunnels was no easier than going in, but I hardly remember it. I lost a couple weeks after that little trip down below, but eventually I came to in my office. Now I stay above ground. I've asked for rescue, but the agency feels I best serve my country by staying where I am, making sure nothing else leaks out. It's fucked, but I think for once they might be right. I've considered sharing what He gave me. Considered even putting it in this bit of writing here. Might even go get the full Testament and upload it, but that'd involve reading it and, like I said, I'm a coward and I don't want to die. Everyone who reads it dies by their own hand.

I guess all I can say is, the Third Testament, it's something of a warning. An outline of what's coming our way. So bad that He came just to offer us a way out. A promise that there's somewhere else, and an acknowledgement that we're going to *need* it. Makes me think of Coates.

Smartest man I ever met, whose first reaction to knowing what's on the way was to try and engineer something to wipe humanity all out.

Given what we did to Him, I wonder if we don't deserve it.

A BITTER LURE

I've always loved the sea. It's not that I'm a sailor or anything but growing up around the coast means I've always felt close to it. My wife and I met for our first date at the beach in Rhodesia and after we returned from teaching abroad in the seventies, we bought our very first house right by the sea in Wales. In that house, we raised two sons, four grandchildren, five dogs, and one stray cat, all over the span of thirty-eight years.

It's been a good life. I haven't regretted a minute of it. Not even as I watched my wife struggle with her chest, and not even when I fell asleep on the sofa and awoke to find her cold in her recliner. Losing her has been the biggest struggle of my entire life. I used to tell her that life wouldn't be worth living without her. It never even occurred to me I might have to face it. Doctors say it was a clot in her lungs, which is a bitter irony. How many years did I smoke? God, it was most of my life, and I never once saw her even look at a cigarette. The doctor said it was nothing to do with that, but it's not really the point. The point is that I smoked and drank and ate poorly and every morning she'd wake up early and do the same exercise tape for the best part of twenty-five years. We even kept a VHS player just so she wouldn't have to get a new routine.

Even now it just seems so absurd that she died first, and so young as well. I thought she'd live to be a 100, just like her mother. But life's funny like that.

After her death, I've spent the last year battling a dark cloud in my mind. My sons have worked hard to keep my head above water, making sure I do simple things like eat and bathe. I lived in a kind of fugue state for the first few months, barely registering who I was speaking to or what I was doing. It wasn't until the girl that things changed for me. I was sitting on my bed—this was about two months after the funeral—when I heard a scream. It was about 1am, I reckon. I didn't sleep much back then. But this scream, it was awful. It wasn't a panicked scream.

No, it was like this agonised screeching, just a short burst of unspeakable agony. Before I even had time to process what had happened, I was limping out into my backyard with a robe on, shouting into the wind-whipped darkness. I remember walking up to the threshold of my yard, where it opens up onto a small bit of forestry before the sandy beach and standing there shivering and scared. I was so scared and confused, even as I shouted over and over,

"Is anybody out there? Hello!?"

The only thing I ever saw that night were the trees lit up by my torch, looking like bright white sticks of chalk against a blackboard. I kept telling myself it was just a fox! But I knew damn well what a fox sounded like, and it wasn't that.

The next day, as soon as the sun rose, I went looking, walking through the woods until I made it down onto the open beach. With the tide just pulling in, and the wet sand reflecting the low winter sun, it felt like standing on a plane of glass that stank of salt and decay. I quickly found a small fire-pit, close to the trees and far from the water. It's not uncommon for teenagers to come and drink and smoke round here, so I figured that maybe some kids had been hanging around that night. The only other thing around was some dead crabs, bits of driftwood, and a braying tangle of seagulls.

At first I ignored them, but as I continued to scan the horizon, I glimpsed a flash of colour between their flapping wings.

I hurried over and kicked them all away. They'd been fighting over her. It was awful. I knew instantly it was the person who'd screamed. She couldn't have been much older than thirteen, I reckon. Although the police won't say for sure because they're still not sure who she actually is. It's just something about the backpack... it looked the sort of thing a younger girl might have. She was probably invited along by an older boy and snuck out without her parents knowing. They do it all the time. Hell, I did.

Sometimes, when I have nightmares, I still see that seaweed covered pile of ribbon-like flesh. My eldest son gave me a bit of a row for going down there on my own, but the police thanked me for calling them. For weeks afterwards, that girl's death haunted me. I couldn't stop thinking about it. I just couldn't get it out of my head. I called the police every day for a week, hoping to hear some updates, but they never gave me anything. It's not that I was hoping for good news. I knew better than to expect good news.

But some answers, maybe... I hoped to find some answers. And yet nothing ever came, at least not from there. What I did then was to start waiting in my backyard each night. I kind of hoped I might see something. A part of me, deep down, deep deep down, hoped I might even be able to stop whatever had hurt her and martyr myself in the process. After a few weeks of nothing but wind, I started walking the beach each morning, worried I might find another victim. I felt like I was the only one who even really cared. I know that's not true, but in that house, all on my own, I felt like I was the only one even trying to stop it from happening again.

It was during one of those walks I first saw the line. I didn't recognise it for what it was. No. It just looked like seaweed. A plump piece of seaweed that lay on the wet sandy shore like half-chewed liquorice, while a black stalk as thick as my wrist ran all the way into the sea. I stared at it for a bit, horrified by the smell and the way it seemed to writhe and bubble in the open air. I thought it might have been some strange unseen animal. I was set to ignore it, but something about the pustule-covered oily surface piqued my curiosity so badly that I grabbed a nearby stick and poked it.

I wasn't prepared for what happened next. I don't think anyone could be. The mass just... disappeared. At first, I heard a loud twang, and then a splash, then I felt a breeze around my face, and then I was just looking at a crater in the sand. But I cannot emphasise just how quick this thing was. By the time my brain had even registered the thing's absence, it was long gone! I didn't even see it move. It just... disappeared. It was like someone had edited a camera to make it disappear from one frame to the next.

At first, I sort of just suppressed the strange experience. I thought it was unrelated to everything, and I wasn't in a very good place mentally, so I just sort of forgot it. I was still hoping I might find out what happened to that girl, and as far as I was concerned, that thing was probably just a weird fish.

Except, the next day, I went for my morning walk, and it was back. This time, there were some feathers sticking out of it. Up close to it, I saw the mangled, half-alive body of a seagull. It looked awful. The bird was squawking over and over, and the brutal, half-broken flapping of its wings made a terrible racket. I didn't know exactly what had happened to it, I suspected it may have become trapped, maybe when it was looking for some food. I've always had a policy of being kind to animals, so I bent down to pull it out and...

There was the sound of something going taut, the thronging of a rope, and then a crack, and then a whoosh, and then I was looking at nothing. It was so utterly bizarre and shocking; I didn't even react at first. I just stood there, trying to process what I'd seen. I decided afterwards that maybe it wasn't so good for me to go walking on the beach during the morning. I half suspected I was going a bit mad.

A few weeks passed after that. The girl was what occupied my mind during that time. I was happy to have a distraction from the death of my wife, and in some ways, I thought that by worrying over this poor dead child, I was doing something nobler than just looking after myself. It remained like that for quite some time, until one day I woke up and looked outside to find my bins thrown around the garden. This sort of thing can happen now and again, of course. What with foxes being quite common.

But foxes don't normally move the heavy wheely bins. It would have been a struggle for me to drag them that far, let alone an animal. Going downstairs, I saw all my rubbish thrown around and initially my heart sank at the thought of having to clean it up, but as I approached one bin that had snagged on a bush, I suddenly noticed that it wasn't actually a bin at all.

It was the seaweed, again. The way the plastic rubbish was dotted around and through it, and the way it looked so shiny and strange... well, it looked very much like a bin bag. It was... well it was convincing. And that's what made me stop. That's what made me scared. There was even a clump of black seaweed at the very top, shaped just like a little knot. Exactly the kind of knot you'd tie at the top of a bin bag. And the way it was nestled in the bush meant that you had to look quite hard to see the twisted stalk trailing off into the woods.

I couldn't understand it. It was terrifying because nothing was making any sense, but I was pretty sure that this thing... whatever it was... well it was trying to trick me. And not just in the way that a moth might trick a spider with camouflage. No, this felt like a very clever trick. For a moment, I actually reached down, ready to give it a quick poke and see what happened, when I heard a creak. It sounded like rope under tension, or wood being stood on. It sounded like something winding up in anticipation. I hesitated, and then just decided to leave it alone and back away. Something about the thing changed when I stopped bending down and moved away. It suddenly began to throb.

It looked a little bit like it had been holding its breath to stay still.

By the time I'd walked up the stairs, I looked out the window and saw that it was already gone. It was a few days before I saw it again. Enough time had passed that I had managed to try and forget at least a little bit of had happened. I'd spent all day watching TV, just like I do every day, and then fallen asleep in the living room chair. When I woke up, the window was open, and the lights were off. I could feel the draft. It felt sharp and cold, and my knees ached from where the blanket had slid down onto the floor. I wiped my face of drool and checked my watch, seeing that it was 2am.

I was groggy at this stage, thinking that it was a little unusual that I'd turned the lights off. Still, my wife had always kept a lamp beside her chair to help her read and I reached over to turn it on when I heard a subtle creak.

I froze and looked across.

It was there. It was smaller this time, probably to help it fit through the window. But it was there. It was bunched around the lamp, steady and waiting. If it wasn't for the moonlight pouring in through the living room window, I would never have seen it. That slick black flesh disappeared utterly into shadow. Looking around, I saw the twisted black stalk, as thick as my arm, trailing across my living room floor and up through the open window.

I stood up, shaking with fear, and I went and then turned the light on, noticing the strange black-purple residue that was left on the switch. That same residue now soaked my carpet, filling my living room with the stench of rotting fish and strange, salty air. Once again, that strange mass had started throbbing once I moved away, looking like it had relaxed its dreadful ruse. I grabbed a nearby newspaper and in anger, I walked over and hit it.

I don't know exactly what I expected, but the speed of the thing... The living room window was practically torn out of the wall, the air rushed in as if displaced from an explosion, and my rug had friction burns! Actual burns charred into the fibre from where this thing had moved so fast it had damn near ignited the nylon! And the newspaper I'd held? It had been snatched out of my hand so fast my skin was left bloodied, and my wrist was sore for days. But what worried me the most, even in the moment, was the sense that it had actively tried to grab me. My eyes had barely registered it, but I swore I saw that thing clamp onto the paper with phlegmy tendrils. If it wasn't for the fact I'd used a random object, it would have succeeded.

After that, I couldn't get the idea out of my head. It was a lure. It was a God damned fishing lure! It was a smart, sophisticated fishing lure and it was trying to drag me into the damn sea! What the hell for I couldn't imagine! But I had a good guess that when it was done with me, it wouldn't be throwing me back. I became paranoid pretty quickly. I started carrying a flashlight with me at all times, and I never left any windows open. But there was this horrible sense... you see, I knew nothing about this thing. But it had known enough about me to switch off the light and then set the lamp up as a lure.

I started double-checking every little thing. Would it rig the toilet paper for one of my many midnight bathroom trips? Would it rig the very rug I walked on to get to the lights? What about my bed? My pillows? My clothes? How often do you wake up, groggy eyed and barely sentient, and shamble into your morning routine?

It wasn't just the fear, it was the false positives. It was the way I'd scold myself if I grabbed something without looking. It was the way I'd live in constant fear of messing up all over again. I made sure I knew just how much luck had saved my skin up until that point, and I kept telling myself my luck would not hold for much longer. That's not a healthy way to live, by the way. It's actually quite exhausting. I just kept hoping it would somehow end, and as the weeks passed, I started to hope that maybe the lure had left me alone, finding me a little too smart.

Looking back, that's quite a laughable idea. If anything, I had drastically underestimated the lure.

You see, I'd always had a fondness for cats. My wife had pre-ferred dogs and while I love all animals, I'd grown up with cats and

I liked their company a lot and secretly I'd always wished we could have had more. It was late one night when I heard a strained meow coming from just beyond my window. It was a stormy night, and you could hear the sea battering the distant cliffs. I ignored it at first, because it's so typical for cats around here to fight and cry. But the sound kept coming. Sitting there, listening to this creature in pain, I couldn't help but get to thinking…

Wouldn't it be nice if I had a cat in my old age? I could find one and help it and call the vets in the morning and then the cat would maybe stick around. I had images of a little ginger tabby cat sauntering around the kitchen as I pottered about. God, I was being so stupid…

I rushed outside and followed the noise. It was almost regular, like a church organ. When I traced it, I found a cat's back-end sticking out of a bush. It looked like a little like it was struggling, almost like it had become stuck. I was so wound up, so broken from the lack of sleep and distressed by the sound of pain that I came so close, mere inches away from touching the orange fur. But something within me told me otherwise. In the moment I hated it. I hated that thought. I so badly wanted to help another living thing that I secretly loathe this part of me that suggested that maybe, just maybe, it was all part of the lure.

I took a deep breath and pulled back the bushes, and what I saw horrified me. It hadn't even found a living cat. Or if it had, it certainly hadn't let it live for long. You see, this thing, this amorphous tendril-wielding lump of tobacco spit come-to-life, had driven long-knuckled fingers that looked like grotesque spider legs deep into the belly of this cat. Before my very eyes, I saw those fingers spread the cat's ribs and then squeeze them shut, pushing a withering and unnatural cry out of the animal's mouth as it did so. It was like some twisted hellish version of a bagpipe.

I fell backwards and screamed. The very sight made me want to vomit. I couldn't bear it. I was so angry I wanted to grab that damn lure and yank whatever the hell was in that ocean out to meet me and face my wrath. It took every ounce of my willpower to stop myself.

That's what made it so clever.

It knew. It knew exactly how to push my buttons. It wasn't about tricking me that time. It was about goading me. It took every bit of strength to hold myself back. But in anger, I stood and screamed at it,

"Go away! Just fuck off and leave me alone!"

With that, the cat's body suddenly slumped and fell down. When I looked in the bush once more, there was no sign of the lure. It had gone, leaving me with the poor animal's body. I buried it that night, sobbing the whole time.

The next morning, I called my son and asked him to take me to a home. One that's far away from the sea. Since then, I've just been waiting. I've been ready to go for days. I don't want to take anything with me. It hurts just to look at it now. All I wanted to do was leave. I thought that maybe if I got far away... But, like always, I just keep underestimating the lure.

I thought that my son would be coming this morning. He was supposed to. He rang at midday, a good few hours after he was expected. He was hysterical. He kept saying no one could understand why. No one knew why.

"Why what?" I'd asked.

"Why they'd dig her up, Dad. Why would anyone take her body?"

And now it's nighttime. It's night and my head is hurting and I'm afraid. I'm afraid of what's upstairs. I'm afraid of the sound of smashing glass that I heard an hour ago, and the strange and dreadful thumping that followed it. I'm most afraid because when I went upstairs to check on what had happened, nothing looked different. It was the most normal thing in the world: a sight I've seen a thousand times.

My bedroom, the lampshade on, my slippers ready. And worst of all, the duvet-covered shape of my wife, her chest rising and falling.

A GLASSFUL

I hope that by sharing this, maybe I can scrape some kind of repentance together. But no one else believes me and it doesn't work unless people believe me. People kept thinking I was joking, but I'm not. I need help and I was told this place would believe me.

I need you to understand just how bad a person I am, or else the confession doesn't mean anything. I think it's too late, but I need to get this off my chest, if only so I have a chance at entering heaven when my time finally comes.

You see, bad things have a weight. They stay with you long after you've done them. I know I'm not a good person, but sometimes I do think it's unfair. I know other people aren't perfect. I have to wonder if I'm really that much worse. I know that everyone must have bad things in their past. Do they all have dark little nasty things they hide away? How do they cope? Knowing all the awful things they've ever done?

I just don't understand how normal people live. I see them from my window. I've spent decades watching them going past. They all look so busy. They have smartphones and cars and cups of coffee and when I look at them I think, sometimes, maybe that's all they're worried about. But then again, I remember what it was like for me. I used to have things too. I used to have a wife and two children and a job. It was so many years ago that it feels like a different person lived those memories. But I did have them, and even back then I was just pretending. I was lying to myself and everyone else. When I was nine, I stole a pound from my mother's purse and blamed a visiting cousin. When I was fourteen, I noticed a teacher's panty line, and I deliberately stared at it, savouring it even as I knew I should have looked away. Time and time again I have wronged, and it's all stayed with me.

But the worst, oh the worst, were the things I could have fixed if I'd just been honest. By now they should just be silly forgotten mistakes, but the longer and longer I left my sins to fester without facing up to them, the worse they became until I have no chance of being saved. I once missed a payment on my school uniform and lied to my parents, saying I gave the money to the school. I spent all year hiding from Sister Mary, afraid that I'd have to tell my parents about the furious Irish nun that the family owed £5. I didn't even take the money! I was so afraid, so guilty, I buried it in the garden. Money my family needed, and I wasted it. My poor mother fretting over everything and I couldn't even care, couldn't even summon a moment's thought of how it affected her until it was all too late, and I was too scared to come clean.

My whole life, it's just been the same thing. Am I normal? Is the difference between me and you simply that I stopped pretending that I was worthless? Or am I broken? I have to ask, even as I know that writing these words proves just how guilty I am... But does everyone have one too?

Does everyone have a spider?

I know it's different for everyone, of course. For them, it's a metaphorical spider. But for me, it's real. It's a spider I trapped in a glass. It's so hateful. I know why. I made it like this. It wasn't always a broiling crawling mass of thick segmented legs. It was once just a spider, a little part of nature. A diligent hunter and its only sin was being big! Isn't that funny? I was never bothered by little spiders, but past a certain size, something about their knotted up silhouette terrified me. At the time, having tip-toed drunk into my own home trying not to wake my wife, I thought I was being a good person by trapping it. I thought it was better than killing it.

When I look at it now, when I see what it's become, I know how pathetically wrong I was. I should have killed it. It would have been wrong, but it wouldn't have been so needlessly cruel. A quick death would have been the lesser of two evils. Instead, I palmed it off, hoping that my wife would come down the following morning and throw it away, only she never had the chance. We all went on holiday that very morning and I forgot about the poor spider trapped in a glass prison, sitting on a shelf in the pantry next to some peaches.

Waiting to die.

We were gone for two weeks. At the time, it seemed so long. I came back and saw him in there and I saw that it had changed. It was angry... it was like all that hatred it had for me had nowhere to go, so it started twisting and changing, poisoned by its own vitriol. Legs had split apart, growing in all directions... Some were as thick as pencils and others as thin as hair, and every now and again, they'd flicker with a hint of life. Its body had grown so fat, betting bigger and bigger until it throbbed with every desperate breath, thick hairs like black paperclips jutting out of hard segmented chitin and writhing like black little worms.

My own cowardice had poisoned it, turning it into something utterly grotesque.

And it wanted to be let out! Could you imagine? I knew could do it, if I wanted to, but I felt so guilty and scared. Letting that thing go would have surely been the end of me! I couldn't possibly risk it. At the time, I thought that two weeks was too long to have left it. It must have been furious at whoever had trapped it and left it to rot. I hoped that maybe if I just waited, it might die.

I waited for forty-two years.

It's funny, looking back to think I could have taken my chances. Two weeks was the best it was ever going to get. It's just, I kept hoping it would eventually die. I know just how cowardly that sounds, but I'm not hiding from how God damn awful I am. I know exactly how bad it was because I did it! I was there. I was there for every single day of the following four decades. And every single day where I chose to do nothing has just compounded my sin, piece by piece by piece.

15,447 pieces in total.

And for every single one, it's just gotten angrier, and bigger. It didn't take long before it smashed through that glass. I've only ever opened the door once after that and what I saw has haunted my nightmares everyday since. There were so many legs. It was like a furry thorn bush with a rabbit sized body tucked deep inside its tangled limbs. I even had to seal the keyhole after its thin legs started to poke through, flailing around, probing the outside, desperate to find me. With each passing year, that paltry barrier looked more and more fragile until it was bulging outwards like a pregnant belly. I always knew that door wouldn't hold forever.

I deserve what's going to happen to me.

Maybe if I'd stopped then. But no. It never ends. My cowardice never ends. I used to let the delivery driver bring the food in and I'd it on his face. He was disgusted by me. They all were. Forty-two I've stayed indoors, but I had to! Anyone could have opened the door, and then what? What if I wasn't around to make sure it stayed trapped? No one knows what that thing is, or the things it will do to me. My wife... she didn't know either. She would look at me now with horror, just like everyone else. She'd see the towering walls of rubbish that surround me, she'd see the ragged cloths I wear, the food I eat, and she'd hate me.

She'd see the real me.

I didn't deserve her. She trusted me so much. Back then, a wife had to be supportive of her man no matter what and she never failed me. As the days turned into weeks and my absence from work raised concerns and whispers became rumours, she worked tirelessly to convince everyone I was okay. How could she possibly have guessed why I stayed inside all day, why I refused to answer the phone or the door, and why I beat my own son senseless when he dared to touch a certain door handle? She lied even as she took him to the hospital, saying he fell down the stairs. But you have to understand, I couldn't let him open that door and risk the chance he'd free the spider.

It's looking at me, even as I type this. It's been days since it got out and it's just look at me the whole time. I can't even move, but I know now just how strange it's become. It defies any natural design now, stretching up and out of the pantry so that it might loom over me as I sit and wait for judgement. Half the house is taken up by it, whole rooms and hallways cast in darkness as a myriad of clicking legs choke the very air, blocking windows and smashing lightbulbs.

But it's changed in other ways too. There's a hideous intellect buried inside that body. I know it and oh God, even worse, it knows me. It knows me through and through. That's why it's waiting, isn't it? It's making me write my confession, but I didn't know! I didn't know it wasn't hungry! Isn't it bad enough that I have to be me? Can't that just be my punishment? Did it have to bring them out here and sit them down? Those hollow eyes are staring at me.

I thought it might be hungry! I heard that dreadful shatter one night and I just... I didn't know what to do! It needed to eat. That's what. It needed to eat. But what? What would be enough? I ran around the house, throwing cupboard doors open, looking for anything I could find. I was screaming, hysterical, ranting and swearing about how it needed something from me. I needed some kind of penance. Something to give it, to appease it.

And then I saw them. They were huddled under the stairs, scared of me. I caught a glimpse of my ragged face and wide blood-shot eyes in a mirror as I approached them. God, I looked like a madman. But I kept thinking that I just needed to feed it.

I tried to take just the boy. He was the youngest. I couldn't lose my wife or my daughter, but I thought maybe the boy... he was just four. They'd have forgotten about him if they'd just listened to me and done what I'd asked, but they didn't! My wife grabbed a knife and cut me when I went to take him, and it hurt so bad. I over-reacted. I know that. But the entire time I could hear that spider slamming into the door over and over and over…

I snatched the knife out of her hand, and I just started stabbing. I didn't even look at what I did. I screwed my eyes shut and fell on top of her, driving that blade down again and again while my children screamed. I reached out to my daughter, trying to calm her, but she struggled, pushing hard and I tried to get her to stop. But it was too late. Things were moving too fast and when I pushed the knife against her throat, it was only meant to be a warning for her to stop screaming. But she moved too much and before I knew what was happening, thick rivulets of red blood were streaming down my hand, soaking her floral nighty, and her voice turned to a ragged whisper.

But I still had to feed it. There had to be penance. Not just for the things I'd done to the spider, but for what I'd just done to my family. I found my son cowering in the kitchen and I dragged him and the bodies towards the pantry. I pulled the door open, so afraid I actually soiled myself even as I rolled the two girls and then shoved my crying child inside. The last thing I saw before I shut the door was that horrible spider rising out of the darkness to take me. I slammed the door shut before it reached me and fell down, crying, hoping it might finally stop coming for me.

If only it had been hungry.

If only that had been what the spider wanted.

But you have to understand… once he was in there, it's not like I could let him out! How was I supposed to know they'd just stay in there, the lot of them, bodies, spider, and the boy!? How was I supposed to know it'd just sit back and leave him be?

It took weeks before he finally stopped crying, his chubby little fists banging against the door the entire time.

Now he's sitting on my sofa, along with his sister and mother, their mummified corpses pulled out of the darkness to taunt me. It's been weeks and weeks, and it won't let me go. I'm starving. I can feel it. I'm sitting in my own filth, slowly dying, and I can't do a damn thing about it! If I do, it corrects me, those wretched legs dragging me back with horrible strength, forcing me to sit and stare at those leering grinning skulls.

They're all going to watch me die, no matter how long it takes.

BOTTOMLESS FUN

I mean, I've worked at this place for as long as I remember and it's pretty weird and even harder to describe. It's your usual family-fun indoor park, I guess. There's a million of them all over the place and they all have different names. We have a shitty little café that over charges for stale hotdogs and then a butt-load of warehouse space filled with random crap to keep kids entertained. There's a jungle gym, an arcade with ancient games, a greasy bowling alley, and obviously there's a ball-pit.

Honestly, it's a pretty cool job although it has taught me that kids, in general, are *super* weird. I remember this one time a random kid came up to me and handed me some marbles and then just started laughing. It took me a few minutes to get it out of him, but he told me that he'd shoved the marbles up his butt, and now I was touching his butt marbles. And he just thought it was the funniest God damned thing anyone has ever done.

Ever.

We have a high turnover rate, that's for sure. We chew through new employees like popcorn, and I think it's because kids have this weird ability to home in on anyone they make uncomfortable and just thrive off the awkwardness. At least teachers and parents get to deal with one set of kids, right? They get to know them over time, and sure those kids will occasionally explode or have prolonged periods of begin crazy high energy, but for the most part, the parents and teachers are there to manage the kids.

But that's the exact opposite of what we do. We're here to manage the centre, not the kids. Every kid here is meant to blow off steam. That's why parents bring them here. It's why they pay the entry fee. We can't make these kids sit down or write lines. We can't threaten or goad or shout. What we have is a revolving door of kids who are permanently psyched out, and we're just meant to keep them occupied long enough for their parents to smoke a joint around the back or cry in the toilets where no one can see them break down.

I gotta say, it's tough. I only stuck it out because I'm in management and that means my job is to get a bunch of teenagers to do all the dirty work. It's like a pyramid scheme, but grosser. Nobody at Enron had to brush vomit out of a crying 9-year-old's hair. Still, I limit my exposure to the kids and for a damn good reason.

They scare the shit out of me.

For one thing, there's always the wrong number. This place is always full no matter how many tickets we sell. Most people don't even stay here long enough to notice, but I have. I've spent a few years now counting tickets and then heads and I know for a fact that there are rainy days in the middle of the coldest winters when we sell ten, maybe twenty, tickets at most. But no matter what, the floor is crawling with kids.

Another thing, kids go into the ball pit and don't come out. Nobody complains, nobody's reported missing. But I know for a fact that not only do some kids never come back out, but some kids that do come out never went in in the first place. I already know what you're thinking, that I'm nuts. But I once trialled a photo-day just to confirm my suspicions. I took pics of the kids and parents coming and going (I said it was for a competition) and I swear to God, I have dozens of photos of parents coming in with one kid and leaving with a totally different one.

I've thought about trying to empty the ball-pit out to see if there's anywhere they could go, like a tunnel I never knew about. I did try to empty it once. It was years ago, and I wanted to clean it properly, so I waited until after hours and started scooping balls out and dumping them into empty bins, but after a while I got scared and stopped. Something about the experience just freaked me out. It was like the more balls I pulled out, the quieter everything got, like the whole place started to anticipate something. All those weird cartoon characters painted onto the wall with freaky eyes that follow you around the room, the zombie-shooter arcade machines that make those stupid fake ghoul noises, the twisty airplane rocket that rocks kids back and forth while blasting obnoxious music… it all kinda faded out. It was like the whole place held its breath. And my head started to throb like the world's worst hangover, and my mouth started tasting all coppery and it made me wanna retch.

It freaked me out, and I stopped and just tipped the balls back in. As soon as I did, the pressure in my head released and the place was full of noise again, like nothing had even changed.

Now I just clean the ball pit out with one of those nets they use for swimming pools. There's always the weirdest stuff in there: dead mice, crushed insects, dog shit, random goo, and what I can only describe as a series of gifts or messed up experiments. I don't know where they come from, but a week hasn't gone past where I haven't had to fish some half-dead, tortured animal out of the depths of that pit. If I'm lucky, the animal dies as soon as I pull it out, but I keep a spare pillowcase around here just in case. I don't know how humane it is to be stuffed into a sack and smashed against an alley wall, but I know it has to be more humane than keeping them alive.

I used to think the kids dragged roadkill in there, but after I started paying a little more attention, I noticed things like badly sutured wounds stitched together with random thread, or even half-healed amputations. I don't think it's even possible for a kid to pull off a successful trepanning on a squirrel and keep the thing alive, half-paralysed, at the bottom of a ball-pit. It just doesn't make sense. But I keep finding them, half stuffed with bugs, eyelids cut off... Jesus Christ, the worst one didn't even have any cuts.

I still don't know who did it or how. I don't know how the ball got inside the rat. It was alive, with no scars or open wounds, but it was like it had swallowed a whole damn ball. It wasn't crying or making any noise. It was just shivering, alive and in shock at what had happened to it. The pain must have been overwhelming, all of its organs crushed, its bones pushed out of sockets... Just looking at it made me wanna hurl. It was the most unnatural thing I've ever seen.

It's just another reason why I couldn't ask anyone else to do this job. I think most people come and go so quickly, they never realise just how weird it is. I'd rather no one start asking questions. I think if I was braver, I'd try to dig a little deeper, and I'd encourage others to help me, but no one else has seen the weirdness up-close like I have and I guess my conclusion is this: if we don't know what's down there, why bother it?

It's clearly best to just leave it alone.

That's why I'm glad we have a high turnover rate. People get super weird if they stick around too long. I've moved a few people on because they started to go a bit loopy. First, we see paranoia setting in. They start looking at you funny, or the kids. I mean, the kids I get, but me? What's wrong with me? Second, we see them starting to fixate on the ball-pit. People who stay too long obsess over it. When you're not looking, they'll sneak over and try to jam a broomstick into the bottom. When they can't find it, they'll start freaking out, talking about foundations and floor plans. Finally, the worst ones will start trying to go over my head to speak to corporate. They go nuts, asking questions and ringing numbers and just bugging me over and over. If you're not careful, they can actually become quite threatening. I know you wouldn't think it, but people get really wound up about this kind of stuff.

One girl I had to call the cops on. She developed a real unhealthy interest in me. She even asked me where I lived! She wanted to know where I slept and ate and who my parents were. Even after I fired her, she kept coming back, even tried to burn the place down. I think this place messes with people's minds because she started talking about how the number to HQ just went to my office, my driver's license was fake, my clothes had someone else's name sewed into them, where did I even go at night, where did I sleep, where was my car? She even revealed that one night she'd camped outside the building and waited for me *like some God damned stalker!* When I confronted her about it, she had no defence. She was completely gone over the edge talking about how the old manager went missing years ago and I was wearing his uniform, and no one had ever seen me outside the centre.

I'm glad she's gone now because she made me really uncomfortable with that paranoid rambling. I still don't know what she was implying. Honestly, just listening to her gave me a really bad headache with the coppery taste.

I still wonder what happened to her. But she's a good example of why we should just leave this thing alone because, sure enough, the next week I found myself fishing one of her shoes out of the ball-pit. I think what was weirdest about that was that it wasn't covered in blood, or anything like that. It just had a small note asking me, personally, for help.

She was so troubled. I tried to tell her to stop, tried to give her some clue. When I'd fired her, just before the stalking started, she had started asking me all these questions about how long I'd been working here and whether I'd seen the bottom of the ball-pit and I kept trying to tell her,

"I've been here for as long as I can remember, and I'm pretty sure the ball-pit is bottomless."

Well, now she can be sure about it too.

THIRD PARTY

"Hey Dale."

"Yes?"

My head popped up from my conversation with a young elementary school teacher. She'd spent the last thirty minutes explaining how going to a swinger party wasn't normally her thing. I'd been listening, but mostly I'd been paying attention to the delicate locks of downy blonde hair that hung around the nape of her neck.

"We could use your help. Allie thinks we've got a creeper."

"Where?" I asked.

"She's in the garage with him now."

"Sorry," I said, flashing a smile at the pretty young teacher. "This happens. I'll just go take a look and I'll be back in a bit."

She giggled some affirmation while I got up. I had to duck my way around one couple groping each other in the cramped hallway before I got there, momentarily stopping to chastise our accountant for not using a coaster on Allie's favourite coffee table. To be fair to the guy, he was getting head at the time, but the table's an import and worth a small fortune.

"She's keeping him busy."

Minnie, our neighbour, was waiting for me by the half-open door. She was a little tipsy, leaning to one side and looking awful concerned. We'd had our fair share of unpleasant guests in the past, but something about Minnie's expression worried me. When I stepped through the door, I found my wife chatting openly and laughing with Jacob and Alex nearby. She was keeping it jovial, commanding all attention with expert control. That alone let me know she'd already had to do some de-escalating.

"Hey babe," I said, stepping up and wrapping an arm around her waist. "What's up?"

"These are our new guests," she replied, gesturing to the quiet man in front of us.

He was younger than he should have been. Twenty-five, tops. Not a bad looking man by any measure, but he seemed about as comfortable as a stray cat in a dog pound. I couldn't tell if he'd noticed the ever-growing number of men around him, but I hoped not. Allie's charm offensives were so effective that most unwanted guests didn't see the door coming until it slammed in their face.

"Nice to meet you...?" I held out my hand and prayed to God this guy hadn't been jacking off.

"Francis," he replied as he shook it. His grip was limp, cold, and worryingly moist. "And this is Nadia."

Here we go, I thought as he moved aside to reveal a foldout chair and its occupant. *There's the rub.*

At a glance, it looked like just a girl in her late teens with a hoodie pulled up and over her face. It didn't take long for my eyes to correct themselves. Her frame was too slight. Her pose was too stiff. She wasn't a *she* at all. She was an *it*, a doll, and this wasn't some cheap store mannequin either. You could see the pores on her skin and a light downy hair along her exposed forearms.

Jacob and Alex snickered behind me, and who could blame them? I had to suppress a smirk myself. It got even harder when Allie gave me a nudge and told me to introduce myself, and I had to talk out loud to a fucking real doll.

"Hello Nadia," I said, biting the inside of my cheek so hard it bled.

"Sorry," Francis replied, "she's not much of a talker."

"Oh, I bet," I said, and there were more snickers from behind me. "Are you comfortable, Francis?" I asked. "We want to make sure everyone here is comfortable."

"Little nervous," he laughed, "but I'm being brave for Nadia. She's always been the adventurous one."

"How did you find out about us, Francis?" Allie asked with a gentle smile and a tilt of the head.

"Nadia knew," he replied. "She wanted to experiment, and we've been talking about opening up a little."

"It's a lot for the first time, isn't it?" Allie asked, leaning forward and touching his forearm. "A lot of new couples like to pop in and look around before committing to anything. Great fun for them, not always for the people being watched. Our lifestyle has meant we're *extra* sensitive to being put on show. We don't like to feel judged."

"Now *that* I understand," Francis laughed nervously. "My parents hated meeting Nadia."

Jacob let out what can only be described as a kind of squeal of laughter before covering it up with a burst of coughing.

"Sorry," he sputtered, "beer went down the wrong way."

He wasn't holding a drink.

"It's not good to feel judged, is it?" Allie said, stepping a little closer to Francis. Without him realising it, she began to walk him slowly to the door even as he nodded his agreement. "And it is so much to digest, all the sights and sounds here, that we have generally found it best for new young couples like yourself to look around and then go away and chew on it. Really think about what participation means."

"That makes sense," he replied.

"You can't un-fuck someone." She smiled as she lifted the doll and placed it in Francis's arms. "It's a door you can't go back through. So, given that you've spent some time with us. Both you and Nadia. It's probably a good idea for you both to give some serious thought about what you've seen. And how you feel about it."

"Oh, of course," he said. "Nadia and I will—"

The door closed, and we all returned to the party in a flurry of laughter.

———

Allie had her head on my shoulder as we watched the video on my phone.

"You could have told me I had a spot on my arse," she grumbled.

"Jacob's a cop," I said. "He's seen worse."

"How was the teacher? Was Sal her name?"

"Yeah. She made a few comments to Jordan that made him uncomfortable," I said.

"How bad was it?"

"The word *urban* was used. Obviously, Jordan's a big boy. I don't think he was too put-off by that kind of thing. But it was still pretty awkward."

"Oooph," Allie winced, closing the video on her phone and sitting upright to stretch. "I'll speak to her next time we go for lunch. That must have been as awkward as talking to Francis."

"Not quite," I winced, cringing at the memory of that strange little episode. "Poor guy. What do you think his deal was?"

"Oh, I don't know." She yawned and pushed herself up off the sofa. "I just hope he doesn't turn out to be some weirdo with night vision goggles and a crossbow."

"He *seemed* sincere," I said. "I don't know if that's reassuring or frightening."

"That he did. Utterly fucking bonkers, but sincere. Come on, let's head to bed. We've got a long day ahead of us tomorrow."

I pushed myself up and went about locking up. I pulled curtains, made sure any old cigarettes were put out, and switched a few of the hungrier appliances off at the plug. Somewhere in the bedroom Allie turned on the shower, and I decided I'd hop in and join her once I was done.

My last stop was the garage. I'd been tempted to walk past it. It was always a little too dark in there, with fluorescent lights that played havoc with the shadows. I'd often catch sight of my own eyeless reflection in my car's windshield and make myself jump, and something about the lingering impression of that damn doll meant I wanted to put the whole place as far from my mind as I could. But when I caught sight of the door at the end of that long hallway, I noticed it was slightly ajar, and a cold breeze was coming through.

Inside, I found the backdoor wide open, and the lights turned off. A cold autumn wind blew through, sending a few dry leaves skittering across the floor. Images of old slasher films came to mind and, as cheesy as they might seem, I felt afraid as I called out and waited for some sign of an intruder.

"Hello?"

No one answered, but that didn't mean no one was listening. I had the overpowering sense I wasn't alone in that room, and I turned the light on, expecting my childish fears to be dispelled. As it turned out I was both wrong and right...

"Jesus fuck—" I cried, barely managing to keep my voice from rising into a scream. Nadia, that doll, was sat across the hood of my car in a disturbingly lifelike pose. Her legs were crossed, and her head tilted to one side like a teenager waiting for her acne-faced boyfriend to get out of work. There was even a cigarette propped up between her lips.

She shouldn't have been there, of course. Not only had Francis no right to break in and leave her there, but it made no sense. The room had been dark but hardly pitch black. It was hard to imagine I could have looked at my car and not seen her, not even as a large black shadow silhouetted against the night.

"Francis?" I cried. "Francis, are you in here?"

I stepped down into the garage, and silly ideas started to rush into my head. I knew I should be looking elsewhere for that boy. I knew he must be somewhere, probably filming me so he could post the video to a shitty prank channel on YouTube. But I couldn't take my eyes off that damn doll. I kept expecting her to turn towards me. She seemed so natural sitting there, and part of me believed without a shadow of a doubt that she was waiting for me and no one else.

"I'm sorry to do this to you."

The voice that spoke was desperate. It was quiet, almost courteous, but it still touched a nerve in me, and I cried out loud,

"What the fuck!?"

My outburst was cut short. Francis stood in the doorway, blood running down his temple and his clothes torn to pieces. He was crying, his right arm shaking from the weight of a revolver clutched tightly in his fist.

"You seemed like a nice couple," he moaned. "You don't deserve any of this."

He lifted the gun and as the barrel passed over my chest, I felt my heart flutter and my peripheral vision go fuzzy. *Allie was right,* I thought. He *is a disgruntled creep and I'm going to die over some innocuous jokes—*

He put the gun to his temple and shot himself.

———

"Holy shit, that's creepy."

I noticed that when Sal spoke, the little tufts of hair under her ponytail bobbed side-to-side. There was a second where I didn't answer and only stared, trying my best to remember what exactly she'd just said.

"I don't know about creepy," I replied when I finally remembered. "I mostly feel sorry for him."

"Yeah, but he was still a murderer," Sal replied. "I read that he'd killed his parents. I mean, that's just fucked up."

"Yes, but I've kind of assumed there was something more going on there. We don't know the full story. I just can't imagine that he went so…" I stopped to make a little twirling motion at the side of my head. "…if his parents were normal."

"I guess it makes sense," Sal said, sitting back in her chair. "So you guys just upped and left for a month? I'm surprised the police let you."

"We have friends in the department. Plus, with the porch camera, there wasn't any real doubt about who did it. Best thing we could've done was just leave. Not to mention we had to hire professional crime scene cleaners. We didn't want to be here for that."

"It was that bad?" she asked.

I remembered the split-second image of his suicide that had been permanently etched into my mind. It was a blur, a mental image devoid of any real detail except the vague notion of skin breaking at supersonic speed followed by the patter of bony shards striking the wall.

"Yeah, it was that bad," I replied.

"Well, I'm glad you guys are back," Sal said, a coy smile on her lips. "I mean, after that first night was so exciting for me… I worried that maybe I wouldn't see you back here again. I felt like I got ten percent into my adventure only for it to suddenly stop."

"Just a short break," I replied. "All of that's behind us now. And you're always welcome to an adventure with us."

"Sounds like fun." She gave me a wink. "Can I ask something, though?" she said, suddenly leaning forward like a confessional.

"What's that?"

"Why'd you keep the doll?" she asked. "It gave us all a hell of a fright when we went into the garage!"

"What do we have?" Allie asked.

"Uh, so Sal saw it, as we know. Frank, Alice, Jake, Al, Jordan, Kim... pretty much anyone who, uh, *partakes* saw it when they all went out there to smoke, sometimes in ones and twos, sometimes as groups."

"And they didn't think to mention it?" she asked. "They just thought we'd kept a murderer's sex doll for... what? Shits and giggles? Did they at least see who took it? Does anyone know where the fucking thing *went* after they were finished getting baked in our garage?"

"They were just having a good time," I said, making sure to sound as calm as possible. "They weren't really thinking at all."

"*Fuck!*" Allie vented, her voice shrill and coarse. "So-so-so what? We have a stalker? Francis had a friend? Who put the fucking thing there!? What did the police say?"

Suddenly, it was like I had a belly full of loose change. I could feel my posture deflating beneath her gaze. I'd secretly been hoping she wouldn't ask, and we could avoid my troubled findings.

"Well, they were initially a little confused about what the relevance of it was."

"The *relevance!?*" she cried. "Someone put evidence from a murder scene in our house!"

"Well, here's the thing—obviously... Jacob saw the doll," I said. "He was there when we first met Francis. But, uh, as for the actual police who were on the scene afterwards... they, uh, they didn't find one."

"What?" Allie cried, her red teary eyes momentarily coming alive with fiery anger. "What does that mean?"

"The Nadia thing. It never really popped up during their investigation. I asked Jacob, and he checked. He went into the evidence locker. He asked around. He looked at all of the reports and... eighteen officers and six forensic guys and none of them saw the doll sitting on that car."

"No no no no," Allie stammered. "No, that doesn't make sense. *They* took the doll as part of the investigation. That's why it wasn't there when we got back!"

"Apparently they didn't," I said. "They assumed *we* did something about it. They were going to ask, but then they found his parents rotting away in that secret basement and it kind of got lost in all the excitement."

Allie covered her face with her hands and slowly leaned forward until her head was pressed into the table. When she finally looked up, I could see that she no longer held back her tears.

"Who took it? And who brought it back!? It wasn't Sal, was it?"

"I doubt it," I replied. "I checked the porch camera, and no one comes or goes that way all night, and it's not like she could've lugged a 60-pound doll through the house with no one noticing."

"So we've got a stalker?" Allie cried, part indignant, part terrified. "It was supposed to go back to normal, Dale. You said it would go back to normal with time and this just feels like the nightmare has started up all over again. And I still haven't heard of Jordan..."

Her voice caught a little on that last part, and it was enough to derail the pace of the conversation. For a few long seconds, the air was pregnant with a heavy silence.

"Why would you?" I asked.

"Well, normally he'd send me a text after a party."

My eyes narrowed.

"Like some memes, just jokes and stuff," she added. "Just stuff we can't say in front of the others."

"Or me, apparently."

Allie swallowed.

"Don't be like that."

For a second, my wife shrank down into a timid creature, a far cry from the strong and free-spirited woman I'd spent twenty years with. The last time I'd seen her look so small it was when she'd been slumped down in some hospital bed getting chemo. Even the slightest reminder of that time softened me up. Maybe that's why I agreed to what she asked next. "Would you mind checking on him?" she said.

"Why can't you?"

"His wife... she wouldn't like that... I mean to say that..."

"I once sat on a sofa with Jordan and watched Kim blow three guys," I snapped. "What *exactly* would she have to be jealous of between you and her husband?"

"He hasn't gotten back to me in a couple of days."

I took a deep breath and let it out slowly, if only to give myself enough time to decide a proper answer.

"What's the fucking point of the rules if you don't follow them?" I said, having failed at deciding anything. "They were *your* rules! No texting! No calling! No secret little friendships!"

"Dale," she said, shrinking even further. "Please? Please just go check on him for me? This whole doll thing just feels like a nightmare. I just want it to be over."

***

Jordan and Kim's cars were both in their driveway, but no one answered when I rang the bell. I tried a few times, even tried banging the door with my fist as hard as I could. But from the looks of it, no one was home. I was left standing there in the rain, ready to leave, when something caught my eye. I could've sworn a curtain on the upper floor moved a little, like someone was trying to sneak a peek without being seen. A part of me figured that maybe Jordan was avoiding me, even though he should've known better than to expect me to come charging over in a fit of jealousy. But another part of me wasn't so sure it was Jordan at all, and without really knowing why, I found myself feeling worried for my friends. I wanted to make sure they were okay, mostly for them, but also partly for me. I couldn't quite shake what Allie had said to me before leaving.

This whole doll thing just feels like a nightmare.

I found their backdoor open—not just ajar, but thrown wide with the lock smashed in and the top hinge broken off. With no lights on inside, it was surprisingly dark, and I struggled to make myself cross the threshold.

"Guys?" I cried, still standing in the doorway. "Anyone home?"

I wanted to phone the police… I knew I should have. But that just felt like it'd prolong the nightmare. What I really wanted was to find my friends, maybe sitting on the sofa laughing, or maybe wrapped up in bed with a stomach bug. It didn't matter. Every second since we'd met Francis, it had felt like the world was spinning too fast and my feet were leaving the ground. Reality felt thinner, almost like it was obedient to my anxieties and fears more than logic or rationality. I wanted to assert some sense back into the world. I didn't want to be afraid anymore.

So, I took a deep breath and pushed myself inside, where I quickly found that none of the lights worked and that someone had left a cup of coffee on the countertop where it now sat ice-cold. The hallway leading to the living room was almost completely dark, as was the rest of the house just beyond. The power was cut, and the heating was off, making it so cold I could see my breath.

I stepped through the kitchen and into the living room where I found the curtains drawn, but otherwise everything was in order. I had no idea what to make of it all. If it wasn't for the shoes by the front door and the cars in the drive, I would've probably guessed that the couple had gone on holiday without telling anyone.

"Hello?" I shouted, facing the general direction of the stairs.

Something *thumped* against the floor upstairs, and I was reminded of the glimmer of movement I'd seen by the front door. *It must be Jordan and Kim,* I told myself, but the words rang hollow. I tried not to listen to the part of me that began to worry. The very notion I might be in danger… It seemed to carry baggage with it.

Thoughts of stalkers, thoughts of Francis blowing his brains out and leaving me spattered with gore. And worse, thoughts of that fucking doll sitting on my car and watching me as I stammered a cry for help.

No, I decided, *they simply must be in bed.*

I was half-way at up the stairs when I heard that same *thump* again. This time I didn't cry out for my friends. I carried on upwards like some kind of clockwork soldier, having convinced myself that I'd find a sensible explanation up there. But with each step, I felt more and more like a hostage of my own rationality. *Surely it makes most sense to turn around and leave?* I asked myself.

But then the nightmare might follow, a part of me answered.

At the very top, I was met with an eerie silence and the purgatorial lighting of a rainy afternoon deep in a house with few windows. I could see that almost all the rooms were empty from where I stood. But not Jordan and Kim's bedroom, which had the door shut tight. Not the room with the window that overlooked the driveway...

Just beyond that door, something moved. I heard it. It could have been a footstep. I wasn't sure, so I cried out once more.

"Jordan, what the fuck is going on?"

There was no response.

"Fuck this," I cried, and upon hearing my own voice quiver with anxiety, I decided to try and seize some measure of control over myself. I barged through the door and right into the bedroom, ready to make any excuse necessary so long as I found my friends safe.

I think deep down I expected to find what I did, but it didn't really make it any easier to see. The room was empty, almost. No Jordan. No Kim. Their phones were on the nightstands. Their clothes lay, still crumpled, by either side of the bed. Even the duvet covers had been slid aside as if they'd only just woken up. Just around the corner, in the bathroom, I heard the faint sound of a leaky faucet dripping into a tub full of water, and I knew it must be full. But there were no living, or dead, people inside that room.

Except for Nadia, who was sat upright on a chair in the corner of the room. A latex and rubber simulation of a person, posed awkwardly upright. She was naked, and I felt a flush of revulsion at the sight of her featureless frame. Everything about her was wrong, and it made my skin crawl to see it all laid bare.

I would've left were it not for the sound of something sloshing in the tub. A thought entered my head – I wondered if perhaps Jordan and Kim had somehow kept the doll and been using to play a kind of joke. Cruel or not, I would've been relieved to know that was the case. Staring at it then as it gazed emptily at their bed, I desperately wanted to be reminded that it wasn't real. It wasn't alive or feeling. It just *was*. A piece of inert matter devoid of everything that makes you or I special and alive.

Because despite everything, it kinda looked alive. It had arms and eyes, a nose with freckles, slender fingers that sat patiently on its lap... I told myself it was some part of the old lizard brain that made me project the notion of a patient predator onto its delicate features. That was what it reminded me of... some deep-sea rock fish waiting for its prey to come floating past.

Plop.

Once again, there was that noise from the tub. The door to the bathroom was barely a metre from the doll. If I wanted to find out more, I'd have to get closer to it.

I kept my distance from the doll as I approached the door. I tried to ignore it but my nerves were up and my mind was focused on where it sat in the periphery of my vision. I could *feel* that fucking thing sitting there, like a heat source blazing away at my subconscious. It was positively radioactive in my mind, triggering every deep-seated instinct I had.

Plop.

I turned the handle and pushed the door, and found the bathroom cold and empty. Dingy looking water sat in the tub, disturbed occasionally by the leaky faucet that sent the water sloshing. I walked over and dipped my fingers into the water, finding it tepid and unwelcoming. Everything about that fucking house was cold, like it wasn't meant for human occupation anymore. I rolled up one sleeve and pulled the plug, pausing for a moment to listen to the water gurgle down the drain.

"Where are you?" I muttered quietly to myself while looking back at the empty bathroom.

"Right here."

"Jordan!?" I cried, almost bursting into laughter, ready to turn and find my friend waiting for me.

The laughter died when I saw who was really there. Nadia had moved, sitting upright on the bed and looking into the bathroom. She was not alone. Two latex figures sat beside her so that three pairs of glassy eyes faced me. One had been made to look like Jordan, the other to look like Kim, and they were all smiling and naked, their plastic limbs resting nonchalantly on each other's bodies.

"Why so shocked?"

Jordan's voice was the same, but when that plastic mouth moved to shape the words, I felt as if my feet had finally left the ground and my mind went airborne. My vision blurred and the skin on my scalp tightened like there was a big screw being turned at the back of my skull. Blood rushed from my brain and went to God-knows-where as every inch of body struggled to reject the scene before me.

"This isn't anything you haven't seen before." Kim chuckled as her head turned stiffly to face Nadia.

I snapped and ran straight through the door, desperate to escape. Only my progress was stopped partway as something wrenched at my jacket. Nadia's plastic arm had reached out and grabbed my jacket, pinning me to one spot like I was an unruly dog with a leash.

"I'll see you this weekend," she said in a husky voice. And then just like that, she let me go and my feet finally finished carrying me out of that room and out of that house, their laughter following me the entire time.

———

"I think we should cancel this weekend's party," I said as I sat opposite Allie. So far, I'd managed to avoid mentioning what I'd found to Allie, but she clearly sensed that I wasn't being honest and had been cold to me ever since. I thought she figured I was hiding something about Jordan, maybe that I'd gone and told Kim and gotten her little friend in trouble.

"I don't want to," Allie replied. She'd spent the last hour sat on the sofa with her knees pulled up to her chest. "I don't like the way this place feels when it's empty."

"I think we should go away again," I said. "We've got the money. We've got the time."

Allie looked at me and almost smiled.

Almost.

"What?" I asked.

"I don't want to do another two weeks in some rainy flat with you," she replied. "Just hiding from all our problems."

"I thought it was quite nice," I said. "Just you and I."

"Dale, we both know neither of us signed up to living in each other's pockets," she said. "I like our life, as it is... I don't want to leave it behind for what could be months, maybe even years."

"No one's even replied in the group chat," I told her. "We don't actually know if anyone's coming this Saturday."

"They're grownups," Allie replied. "They know it's every other weekend. It's not like we need them to RSVP."

"No one is this quiet for this long," I said.

"Well, they're our neighbours, aren't they?" she cried. "Sal lives like eight doors down. Jacob's around the corner and you saw him a few days ago. Just go knock and see what they're doing."

"Sal?"

I knocked on the door and waited, looking anxiously in the direction of Jacob's house. I'd last spoken to him in a panicked phone call after seeing Jordan. He'd come quickly to where I'd pulled over on the side of the road and was mostly a good friend. I say mostly... I asked him to make an official report on what I'd seen, to go get help from his friends in the station. He'd refused, looking at me in a kind of sad way that broke my heart, like I was an elderly dog that was due one last trip to the vet.

After that, he stopped returning my calls.

"Sal!?" I cried, suddenly desperate to break my train of thought. "Sal, please open the door?"

No one came, but on a hunch, I tried the handle and the door opened easily.

Inside, I found a familiar scene. The rooms were cold. The curtains drawn. There were a few signs of an early morning start for the young teacher who lived there. A blouse was hung up on the kitchen door next to an opened ironing board. A mug sat by the kettle with a teabag already inside. And the washing machine door was open, with a few damp towels left to dry on a nearby clothes' horse.

"Sal!?"

This time I didn't shout. It was more of a whimper. Something was wrong, and I already knew what. I could feel it in the air. Upstairs, I found two locked doors, not one. And I was reminded that Sal shared a rental with her close friend, who she'd talked about a fair bit. I hoped to God that both of them were safe.

I tried the nearest door, and for the first time since entering, I felt something like relief. There was no one there, just a rumpled bed and a few photos of Sal, and some people who bore a family resemblance to her. Without meaning to, I laughed, and began to seriously entertain the notion that I really had been seeing things back in Jordan's house. Seeing that young man's death had left me seriously on edge. Maybe everything I'd seen had just been trauma? For weeks, it had felt like my mind was fraying at the corners. And while this line of thinking was hardly comforting, it did give me the courage to try the final door.

"Oh, shit!" I cried, shocked and embarrassed at the sight of a naked young woman standing with her back to me. I immediately pulled the door shut and began to stammer out an apology. "Oh Jesus! I didn't mean to break in! I'm just a friend of Sal's and the door was open, and I had this ridiculous idea that something bad had happened to her and..."

Slowly, it dawned on me there'd been no cry or gasps or shouts. I'd never met Sal's friend, but whoever was in that room, their reaction to having their privacy invaded by a total stranger hadn't been to scream or threaten me with the police. It had been silence.

Well, I realised as I held my breath and listened, *not quite silence.* Something was creaking on the other side of the door, like wood under strain. It made me think of tightening rope and badly-oiled metal.

"Are you okay?" I asked as I opened the door and saw once more the young woman standing naked with her back to me. Her downy blonde hair was short and messy, but something about her was all-too familiar. I figured it couldn't have been Sal, despite the resemblance. She was too different, as if she was Sal reduced. Her waist shrunk down. Her shoulders made diminutive. Gone were the faint dimples along her thighs and bum, the faint blue webbing of veins by her ankles. Everything I saw now was smooth and blemish free. So grossly devoid of character as to betray itself as dead and lifeless, a homogenous slab of nothing carved to look human.

"S-s-sal?" I stammered.

She turned to face me, her head rotating effortlessly without her shoulders or feet having to move.

"What an adventure!" she giggled, bending one elbow in the wrong direction to have a hand awkwardly cover her mouth. Her eyes, enlarged to the size of golf balls, moved independently to look at me.

"What happened!?" I cried.

"Would you like a threesome!?" she cried in an infantile voice. "My friend and I are ever so keen!"

There was maybe half-a-second between her shrill giggle and her launching herself over the bed and right at me. Even with my hand already on the handle, and with my nerves so fraught that my reaction was lightning fast, she reached the door before I had time to slam it. Three fingers that looked like cheap Halloween decorations poked through, and she wrenched the door back open with such little effort that I was thrown head-long into the room with it.

"Come see her!" she screamed, grabbing me by the hair and lifting me. Somehow, even though I'm not a small guy, she lifted me off the floor and walked me into the bathroom, where she showed me what she had trapped in the tub.

"She's the shy one!" Sal said, tilting her head to one side in some twisted affectation.

Jesus... I stopped struggling when I saw what lay in the bath. There was a young woman pinned down beneath what looked like sheets of heavy skin-coloured rubber. Silently she writhed beneath a sloshing mixture of featureless flesh and discoloured blood that coagulated along the edges. Two red, swollen eyes pled with me for help, like she wanted to scream but couldn't. With mounting horror, I realised why.

She wasn't *beneath* the sheet of rubber. She *was* the sheet of rubber, or at least bits of her were. Where it buried itself into her skin, it would melt what came beneath in what must have been an agonising process of slowly flaying flesh. She could not scream be-cause her mouth had been lost to the biological stew that consumed her, and even as I looked, a fake-looking pair of lips rose up from the clay-like substance that engrossed her and smiled.

"You are so handsome!" It cooed. "Can I call you master!?"

Something about it... about the words. It broke me. I no longer tried to unfurl Sal's cold fingers from my hair. Instead, I grabbed her wrist and pulled, deliberately tearing a massive chunk of my scalp free in the process. It hurt like nothing else I'd ever felt, but it was worth it just to feel my feet touch solid ground. Sal made no effort to grab me.

"See you at the party!" she cried.

"Oh, I am *so* excited for the party!"

I nervously combed over my hair for the thirtieth time, hoping the patch missing from my scalp wouldn't be too noticeable.

"Why don't you pop down and see how everyone's doing?"

I'd been dreading this for quite some time.

"I thought I'd wait for you to finish getting ready?" I cried. Hearing how close my voice was to breaking made me wonder how I would possibly make it through the night.

"Oh, don't be silly!" Allie laughed as she shuffled about in the bathroom. "Go on. I'm sure Sal's waiting for you. You two have been getting on like a house on fire lately, haven't you?"

Gently I touched my head and winced.

"I suppose."

I straightened out my shirt and opened our bedroom door. The sound of clinking of glasses and braying laughter from the guests downstairs reached me in the hallway and I stopped, momentarily taken aback by how easily things might seem normal.

"Don't keep them waiting!"

Allie sounded tense as she slammed the door shut behind me.

I straightened my shirt once more as a nervous gesture before taking the stairs. The first guest I encountered was Minnie, sitting on the bottom step with a glass of wine beside her.

"H-h-having a good night?" I asked.

She rotated her head stiffly and looked at me with lifeless eyes. Burgundy-painted lips curled upwards in a mischievous smile as she winked at me. When she went to raise her dress with rubber fingers, I turned away and rushed out of her reach.

"Let me find you another drink!" I cried, desperate to make any excuse I could.

In the dining room, I found Jacob and Alex watching their wives caress and kiss each other, their plastic limbs squeaking under the friction. When they noticed me, all four of them turned in silent judgement and stared. None of them spoke. They only smiled, waiting for me to join in.

Unsettled by their gaze, I hurried away, stumbling across one bizarre scene after another. All of our friends had come, and the party was in full swing. People kissed each other hungrily and fucked openly in the corridors. Plastic toes and fingers explored rubber joints, and frighteningly lifelike bodies leered at me with suggestive thrusts. Not all the bodies were anatomically correct... it seems imagination had started to overtake the reality of the human form, and I was left reeling from one room after another as I fought to hold off a full-blown mental breakdown. It was a living nightmare and without realising it, I shepherded myself away from one grotesque orgy after another until, somehow, I stumbled through the garage door and slammed it shut behind me.

"Oh, I am so glad you're here!"

The voice was all-too-familiar.

Nadia was sat on her little foldout chair, as disgustingly realistic as she had been the very first time I met her.

"I was afraid Allie wouldn't convince you to keep the party going."

"No no no no no," I sobbed.

"Yes yes yes," she said, her monotone words dripping with sarcasm.

"What the fuck are you?" I cried.

"I don't know," she said, and this time she genuinely seemed a little sad. "I clawed my way out from that basement, thinking I was free, but... I was already dead. I didn't even get to take my body with me." Gingerly she touched a finger to her own face, depressing the plastic to make a little dimple. "I had to get a new one. It's not always *God* who answers prayers, you know? Just ask Allie when you see her. It was *her* cancer that called to me. I was hardly the answer she wanted."

"No. S-s-s-she beat it," I said. "That was... Jesus, that was over fifteen years ago."

"Now you're being deliberately dense." Nadia shook her head. "They say remission for a reason, Dale. They don't say *cured*. It had come back, and it was tearing through her one organ at a time, and she could feel it. So could I, for that matter. I decided to offer her the one thing *I* never had. Never. Not once. I offered her a choice. A way out. Not the ideal way. But at least the party could keep on going."

From behind me, the door opened and closed, briefly letting in a flourish of the nightmare that still raged on.

The hand that rested on my shoulder was cold and firm.

It was also plastic.

"Hi Allie," Nadia said. "How do you like it?"

"I feel cold."

"Well, you better find someone to warm you up," Nadia replied while winking at me. The hand on my shoulder tightened.

When I risked a backwards glance, Allie looked down with eyes that curdled my blood.

"Did you really sell yourself to this monster?" I asked.

"No," she said, and for a second, I could see that her eyes were almost overcome with heartbreak. That only made the words that followed a thousand times more painful.

"She sold *you*, Dale," Nadia said, rising out of her chair and walking towards me. "I'd like to meet new people. And I'd like these parties to keep on going for as long as they can. Arrangements must be made, Dale, and having you around to bring new faces and keep the old ones happy... well, it was just about the *only* thing your wife could offer."

Nadia bent down and stroked my face.

"You know Francis was right about one thing...

"You are a nice couple."

DO NOT PRAY TO THE GOD IN THE DESERT

*N*othing gives us the right to be this cruel

The words greet me every day on my way to work. It takes me two hours of driving alone through the desert to reach the abandoned chicken farm where they are sprawled across the front entrance. Used to be they had a driver pick me up and take me, but after Hector, I asked them to stop sending one. I liked Hector and didn't fancy going through it all again. Besides, I've been doing the job long enough so they can trust me. Don't need anyone standing over my shoulder. Most people they tried getting to do this job didn't stick to it more than a few weeks. Some found it too boring. Others found it a little too exciting.

Job's easy enough *if* you have the right frame of mind. All I gotta do is paint a wall. It's not far from the farm, technically on the land, but in reality belonging to the desert. Ten feet by ten feet. A slab of solid stone. Every day I drive out and paint that wall top to bottom with a mixture of resin and tar. I try not to think of who put the wall out here, just like I try not to think why a non-existent branch of the US government pays me six figures to paint it. But I do know I ain't hired to paint this thing for aesthetics. I'm hired to cover whatever's under there. Whatever's drinking the resin and tar I slap all over it day after day because even though I've been doing this for twenty-five years, when I come round every morning, I can see the last coat starting to fade away like it's been on there a hundred years. So I paint it again. Cover it top to bottom. Day after day.

Something's on the other side and it's drinking the foul concoction layer by layer.

I try not to think about it.

Whoever's paying me to do this has the right idea. Paint the wall. Forget about it. Don't dwell on it. Just cover the fucking thing, keep whatever's lurking under all that heavy tar out of sight and out of mind. People come sometimes and make offerings to the wall and that's a bad idea. If they come at daytime, I shoo them away, but it don't always work. I tell them not to pray to the wall. It only brings bad luck, but they do anyway. They kneel in front of it, heads pressed to the sand, and they pray to that rotten slab of stone, thinking it was sent by a loving God. After that they drive away and if I'm lucky, I never hear from them again.

If I'm unlucky, they're on the news the next day, what's left of them. Sometimes they come at night to make their little offerings. I know they've been because their cars are still here come morning. No sign of the pilgrims though, just the trinkets and prayer beads they leave behind. Maybe some scuffled sand in front of the wall or a trail of clothes leading into the desert. One time there was a baby carrier but no baby. Used to be I'd call the cops, and they'd come tow the cars away and file missing persons reports, but now they tell me to just roll the cars out the way so they can come get them at a later time. Only they never do. I park them up a quarter mile out West and I'd say there's about a couple hundred of them out there now. It'd be a pain to store them if there weren't so much room.

No one's running out of desert.

The cars sit squat and idle in the heat, day in, day out, faded pastel paint jobs robbed of their gloss by the harsh desert winds. Fuzzy dice. Key chains that jingle still hanging from the ignition. Tiny virgin Mary figurines glued to the dashboard. Hector used to take spare parts from them, but he stopped after the third accident. Eventually came to the conclusion the parts were cursed like everything else around here. It's that wall. It hurts everything around it. Even the soil is poisoned. Wouldn't surprise me if it's the real reason there's a desert here. Ain't nothing to do with geography. It's the wall sucking the life outta everything around it like a black hole.

Just look at the old chicken farm with its gates covered in graffiti. It's where I lunch, where I park my car up under the shelter of old corrugated roofs. The owner didn't think anything of taking his business out here. Thought the heat and the isolation would make it harder for the animal rights activists to follow, but it only pissed them off more. Like so many others, he saw the free-standing slab of cement in the middle of the desert and figured it was a quirk. A remnant of a forgotten building that just so happened to be on his land. Didn't realise it was a poison well that would leave him hanging in a rundown jailhouse.

The fire that shut the farm wasn't even that big, but a fire doesn't have to be big when it starts in a room with four thousand chickens and a couple hundred men and women, many of whom don't speak English. Didn't stop the two supervisors in there from screaming at them like they did, throwing fuel on the panic and making it a hundred times worse. Add on the fact the fire exit was padlocked and very few made it out alive. The crematorium soot that now carpets the floor absorbs any sound you make as you walk. Lends the place the hushed vibes of an old church. Can't escape the feeling that something in there don't wanna be disturbed.

The owner blamed the activists who protested there every single day. Said he had to lock the door to keep them out. If there'd been plenty of survivors, he might've gotten away with that kind of excuse. But as it was, only forty people made it out alive, so they pretty much had to throw the book at him. They even reckon someone fell in the macerator during the panic. The gnarly looking machine they used to churn up male chicks, so no meat went to waste. I looked into it once and noticed a lot of the blades were chipped and broken, like something a little too heavy for the machine's specifications fell in. It wasn't built for something as big as a person. The motors would have struggled. The blades would have dug in only so far before stalling and trying again and again and again...

Removing him would've been like clearing a paper jam. It would've been better to just go through all the way in a single go. Head first. At least that's what I think.

When I asked around, some of the workers remembered the wall. Always visible against the wavering lines of the heat-struck floor like a little door to nowhere. It's funny. If you press people on it, they'll say it's just brick and mortar, some old building that didn't get torn down properly. But they'll change the subject quickly. Won't postulate on its origins for longer than a second at most. At least I found that even back in the day there was a guy who hauled ass up there to paint the thing top to bottom. Just goes to show this job of mine goes back a while.

The wall spoke to Hector before he went missing. It's spoken to me a few times too, usually in the morning when I first arrive and haven't had time to apply a new coat of tar. It's a struggle not to listen, but Hector found it harder than most. Something about that farm just bothered him, made him easy pickings. He hated it. Hated what it represented. Industrial farming. Humans at our worst. You'll know what he means if you ever see one of these places up close. Those cages, thousands of them all lined up in row after row, they're still there and the fire didn't burn it all away. You can smell the rot of infection on them. Sickly sweet and foul. Feathers still clinging to rusted metal bars, living things pressed in so close the wire frame metal would sometimes flay the skin like cheese wire and leave raw, swollen flesh exposed to hot desert air.

Hector said the wall put that idea in the farmer's head and from there it spread across the world. When I argued that people have never needed help being cruel, that we as a species have been fucking evil for a lot longer than the wall's been around, he pointed out that I didn't know how old it really was. Maybe it's been standing for as long as we have, leaking its infection into our species like a splinter in hot flesh. I don't know why, but that scared me. The thought of my neolithic ancestors banging rocks together while that thing stood alone in a desert half-way round the world just waiting for me to come to it. Knowing that the tumbling passage of history would eventually bring the two of us together. That whole line of thinking scares me shitless.

Something about the wall broke Hector, but out of all of us, I think he understood it the most. At first, he thought it was a joke. Spent months pouring over the farm obsessed with finding cameras. He later admitted he was having nightmares. So was I. But they fucked with him something special, left him sobbing on the bathroom floor while his two little girls and wife struggled to understand what was changing the man they loved. He would've given anything to find out it was all a hoax, that he'd just let his imagination get to him and that the dreams didn't really mean anything. Never told me what he saw in those dreams, but if they were anything like mine, they were shapeless narratives of violation that left him squealing like a pig in his bed, drenched in sweat and piss.

Despite all this, he lasted the longest of any driver I ever had. It was like that thing had its hooks in him good and proper and it wasn't gonna let him off easy. Most guys who had the job before him simply disappeared. The very first guy was like that. He was a big man and much older than me. This was back when I first got the job, when no one was sure I'd last at the job and the driver was there to make sure I actually painted the damn wall and didn't run off screaming into the desert after the first five minutes. Part-bouncer, part-chauffer, he would stand behind me with arms crossed and a cigarette between his lips. On the eleventh day he left me so he could go take a piss and never returned. He couldn't have been twenty feet behind me and there wasn't so much as a peep to indicate a struggle. All I found of him was a wet patch of sand, two footprints shoulder-width apart and a strip of skin about a foot long that could've come from anywhere.

Most of them don't even leave that much behind. Sometimes they get bored and go exploring only to never come back. Other times they'll turn a corner as they walk just ahead of me and when I catch up, there's just empty air where they were standing seconds before. Not all of them are that quick and clean, though. A few have left big messes. By far the worst was Hector's predecessor. Didn't even last two days. Silly man took his friends up to the farm at night. *Camped in it.* Showed them the wall and let them all get drunk and play games.

When he didn't turn up for work that morning, I drove myself up and found the remnants of their little party. One guy, still alive, was using the beak snipper to amputate his arm one inch at a time. Little cubes of himself lay at his feet, many of them still moving. Another, some poor girl, was all tied up in the outer fence. At first it looked like she'd tried running and got tangled in the waist-high wires, but when I got closer, I saw that a whole load of the stuff had been bunched up and was now running through her mouth and out the other end. No sign that it was ever removed from the post, so God knows how it got worked through her digestive tract like that, but at least she was dead by the time I found her. Although judging by the finger marks she left in the sand, she'd hung there suspended for a good while, scrabbling at the dirt, desperate for purchase.

The worst was the girl who'd been crammed into the cages, and I do mean plural. One cage, less than one foot square, had her torso all bent up and crammed in there. Wireframe squeezing her belly fat and making shallow cuts that repeated over and over like the lines of a sketch. Another cage had her right arm, head, neck and shoulder. The ball and socket joint was dislocated so badly it nearly broke the skin. Beside it was another cage with her other arm and most of her back that had been whipped so bad there was hardly any skin left. Another cage had her pelvis. All in all, she was split across eight, maybe nine cages, some of which were all the way on the other side of the room.

And somehow, I don't know how... *she was still alive.* All of her. All of her at once. She was like a doll that'd been taken apart. I don't know it was possible. She was even stroking her own face with an arm that wasn't attached no more, the fingers reaching through the bars as she quietly snivelled and sucked on her thumb. Broken glassy eyes fixed on me, but there was nothing behind them except despair.

And the driver... All I found of him was a single foot sticking outta the wall. Acting on instinct, I grabbed his ankle and pulled, and the damn thing came away like I was carving up a well-cooked turkey. It just fell off, leaving a little bloodied nub of leg sticking out of the tar that kept on wiggling, letting me know its poor owner was well aware of what had just happened. There was no helping him though, I knew that much. So I called my boss to pick up the others and got to work on my job because something that boy had done had agitated the wall. The tar was fading fast, like water on hot sand, and I knew that if too much of the stonework underneath got exposed, then it'd be all over for me. So I grabbed my tools and got to work and tried to ignore the way what was left of his leg would thrash every time the hot brush touched it.

Stayed like that for weeks, wriggling each time I painted the wall. You'd figure he'd suffocate or die of thirst eventually, but no, his leg just faded slowly over the course of a month or two, sensitive to the brush right till the end.

If I had to guess, he's still on the other side.

That's its secret, you see. The walls. Just one of many secrets it has, but that's the one it plies you with and it's the one that *works*. Mortality is just a bit of clay for it to play with. Life. Death. Don't mean nothing to what's on the other side. Hector told me he was a God-fearing man. Told me death didn't scare him. But the wall doesn't brook fables and fairytales. You try standing in front of it and saying you don't fear death because you're gonna go up to some grand old VIP afterparty where humanity's long-lost dad'll keep you safe, and you'll feel the faith just drain right outta you.

And in its place, there's the wall and the things it can show you.

It took Hector's faith. First time I told him there's nothing after death, he called me a cynic. Two years of staring at that wall, at the shifting patterns in the obsidian filth, he changed his tune. Told me nothing was the best we could hope for. Told me he saw what was really waiting for us, got shown it in his dreams. I knew what he meant. I'd been there too. Glimpses of what waits for us after death. Makes the things we do to our livestock seem gentle. It's nothing but filth and misery. Subservience and suffering. A despair that stretches out in all directions, past, present, future. It consumes it all. Time has no meaning in those nightmares. It's like tracing a mobius strip with your finger.

I wanted to say the wall was lying, but... well, those dreams... it didn't *feel* like a lie.

I knew things were bad when Hector started driving up on his own. I'd turn up and find him there, just sat in front of it. He didn't whisper or pray. I guess at this stage he was just listening to find out more. Bargaining. Negotiating. If I had even the slightest idea what he was planning...

I'm not sure how he even found the barrels, but he did. I turned up one day, and he was there sitting cross-legged with a massive steel drum barrel laid out horizontally just in front of him. I knew the story behind those barrels, just like I knew it ended with them being welded shut, padlocked, driven out ten miles into the desert and buried as deep as ten men could dig in a single day. How the fuck he got one out and rolled it all the way back to the farm I'll never know, but the sight of it turned my blood to ice.

"Hector," I said as I wandered over, "you need to step away from that thing."

"You know what it is."

He didn't ask. He just knew.

"Yeah," I said. "You know, I dug around a bit back in the day. Got a lot of stories about this place."

"Never told me this one."

"Didn't want to," I replied.

"Tell me now."

"I don't..."

"If you tell me, I'll leave. If you don't, I'm going into my truck and getting my tools and I ain't leaving till it's opened."

Something about the way he spoke let me know he was telling the truth.

"Alright," I said. "It's just a story, that's all. Those barrels were left behind from the farm," I told him. "Back when it was still up running, they'd take all the chicken shit, pack it up, and sell it on to other farms who used it for fertiliser. This stuff would spend weeks baking in the desert heat sealed in metal barrels before it finally got put on a truck and sold. It wasn't a priority. Just a cost-cutting measure. Loading them up on a pickup truck that came once a month was the sorta job they gave to newbies or guys who didn't look busy enough when the owner came round. Usually it was a group job, but one poor guy had the bad luck of being called up on a particularly hot day to do the loading all by himself. Maybe he pissed his supervisor off. Maybe the usual guys were off sick, and they were shorthanded. Doesn't matter. Poor fucker spent hours all on his own round back of the farm, away from all packaging and processing and all that noise, struggling with these big old barrels full of rancid chicken shit.

"Each one damn near took him fifteen minutes to move," I said. "Terrible job, and he had no help. He was about half-way through it and struggling with one particular barrel, doing his best to lift it onto the truck with the hot metal pressed against his face, when he heard something, he'd never heard before. A little *tap tap tap* coming from the inside. His first reaction was to cry out and drop the drum, letting it hit the sand with a bassy thud. By the time the dust had settled, all he could really think was that it was good no one was around to hear him shriek like a little girl. He laughed it off, as you do. Figured it must've been something that had come loose and was knocking about. A bit of metal off the rim, maybe. So, he took a breath and was just about ready to bend over and get back to the job when it happened again.

"*Tap tap tap.*

"This time he kept his composure, but the fear stuck around. Something about the rhythm of the knocks didn't sound right. He froze. Couldn't bring himself to get any closer. He just stared at the thing, sweat running off his brow as the seconds ticked on. He was thinking something crazy. He knew it was nuts, and he knew it was only really bothering him because he was all alone, and his imagination was running wild. Whatever was making that noise it couldn't be anything to worry about, he told himself. That barrel had been filled and sealed three weeks before. Nothing... *nothing* could be alive in there. So, to put this idea out of his head, to prove his own imagination wrong, he walked up to the barrel and with a curled knuckle he rapped out the first part of two shaves and a haircut.

"*Tap tap-tap tap!*

"And when he heard a response...

"*Tap tap!*

"...that was when he started screaming like crazy. Drew the other workers over and when they heard it too, they decided to call the cops. The official story was that those men turned up and found a body. A vagrant, they reckoned, who'd tried sleeping in one of the barrels but had the misfortune to still be there, passed out from booze, when it got filled up and the poor fucker drowned without ever coming to. The tapping sound was just his head knocking against the inside of the barrel.

"It's just another story of suffering," I added as the silence drew on. "The wall attracts them. You know that. Lots of people die around that thing. Accidental deaths that are nasty as hell, but accidental nonetheless."

"There's more to it than that," Hector muttered, his voice dry and hoarse but strangely loud in the silence of a desert morning. "When it was all done, they shut the farm down for the day and those police and a couple of strong workers drove every barrel in that shipment out into the desert and buried them deep, deep down in the middle of nowhere. Now why would they do that?"

He laughed, and he'd never looked so crooked and broken in his life. He looked ill and my heart sank just to see it.

"Hector…"

He was still laughing when he raised a fist and struck the side of the barrel.

Thump thump thump!

Silence. He stopped laughing. I couldn't bring myself to move a muscle. I was so scared. We both just waited for the inevitable.

Thump thump thump!

There was no denying where that sound came from. Something had responded from inside the barrel. Coulda sworn that knocking sound echoed around the empty valley so loud it shook the sand beneath my feet. The kinda hollow booming that swallows you up whole. Felt like it took a whole minute just for the echo to die down.

"Fucking vagrant." Hector chuckled as he stood up. "Weren't no vagrant. Weren't nothing so simple. It was an acolyte. A follower. He crawled in and waited on purpose because of what the wall had told him."

"Hector, you're fired," I said, certain that I should've done this a while ago, but he just laughed so hard he was nearly sick.

"Fine! Fuck you too," he said. "It enjoys it, you know? The wall. We ain't tricking it or trapping it doing what we do. We think we can keep it at bay by what, covering the doorway? It *likes* it. It likes that we come out here and that we do this to it. It's like fucking foreplay for the thing."

"You've got kids, Hector, a family. Just go home. I'll take it from here."

"Tell me the rest," he said. "You know the rest of the story. Tell me."

"I think you already know," I replied.

"*Tell me!*" he screamed, and his fists clenched. Hector was a wiry guy, but I knew he had a history that made men like me look soft and gentle. Time had smoothed out his rough edges, and at heart he was a decent guy. But he was a fighter, an experienced one, and I had no hopes of beating him.

"Alright," I said. "You're right. I spoke to the cops. I found them and spoke to them, and they told me what they saw. They told me that they took the call and made the long drive out here, not expecting much. First thing they saw when they turned up was just some poor guy in his undies out front being comforted by half-a-dozen workers. He'd pissed himself and they didn't have clean clothes. Cops thought this was pretty funny, but the owner of the farm was nearby, and he seemed to take it seriously, so they thought they'd at least give it a look around. They walked out back, found the drum and a crowbar, and pried it open. Not wanting to actually look inside, they kicked it over, a baking hot barrel of chicken shit, and emptied its contents onto the bone-dry desert floor."

Hector seemed to get excited by this part of the story and he seized the opportunity to finish it for me.

"And as they watched the bubbling brown goo disperse into nothing, they saw it," he hissed gleefully. "A nightmare. A skeleton of a man, his flesh steaming and skinless. A living figure who was somehow, against all odds, alive and reaching for his throat, gasping desperately. Those cops stood frozen with terror as they watched the man clear his own windpipe, digging shit out of his oesophagus with his fingers, before he took a desperate breath and started screaming. And screaming. Gibbering and howling and not just about nothing either. He told them about the dark secrets he'd learned as his flesh fermented in oily shit. Secrets about that desert, about the world and man and his place in it, and the doorway not far from where they stood that could tell them all about it if they only wanted to look.

"It's right fucking there!" he screamed so loud that he went red in the face. "A way out. The wall is the *only* thing that can stop us from dying and crossing over into that fucking endless nightmare."

"It's a trick," I said. "You can't trust that thing."

"I don't have to," he said in a dreamy whisper. "I've seen it. And if you were honest, you'd at least admit it scared the shit out of you too. There ain't no fucking heaven and hell. There's just that fucking farm only we're inside the cages, and our cruelty doesn't even compare to theirs. Death is just a fancy idea they put into our head for fun. *This...*" he gestured to the desert around us, "*this* is a fucking dream and it's not even a good one. A rock in the middle of an infinite abyss? The smartest, strongest animal alive. Build skyscrapers. Build space stations. A little garden of Eden just for us. It's a joke! They're laughing at us. They want it to hurt when we finally wake up. The best any of us can hope for is to put as much as space between us and what's on the other side. Every second spent *here* and not *there* is a golden victory to be treasured. That's what that man came out of the barrel to scream about. That's the secret he was telling those workers.

"He was saying *get in the fucking barrel too, because it's better than what's waiting for us.*"

And with that desperate breathy rant, he gave up, doubled over, vomited what looked like the same tar and resin we painted the wall with and passed out. I could tell by the way he shivered and went all pale he needed to see a doctor. Something perverse was going on inside of him. I dragged him to my car, loaded him up, and drove him to the hospital. All the while doing my best to ignore the fact that I'd left the wall looking pretty bare. By the time I got him there and spoke to the doctors, it was already two in the afternoon. But I couldn't just leave him to rot in the waiting room. I had to get him set up, and it was only then, when the day was already reaching four o'clock, that I managed to get out of the hospital and back in my car.

I drove through the desert at a reckless speed. I'd never let the wall go more than twenty-four hours without another lick of paint. This job was about more than the money. It was about keeping something locked in. Something so dangerous it had already poisoned the lives of hundreds, and I knew it could poison so much more if allowed to.

The sun was already setting by the time I arrived. Strange lights blared from the farm, noises that sounded like celebration and hysterical screams, so I swerved to avoid it entirely. I came off the road and mounted the desert itself, veering around the farm and heading straight towards the wall. When I found it, it glowed black in the darkness. I don't know how else to describe it. It glowed a sort of radiant oily darkness. A shadow within a shadow.

The drum was where we'd left it, only now it was shaking like crazy. I did my best to ignore it as I grabbed my tools from the car and began to paint the wall lit only by headlights. Up close, it looked a funny sort of white. I mean, it was black, but it was like it was lit up from within by a different light, something else underneath it. Never seen it look like that. Made me think of the moon. Pale dust and craggy features glimpsed from afar. I never painted the fucking thing so fast in my entire life. I practically threw the brush around like a knife and towards the end, as I started to feel a sort of tingling electric charge in the air that scared the living shit out of me, I gave up on the brush entirely and just grabbed cans of paint whole and threw them on there.

It was a messy job, but in the end, it seemed to work. The air calmed down. The lights from the farm faded. And when I looked back at the wall, it looked like just that, a wall with a bad paint job. It had all happened so fast and in such a rush I didn't even notice I had burns all over my hands just from letting them get close to it. Hurt like hell as the adrenaline rush faded, but it was fucking worth it just to close that thing up before it got any worse.

I started to laugh. I'd never had a close call like that. Never let it go that long without a coat. The relief was almost orgasmic, even if I'd fucked up my hands and ruined my car's suspension.

I was still laughing when the lid popped off the drum behind me.

Jesus Christ, the noise as it emptied... I stood facing the wall and just listened to that god awful sound. *Gloop gloop gloop...*

When the smell hit me, I knew I'd have to turn around. I did so only to find myself blinded by my car's lights. *Dumbass,* I thought to myself. I couldn't see shit and I had no torch, either. But the faint sound of something groaning and thrashing let me know I wasn't alone. I sprinted to the car and dived in through an open window. I was upright and in the driver's seat before I even had time to think and next thing you know I was looking up at the wall, lit by my car's lights, and in full view like it was showing off, I saw what had come out of the barrel.

The stories didn't do it justice.

Decay is transformative. All death becomes new life. You ever seen what happens to a whale at the bottom of the sea? But death, decay, even as it fertilises and nourishes, it is still at its core entropic. Something organised becomes disorganised. The body turns to mulch, even if for a while it flourishes with the new life of maggots, worms, bacteria, and fungi. It's an arrow. It goes from A to B. But the thing in front of me, the man who had stewed in oxygen-deprived animal shit for two decades... it was like that arrow had become a circle. Like the maggots and the fungi had fed freely but he had stayed *organised.* He had not dissipated or dissolved.

He was alive.

And he was screaming.

And he ran, still screaming, right towards me and I managed to fumble one foot onto the accelerator just in time to realise I'd never put the car in reverse. The car jerked forward, hit him hard enough to prove what was stronger, and by the time I backed up all that was left was a smear on the hood the colour of a smoker's spit, and what looked like strips of beef jerky in gravy strewn all over the desert floor.

He kept screaming even as I backed up and fled. I kept the car in reverse for a full two miles before I finally calmed myself enough to pull over and turn it around. Without even realising it, I drove the rest of the way to the hospital to check on Hector. By the time some kind of lucidity came back to me, I was sat beside him with my head in my hands, wondering if it was time to call up my boss and tell them to find another idiot to do this job.

"Are you his family?"

I looked up and saw a doctor looking at me.

"No," I replied. "I gave the hospital his wife's contact details when I dropped him off earlier."

"Oh," the doctor mused. "Hmmm. He hasn't had any visitors. You sure you gave them to front desk? Maybe check the details are right. The infection in his blood is serious, and if he has family, they really ought to know where he is."

"No one's visited him?" I asked. "His phone... no one's called it? No one's come looking for him?"

The doctor shrugged and shook their head.

"You're right," I muttered. "Must've given the wrong number. I'll go check on it now."

The doctor accepted this and left me and Hector alone. I took out my phone a couple of times. Thought about calling his wife's number but I wasn't sure I wanted to know the truth. I knew for a fact it was the right one. He used it all the time to call me all the time when his own didn't work, which was often.

"What the fuck have you done..." I whispered to myself as I stared at her number.

"I found a way."

Hector was awake, his eyes fixed at the ceiling but glassy and blank. He didn't look at me, not even when he kept talking.

"What did you do?"

"I prayed to the god in the desert," he said. "And it was kind enough to show me a way. Not for me, but for *them*."

I could've died of heartbreak looking at him there and then. He was broken. The wall could've just taken him like the others, but it didn't and somehow that was worse, seeing him reduced and made so low. I didn't speak to him again. I left him there in the hospital. I don't even know if he died or if he's slinking around the streets doing God knows what. When I returned to the desert the next day, I found the remnants of the old barrel and the stain on the sand from its contents. What was left of the man inside had been scattered by the wind and scavengers.

Back on the farm, I found what Hector had left behind. Three barrels, brand new. One big, two small. Nothing like the old ones. He'd sourced these himself. It was on a dark impulse that I took out my phone and tried his wife's number. Shouldn't have been surprised when I heard it ring on the inside, a muted digital tinkling. The sound woke up the woman inside and the barrel shook as its contents tried violently to escape. But they'd already been in there for a day, stewing in God knows what because it wasn't like Hector could've used chicken shit. And the wall wasn't far away, its effect radiating out as surely as heat from a fire. They couldn't be alive in there... not *alive,* as you or I understand it. They belonged to the wall now, and like everything else about it, they'd be best forgotten about.

So I called my boss, and we organised another dig out in the desert.

And when we were done, I painted the wall.

CLAY

"You can understand why we weren't exactly expecting this."

Dr Greaves had been talking for hours, but I'd barely been listening. I was fixated on the windswept arctic plain beneath me. The turbulence this low down was rough, and the inside of the plane was close to freezing. But the view it offered was astonishing. It was like looking down on an alien world; an infinite white sheet broken by gargantuan clumps of black volcanic rock.

"Most of the team down there are geologists and meteorologists, so for the longest time they never really considered the possibility that we'd need an archaeologist," he said. "The ice sheet is miles thick and over firm bedrock, and the team's primary concern... well, up until a week ago, was to investigate the effect of global warming this far in land." The doctor's breath turned to mist with each excited word. He was smiling even as his nose turned blue.

"What did you think it was?" I asked.

"Well, sonar showed it was hollow, but parts of it were clearly wood and metal. But the size of the thing... I guess the simple answer, Dr Rollet, is that we didn't know. We aren't keen on making guesses, as you know it can lead to bias, but I think if it wasn't for the fissure, we would never have never guessed the full truth.

Current samples put the trapped air are over 85,000 years old! A ship like this rewrites everything we know about our history."

"Quite a bit of luck," I said.

"Well," the doctor replied. "If you work here for long, you'll quickly learn that the ice sheet is degrading faster with each year. The warmer it gets, the more liquid water there is to weather out old caves and expand them, or even to create new ones. It was exactly that process—and our looking for it—that led us to the discovery."

"The effect is the same, though," I said. "A new cave system opened up within days of your discovery, and it led you right to it. As if the original find wasn't bizarre enough."

"Well... yes," Dr Hargreave said. "It *is* a miracle. That's what I've been trying to get at. Chances like this aren't just once in a lifetime, Dr Rosset, they're once in an epoch. It makes winning the lottery look mundane."

I couldn't quite stymie a chuckle, and I had to shake my head apologetically to the doctor when he took offence. "I believe you," I said. "I do. It's just that exact same good luck has landed you in a rather... *strange* position."

"Everyone thinks it's a hoax," Dr Greaves cried, slumping back into his seat like a scolded boy. "They've sent three different researchers from my own university and even after they've all confirmed the find, I'm still being treated like a fraud."

"Proof is in the pudding," I said. "You know the truth."

"See," the doctor said, cheered slightly by my words. "If anyone would understand, it's *you*."

I was saved from the need to reply further when a light chimed overhead, and the captain's words rang out over the speaker. The doctor straightened in his chair and Ryan, my assistant PhD student, finally woke up. I returned to the window and watched, breath held, as we finally made our descent, sinking into the fine white mists below.

Basecamp was filled with busy students shuffling back and forth. In the distance, two young men argued over a half-dissembled ice drill while nearby, three people worked to feed a small pack of sled dogs. In the centre of it all was a small table where two men around Hargreave's age assembled various picks and other tools. I made towards them, dodging half-a-dozen people carrying boxes along the way. Everyone looked exhausted and utterly disinterested in my arrival, and it was only when Dr Greaves caught up with me and called out to the two men in the centre that they looked up and paid attention.

"Ah Dr Rosset," the oldest called out, fat and plump with red cheeks like Santa. "Good to see you. Bloody tough going, isn't it? Bet *you've* never flown anywhere like this before."

"It's certainly something," I answered as he took my hand and shook it.

"I am Dr Whittle, this is Professor Shauley," he pointed to the whip-cord thin man beside him, who looked very much like the classic ideal of an aged adventurer. "And obviously you're acquainted with Dr Greaves." The moustachioed man beside me smiled and gave a small nod. "Now we've had a few of the staff put aside what data we've managed to collect so far and put it in your tent, which you'll find hopefully to your liking just over there." He pointed to some far corner of the camp and smiled as if that was all the introduction he needed. I ignored him, instead paying close attention to the rope coiled around his shoulder, his spiked ice boots, and the bundle of tools both men carried at their back.

"I'd like to see it," I said. "I'll gear up now and join you."

"Oh well, we sort of hoped you'd…"

"No need to worry about my schedule, gentlemen." I smiled. "That's my job. I'll be with you shortly."

I picked up my things and marched towards my tent, taking only brief notice of the small cot and heater I'd been provided. I hadn't arrived unprepared, and despite what Dr Whittle might have thought, I'd spent years working in the arctic circle and was just as well equipped to deal with the climate as the best of them. By the time I was unpacked and ready, barely half-an-hour had passed.

And yet, when I left my tent, I saw that the three doctors were nowhere to be found. I pulled aside a young woman making her way past and asked if she'd seen where they went, and she told they'd announced their descent just after I'd entered my tent. I was seething at the news and had her show me the entrance to the fissure. Sure enough, there was fresh rigging buried into the ice, slack rope hanging loose over the edge.

"Thank you," I muttered and attached my own safety line to the rigging, accepting that I'd be travelling solo. The girl tried to talk me out of it, but I was already a metre down before she could finish her first plea.

I can't say exactly why I did it, except that I'd been pulled into this venture at the last possible minute, and I wasn't very happy about it. From Dr Hargreave's behaviour on the plane, I thought, perhaps, that the researchers on site would be friendly enough. But it seems they figured out what I'd known right from the beginning; I'd been brought in by the university to harm the project's credit, not bolster it. I was a black enough sheep that from time to time my name would be stapled on to risky papers—willingly or not—to help ensure they sank in unfavourable journals. I'd learned to accept my fringe status years ago, but to researchers only just learning about the death of their career, I was about as welcome as a leper in a hot tub.

Thankfully the vertical drop wasn't all that severe, and the journey down was short. The fissure penetrated a small cave system below the surface and after a few dozen feet I landed on flat ground. I'd previously worked in ice caves close to the edge of the Canadian coast and most of them have a floor made of bedrock, but in Greenland the ice sheet can reach 3km in thickness and there was nothing but water-worn ice for my feet to find purchase. I felt a kind of vertigo imagining myself hovering two miles over the Earth. It was like another world down there. Fine motes of snow drifted lazily down from the breach above and the gale-force wind—ever present on the surface—had been whittled down to a distant whistle. It was not dark as you might expect because the crystal blue walls turned any torch into a dazzling light display. The effect was one of insulating warmth and uncanny beauty. But it made me feel small, too small to be mucking around in a continent-sized lump of ice where even the minutest shift in material would leave me crushed like a gnat.

I pushed on regardless, and the cave system opened up after a few dozen metres, but the vast empty spaces only doubled that feeling of insignificance. Thank God there were clearly marked guidelines to clip onto. I must have fallen half-a-dozen times and one of them brought me frighteningly close to tumbling into a bottomless chasm. Without those safety lines, I would have slid right on over the sloped edge and died. But if those three old dolts could manage it, I knew I could too. It was just a matter of following the trail and staying clipped on.

By the time I arrived, I was red-faced and sweaty and had more than a few bruises hidden by my thick clothes. The three men couldn't see any of those, but they raised an eyebrow at my breathless state and I'm sure I heard Dr Whittle make some shitty comment beneath his breath. I was getting ready to really start tearing into them when finally, I saw it, and I wasn't in much shape to do anything afterwards except gawk.

It really did look like the photos. And in fact, for a second there, I didn't believe my own eyes. I just, well... I just couldn't piece it together as something real. If I had taken a picture, you would have called it fake. If had I sketched it, or painted it, you'd think it a pretty picture of a dream, but nothing more. I have seen photos of glacial ice bisected by sudden geological change, seen the clear blue crystal standing tall like an impossible snapshot of the ocean depths but this was something else. Just a few metres away from where I stood, the wall of ice began, and a few metres further, the prow of an enormous ship was clearly seen, frozen perfectly in time. Impossibly large for any wooden vessel I've ever seen, it was like a jagged piece of rock or wood that jutted out of the darkness towards us so that only the nose was visible. It looked like some colossal aquatic predator with its face pressed against a sheet of glass and you couldn't help but feel a little afraid looking at it.

"How big is it?" I said, stammering the words out like a frightened child.

"The air pocket is around 800m."

I looked towards the three men. I didn't even remember who'd spoken, but my face must have said what I was thinking, because Dr Whittle spoke up quickly enough.

"The nose which is clearly visible is about 100m tall. Whether the ship behind it is 800m long, we can't easily say. But the sonar shows the cavity it's trapped in is 800m long."

"It could be half that," I said. "And still piss all over everything I've ever understood about the limits of ship building. The largest ships currently in existence reach around 4 to 500 metres. This... this is a city that floats."

"It shouldn't exist," Professor Shauley snarled, and I realised the sour faced adventurer wasn't making the comment out of awe or even curiosity. It was more of a flat statement, with the emphasis on *shouldn't*. Dr Whittle and Greaves both noticed this, and something of an argument quickly broke out.

"Well, it does exist Garett!" Dr Whittle cried. "That issue has long been settled!"

"This is the opportunity of a lifetime," Dr Greaves said. "Please gentlemen, this is truly something special."

But Professor Shauley was obstinate and difficult, and he never fully stated his case while I was present. Instead, he skirted around the idea that they should have never reported it, that they had somehow breached their scientific responsibility by not ignoring the evidence of their own eyes. In the meantime, I returned to the ship, absolutely breath-taken by its imposing size and jagged outline. It looked unlike any ship I'd ever seen, pitch-black and full of blunt hard angles, like an oil-tanker made out of burnt matchsticks.

"This won't reach the outside world," I said, my loud voice cutting cleanly through their bickering so that they all looked towards me. "I'm sorry to say this, Dr Greaves, but you won't be recognised for this kind of discovery, or in all likelihood any others. Some truths are a little too big, and this is one of them."

"You can't say that!" Dr Greaves cried. "We've had visitors from at least a dozen universities, and they've all seen this very thing right in front of you."

"And they won't be recognised either." I smiled. "Some things break the scientific method, and this is... hoo boy, this is a big one."

"But we have to try!" he cried. "You said it yourself: the proof is in the pudding."

"I'm not surprised you're trying to pull us into your silly conspiracy peddling," Dr Whittle snorted.

"None of you will see this work published," I told them, ignoring Dr Whittle's remark. "Not even in the small journals. To be honest, I thought it was all a hoax, despite the things I've seen, and so does everyone else, and they don't have the benefit of my experience. The fact you so readily called in help will only make this worse for you because the sooner it becomes clear you really do have something, well, that's when *they* show up."

"They are welcome to it," Professor Shauley said, a glint of defeat in his eye. "I never wanted to be Galileo."

"I don't blame you," I replied. "But there are worse hills to die on. As it stands, I'd say you have a week or two before some very stern-looking people turn up and start taking everything you have. At least, that's my experience."

"Of course!" cried Dr Whittle. "Here we go again. The strange men in suits, the inexplicable stalling of a bright young career, threats and even direct coercion. The difference here, Dr Rollett, is that we have *proof* of our claims instead of parading some nonsense theory about prehistoric civilisations."

I left that last part unanswered and instead cut to the chase.

"You have 7 to 14 days," I said. "Your careers are dead. There is no acclaim to be had, no place in the history books. I am truly sorry, but sooner or later you must mourn the death of your life's work because it's happening one way or another. Why else would I be sent here to taint you all by association? Any of your colleagues who openly support you will quickly find themselves out of pocket for all sorts of reasons. Dismiss it as conspiracy all you want. I'm long past arguing it. But all you have going for you is that the people who matter still think you're lying, and that buys you time."

"Time to do what?" asked Dr Greaves.

I pointed to the ship.

"To go take a closer look. There will be no credit, no claims, no glory, no acclaim. Just the truth, for you and you alone. Scream this news from a mountain top and all you'll get is struck by lightning. But for those of us who value knowledge for its own sake, there will always be the truth of what lies in that ship. So," I rubbed my hands together with barely contained glee, "who wants to crack this thing open?"

Ryan was fiddling with the lighting on his camera, but I didn't have the heart to tell him none of it would leave the camp intact. Still, his expertise on remote camera rigs was very helpful and there was something strangely funny about watching him explain the concept of a GoPro to Professor Shauley. As it was, we'd managed to jury rig a pretty half-decent solution to just about every problem that had popped up in the last four days and with the recording equipment all set up, we were good to go.

Now the cave was almost always occupied, as various engineers and mechanics had worked tirelessly to first drill into the ice and then establish a safe corridor to the ship's hull, all under sealed airtight conditions. Tents were set up and quarantine procedures established, and standard hazmat deep-pressure suits were hanging by the improvised bulkhead. Turns out that my connections weren't so unwanted after all, and by the time I'd had a drill flown in that was worth over £250,000, Dr Whittle finally started warming up to me. Professor Shauley remained distant, but he broke one quiet evening while I sat outside my tent and smoked, coming over to ask how I'd possibly known the head of the company well enough to work that kind of favour.

"Proof is in the pudding," I said with a smile. "My theories went down in flames, but the truth is still worth something in the right places. How do you think I fund my research? Some people will give anything to know what no one else does, and they'll pay even more to tag along or play some vital role in digging it all up. But then, you'll find out soon enough." He said nothing in return and simply stomped off in silence, his footfalls crunching in the snow.

But whether he liked it or not I'd played a vital role in making this all happen, and I watched Dr Whittle and Professor Shauley suit up with a kind of glint in my eye. The professor caught it at one point and turned visibly red, and I had to look away to stop myself from laughing. This couldn't have happened without me, and I stopped just short of openly revelling in it.

Once Ryan had the remote camera feed all set up, they pulled on their unwieldly helmets and started the long waddle to the bulkhead. I had felt a powerful sense of accomplishment all throughout this day, and yet the sight of the two men approaching the door with the ship looming overhead left me frightened for them. The ship was a pitch-black splinter in the abyssal depths and nothing about it looked welcoming – a floating city of tar too large to imagine moving around the open ocean. My own experiences taught me that there were old things buried deep in the Earth that do not like being woken up, and the question of who had built this ship and how remained hanging over all our heads. When I took the time to consult a few marine architects, they all practically laughed me off the phone at the suggestion of an 800m long wooden ship. Even with all the luxuries of modern technology, they said, such a thing simply isn't feasible. One, only one, had floated the novel idea that it might somehow be workable if the wood scaled in size as well.

"But of course," he'd laughed. "That'd require a tree over 800m tall to create a really solid structure with any hope of surviving the stress. And gravity puts a hard limit on how tall trees grow."

I hadn't liked to think too much on that. I wasn't sure how to file it away in my brain, so I left it floating around until it came back to me in that moment as I watched the doctors enter the bulkhead and disappear from view. It was a question that should have inspired awe and fascination, but that ship looked all too hungry, and I turned to the remote feed with a feeling of intense anxiety. It took hours for the two men to finally cut an entrance into the hull, and the whole time, a small army of students waited on hand to take away the steady stream of samples and begin testing.

By the time they cut the final section away, Dr Greaves had joined me, and we waited with bated breath.

"Here we go," Dr Whittle muttered to himself, and I watched as he plunged ahead.

The entrance was about two feet off the ground, and one of the men leaned forward into the darkness. His light was pale and chalky in the gloom, showing a floor coated in thick layers of dust that flared bright white in the camera. Debris littered the floor, buried under the blanket of dust like cabins in the snow. When one of the men started to climb upwards, his movement disturbed a flurry of ashy flakes that swept across the screen like a blizzard. They flashed brightly in the camera's glare and visibility was poor. We could see no walls yet, just an empty space.

Hesitantly, Shauley took his first steps and swept his head around to gauge the size of the room. It was enormous, though the ceiling was low, and the shadows felt claustrophobic. We hadn't had time to arrange for proper medical monitoring, but I could well imagine both men's hearts were racing. Their breathing filled their helmets and, more than once, they swallowed too loudly for our comfort. They walked onwards until, after a few metres, something came into view. It swept past the camera at first, and before any of us could tell him to swing back, he had already done a double take and brought the object into full view.

It was a cage filled with little more than a pile of white dust and beside it was an identical one with similar contents. A few feet behind it, a wall came into sight, and the men's torches caught sight of other crates all lined up in a row. Their exact number was lost to darkness, but even with our limited sight we saw that they were arranged in a repeating pattern of pairs.

"Two by two," I muttered.

Dr Greaves was pink, his face a puzzle I couldn't crack. Ryan's expression, at least, was familiar.

"What the *fuuuck...*" he groaned.

I turned back to the feeds and watched the two men follow the wall. The going was slow, and both scientists stopped often to collect a few lone items resting on top of some of the crates; they were knives mostly, but one looked oddly like something the Egyptians used to remove the brain prior to mummification. One by one, they were bagged and put away into various pouches along the men's suits. They were meticulous in detailing what little they found, so the going was slow, but eventually, a break in the wall appeared. It was a rounded doorway and looking through it, we all saw a set of wooden steps rising into the darkness. They were wooden planks fixed to the wall with no sign of rails, and the thought of ascending them turned my stomach.

"Did you see that?" Dr Whittle cried and everyone in the small crowd that had gathered around us jumped all at once. From the back, laughter could be heard, but my eyes were wide and fixed on the screen. He was staring straight up at the stairs, desperately trying to see past the gloom.

"Did you see that!?" Dr Whittle cried again, his voice suddenly frail.

"I did," replied. "I saw it."

"Something moved!"

"That's not possible, Doctor," Dr Greaves said, grabbing the speaker.

"Check the audio readings," Professor Shauley said, his voice grave. "I didn't see anything but I'm sure I heard it."

Ryan was already on it. While we had access to two standard radios, the suits included extremely sensitive recorders designed to pick out the faintest noise. I didn't tell anyone on site, but they were actually specialist items used by ghost hunters to detect EVP. At the time, I'd found the irony delicious. Sitting there as Ryan skipped through the first twenty minutes of recording, it wasn't irony I could taste but instead the acid wash of terror that stung the back of my throat.

We saw it before we heard it, a rising peak in the waveform that stood out from the other noise. When it reached playback, it began as some ill-defined shuffling, briefly pierced by a loud and clearly defined thump, followed by fading drumming sound akin to footfalls retreating into the distance.

For the last few minutes Whittle had refused to take his eyes from the stairway, but Shauley's feed was roaming from side to side. He had focused on a doorway that appeared in the corridor a few metres down. I imagine he was terrified just like the rest of us, but it was clear he couldn't stop curiosity getting the better of him. He peered through the doorway and found an identical room to the last, filled with rows and rows of endless pale cages.

"What's that?" he said and approached one a few metres away. Whatever he saw, our cameras couldn't make it out until he was right by it.

This pile of white dust had a face. It emerged out of the mound like a primitive face carved into a volcano. Attached to two bars on either side of the cage were hands, frail and thin like a shrivelled monkey's paw. Of the arms, there was no sign.

"Looks almost human, doesn't it?" the professor said.

"It does," I replied, my voice like paper. "Is there anything under it? Or is it just a pattern left by the dust?"

"Why don't we find out," Shauley replied, and I watched as he knelt down and pushed his arm between the bars. He gently poked the surface, and it yielded to his fingers, but he must have felt something nonetheless because he spoke. "It's not all dust," he mumbled, before pulling out a small section of skull that included some brow, eye-socket, and cheekbone. He sifted through a bit more and found a few teeth that were too sharp and long to belong to a primate, and he deposited them safely to the excitement of us all.

"Wait," he added, "what's this? That wasn't in the last room?"

He went further into the darkness until a small flat surface unveiled itself on the far wall. It was looked like a kind of workspace, little more than a stone slab with a few large jars huddled around the floor beside it. One of the jars, about two feet tall, had been hauled onto the top and was open.

"Be careful," I said as he approached it, suddenly aware of how far into the darkness he'd gone.

"Dr Whittle," I added, turning to the second screen. "Are you okay?"

His eyes were still fixated on the stairs above him. His breaths were quivering, desperate, and no matter how hard I tried, he refused to reply. "Professor," I said, returning to his feed. "I think you need to return to Dr Whittle."

He was standing over the pot staring down into a featureless pile of white clay-like material. It was soft, yielding like soil to the small scraper he used to collect a sample. "Professor," I repeated myself. "You need to check on—"

The speaker beside me exploded into a cacophony of screams. The professor's own feed cried out as well so that the whole workspace was filled with duelling copies of the same shrieking horror. I snapped my head to the side and tried to see what was happening, but the doctor's screen showed only darkness while the professor shuffled quickly to the spot where his colleague had once stood. He found only a lone strip of the doctor's suit, but no sign of the man himself. I was already shouting at Ryan to playback the recording of the doctor's feed while Dr Greaves grabbed another screen and stared at the audio recording. He was pressing one side of a pair of headphones to his ear and his face had gone white with sheer terror.

"What is it?" I asked, but he didn't reply. He looked at me and I saw he was close to passing out. "Professor," I yelled, grabbing the radio. "You need to leave!"

Shauley's speaker burst into protest, but I ignored them and turned back to Dr Greaves. "What is it?" I cried. "What can you hear!?" Ryan, hovering just behind me who could no longer bear the tension, leaned forward and tore the headphone jack out of the computer. Both the doctor and I cried out at once:

"No, don't!"

But it was already too late. The camp was filled with the sounds of wet and painful splutters. Someone was hyperventilating close by, short sharp desperate breaths, and occasionally those deathly shudders turned into small gentle moans of dying protest.

"No," the Dr Whittle whispered. His voice was distant, but he repeated the word a few more times. "No...

"Please...

"No."

There was a terrible crack and some of us winced. The hyperventilating stopped, but the frantic gurgles and wet animal panting continued. I turned the sound off with shaking hands. I could see that Professor Shauley was close to the stairs, one foot raised to go looking for his friend, and I cried out.

"Professor Shauley!" I said. "You need to leave."

"I have to find him!" he roared. "You can't be serious! We can't abandon him!"

His voice was so loud it hurt the speakers. It was a sobering outburst. As his words died, the whole cave become silent until only the sound of dripping water and radio static could be heard. Suddenly we were all aware of how alone the Professor was, and so was he. I could see him looking around, surrounded on almost all sides by aching shadow. This was an impossible nightmare carved out of tar, disorientating and distressing in ways that reeked of the uncanny.

"Leave," I whispered, and this time he didn't argue. He nodded, probably more to himself than to me. And at last, he turned back the way he came. It was awkward to walk in the suit, but I willed him on to go as quickly as possible. I don't know if it was our imagination, but during such tense silence, the white hiss of the radio seemed full of spectral bumps and shuffles. And I could see the paranoia and fear affect Shauley; his feed was constantly moving from side to side and occasionally he jumped at something none of us could hear or see.

"I'm close to the entrance," he said at last.

"Come on, come on, come on!" I whispered.

Shauley was no more than ten or fifteen metres from the exit when something shifted in the pixelated shadows on either side of the blinding white portal. The professor stopped dead in his tracks and froze like a deer in headlights. In defiance of everything I knew possible, something stepped out into the light and barred the professor's way. It was tall, stooped against the ceiling in a blurry humanoid silhouette. The professor cried out and so did we all. The shape of this thing, the way it moved, sent shivers down my back. I felt like I was watching film from another world, but a part of my mind reminded myself the events occurred no more than a hundred metres from where I stood.

The professor was trying to back up when this thing reached out towards him. Its giant misshapen hand filled the screen and the professor's cries rose to a crescendo. There was a sound like a tree falling and the screen went black, and the professor's screams stopped. For a moment, I thought he was truly dead until Ryan looked up from the workstation. His eyes were red, and I could see he was crying, but it took me a moment to realise what had caught his attention.

The professor's screams *hadn't* stopped. The microphone had been disabled, but we could still hear him. His voice was now tinny, faintly audible through the distance, ice, and thick airlock doors. But we could still hear him, and he was squealing like a pig. I was barely able to stand, but I managed to approach the door. I was close enough to touch it when the screaming finally stopped for real this time. In those final few seconds, I was just about able to make out what it was he was saying.

He was pleading for it to stop.

"Is the air safe?" I asked.

"Yes, quite safe now. We've pumped oxygen into the cavity," Dr Greaves replied.

My face was pressed to the bulkhead's window. From where I stood, I could just about make out the tattered remnants of Professor Shauley's suit, sitting a few feet inside the hull of the ship.

"How long until the security detail arrive?" the doctor asked, his head peering over my shoulder.

"Days," I answered. "We're pushed for time. I want what's left of that suit."

"You... you can't be seriously going through with this?"

The camp was quiet. After the previous day's events, I'd forbidden anyone from sleeping in the secondary site and insisted everyone make the hike up to the old one on the surface. It wasn't just about safety; the doctor and I had devised a plan to snatch the suit and hopefully whatever few samples remained, and I wanted no one around when we did it.

"For the thousandth time," I told him. "I am deadly serious. Good God I could sprint there and back in less than ten seconds. Just keep the lights on, the door open, and that shotgun pointed firmly at that hole."

"This isn't very scientific," he groaned.

"And dolphins don't look like mammals, but they absolutely still are," I said. "Sometimes science isn't very scientific."

I didn't wait for him to reply. I opened the door and stepped forward. I wore no suit for this encounter and took a deep breath—stifling the urge to dwell on the exact nature of the air I breathed—before breaking out into a sudden sprint. I felt like a kid running past the closet to get to the bathroom late at night, except now I was running right towards the darkness, not past it.

I cleared the tunnel quickly, reaching the entrance in a few seconds. I wanted this to be over. My heart was in my throat, my scalp felt ice cold, and my stomach was like a lead weight holding me down. I was so scared I could have easily forgotten to breathe as I reached my arm into the shadow and grabbed a hold of the suit's cuff. I could feel myself losing control, but I couldn't stop, not now. I pulled at the material and cried out in despair when something tore, and I was left holding nothing but a small clump of thick vinyl-like fabric.

"Shit!" I cried, snapping my head back towards the petrified doctor. "Keep that fucking door open!"

I reached my hand out into the darkness, so far that my chest touched the floor and every single cell in my body started screaming at me to me leave. Without the suit, my perception was crystal clear, and I could hear every creak and groan of that wooden superstructure. But I wouldn't back out, and when my hand failed to get a proper grasp of Shauley's old suit, I actually took a small running jump and threw myself into the dark. All that remained outside were my ankles, but this time both my hands grabbed the suit and when I leaned up onto my elbows and started to haul it, I felt the satisfying weight of heavy equipment drag along the floor.

The brief flush of victory lasted barely a second. I shuffled back slowly until my feet touched the floor and looked up to inspect my haul when I saw a large white oval floating in the dark. It looked almost like a bowling ball, if one of the holes was a little larger and further apart than the rest. When two of those same holes blinked, I finally realised what it was I was looking at.

It was a face as large as my torso, and the body it belonged to was cloaked with shadow. It was so still it was uncanny, exuding no emotion or thought or intent. I didn't know if it was scared of me, curious, or hateful, and it made the sight all the more terrifying. Sooner or later, something would give, but I wouldn't leave the suit behind, so I maintained eye-contact—even through the tears—and moved as slow as continental drift, back, back, back out of the entrance. About half-way there, I snapped into action, whipping the suit over my shoulder before springing like a madman towards the exit. For a moment, the doctor looked confused, but then his eyes fixed on something over my shoulder and I knew it had come out into the light. Thankfully the distance wasn't that far, and I flew past the doctor like a sprinter passing the finishing line. I threw myself onto the ground and screamed,

"Shut the door! Shut the fucking door!"

I relaxed only when the doctor heaved it closed and turned the handle with a satisfying clunk. He had yet to look at me, instead fixated on whatever had been close behind. When I finally got back up from the ground, I jostled him aside and stared through the window. That alien face—no eyes, no nose, nothing but three aching cavities in a pale white disk—was staring at us from the hole in the ship's hull.

It was dead still for the longest of times, all three of us locked into each other's gaze. When it did finally move, it was to tilt its head perfectly to the side like a turning wheel. There it stayed for a few more seconds, watching us like a curious dog, before sinking back slowly into the monstrous ship.

———

"It's fungal," the young woman said, holding a sample of the clay. "Unlike anything I've ever seen except in some ancient fossils and even then... nothing quite like this."

"Food, perhaps?" the doctor asked.

"I wouldn't eat it," the biologist squirmed. "It's going nuts under this petri dish. It may look inert, but whatever's going on under the surface, it's doing it at an astonishing rate. In the time we've had it, the sample has undergone tens of thousands of generations."

"What about the dust?" I asked. "And the skull sample we retrieved."

"Similar makeup, but different. I'm not sure, some of them are corrupted with the fungus but just like the sample from the vase, it's inert. I'd say it's contamination, but... well, it looks different."

"What do you mean?" the doctor asked.

"I don't know," she replied with a shake of her head. "In some of the samples they share similar features. Dry air helped to preserve some cell samples in the skull, but that's even stranger. The marrow itself is fungal in origin but there are blood vessels that look distinctly mammalian, not to mention the cranial structure is definitely primate."

"I don't suppose you can shed any light on this?" Dr Greaves asked, turning to me.

I walked over to the sample and took a small piece of it onto my finger. Both the doctor and biologist hissed endless warnings at me, but I waved them off. I crushed the small piece between two fingers and then rolled it back into a single ball. I even took a moment to smell it.

"It's clay," I said. "Or rather, it's something that anyone without a microscope would call clay."

"What does that mean?" the doctor asked.

"The deluge is the oldest myth in the world. Noah and his ark are found in the oldest recorded civilisations, creeping through Sumerian, Mesopotamian, and Babylonian cultures. It's part of nearly every single creation myth, whether it's Hindu, Greek, or even Welsh," I said. "And yet, what does old even mean? The oldest officially recognised version of Noah dates to around 2000 BC. So what? Current estimates say the human race is a million years old. Humans, as we would recognise them, anatomically modern humans, reach back anywhere between 100,000 and 150,000 years. The bulk of my work has focused on uncovering the truth of those lost epochs where conventional science would have you believe we lit fires and chased ox. We certainly did those things, but I have spent my life trying to prove that we were not idle. That many people in those times achieved great heights, some even greater than ours."

"You believe this ship was built by the very civilisations you claim—" Dr Greaves paused briefly to correct himself. He couldn't treat my research like some fringe conspiracy theory anymore, not with a floating city frozen in ice a few hundred metres away. "The civilisations you found evidence of?"

I shrugged. "Maybe. I have certainly come across the deluge myth in some of the works I uncovered in the Canadian wilderness. I would have tried publishing, but I was long past that sort of thing."

"What did the myths say?" the biologist asked.

"They wrote of Dyr-un-anash, a man compelled to construct an enormous ship at the behest of his gods. It was to be a test of his character, of his faith. And just like our versions, he was to use this ship to repopulate the world after an apocalyptic flood that did, indeed, arrive in some form. But unlike all the other versions of this tale, Dyr-un-anash was not a hero. He was a sculptor of clay, perhaps the greatest in the world or to have ever lived. And the gods resented his arrogance. So one night they approached him and said his gift for sculpture was so magnificent it exceeded even theirs. And even though the world was due to end with a terrible flood, they wished for him to be the benefactor of the blank slate that would be left over. He was to take a gift of clay, the very clay used to create all living things, and spend his time aboard the ship fashioning any and all manner of life he desired.

"Dyr-un-anash was only too eager to fulfil his destiny and drove his family into ruin building the ship. But when the flood came, it carried him and his ark away, but left the world untouched, although Dyr-un-anash could not see this. He carried on with his plan, not knowing that the clay he had been gifted was cursed and corrupted. How exactly, I don't know. Still, the gods were laughing at him, and so was the whole world. The moral being that the wise shouldn't trust gifts from the gods."

There was a long silence. I continued to fixate on the small lump of clay-that-wasn't-clay. My heart was pounding. My chest felt tight. A thought had entered my mind while I spoke, and I couldn't shake it. I couldn't get it loose. I wondered if for a moment this really was...

"What are you doing?" the biologist asked, but I didn't pay any attention. I brought the tip of my finger close to my mouth and gently breathed, just like I'd imagined God doing when I was in church hearing about Genesis.

For a short while, nothing happened. I think Dr Greaves said something. I didn't catch it. My finger was starting to tingle, and I squinted so hard it hurt my head. Slowly at first, but with gathering certainty, the small piece of clay started to squirm. It was moving. From beside me the young woman started to laugh a gasping ex-ultation of awe. She had moved in to take a closer look, but Dr Greaves stepped back and cried out in terror. I still didn't speak. I kept the lump on my finger and approached a table where I placed it gently and we all stood, watching it crawl like a caterpillar.

"Get it under a microscope," I said to the young woman. "Hurry!"

She snatched a pair of tongs and went to gently pluck the small worm—no larger than a grain of rice—from the table. The metal had barely touched it when suddenly something white and veiny shot out of the worm and groped around the tongs. It expanded and branched like the tongue of a ribbon worm, forking across the table in pale rivulets so quickly that the biologist was forced to drop the instrument with a cry of terror. She jumped back just as a proboscises left the table and tongued the air, roaming, grasping for something else to take.

"Kill it!" Dr Greaves cried. "It's growing."

He was right. In less than thirty seconds, its tendrils had reached out across the table, and we watched as it grew to cover three quarters of the table. Thankfully, the biologist had her senses about her. She started to splash something on the writhing pile of snow-white flesh, the beaker she held was filled with all sorts of flammable chemicals. I snatched a few with the same universal warning symbol and began hurling them until, at last, I felt some kind of satisfaction that fire would find purchase.

By the time I stopped, the worm had started to grip and pull down one of the tent walls. Dr Greaves took the initiative and ran forward, throwing a burning rag right at it from just a metre away. The fire went up with a loud whoosh and the mutated lump of clay began to change and bubble. The chamber we were in was large enough to house a small building, so we waited nearby as the fire raged onward and took not only the creature but the tent as well.

I took the time to steal the important samples away, but the young woman grabbed my arm before I could leave and made sure we checked the seal of each one. We couldn't risk the rest of that stuff exploding into life. I suppose that was the scientist in her. But standing there as that tent went up in flames, I felt the scientist within me die. The worm screamed in agony in its final moments, and we all watched, our faces twisted into disgust and fear, unable to turn away or block out the sound.

It was screaming in my voice.

———

"You know you shouldn't do this?" the biologist asked. Since the fire, she had risen to replace Dr Whittle and Professor Shauley in their absence, proving herself to be a capable manager of the scores of students and staff and an excellent scientist. I hadn't expected to need a biologist for what I'd figured to be an archaeological problem, but I was glad her expertise was on hand.

The four men beside me were arming themselves with shotguns, the kind used to blow out door locks during police raids. They were small with good stopping power, and my hope was that in such a large space they'd run little risk of doing too much damage to anything we weren't aiming at. All of the men worked for the same company that had provided the drill, and the team had a long history in corporate sabotage and all sorts of shady things. They were used to knowing very little, but I had given them a brief overview of what had happened to the last two men to enter the ark. By the time I'd finished, they all looked at me with acidic glares.

"Fucking spook," one had hissed before spitting on the floor.

But they didn't have to like it. They just had to aim and shoot if the worst should happen. I thought our best bet was to hope that our numbers would discourage attack and allow us to roam in peace. Neither the biologist nor Dr Greaves shared this view. They thought this was madness, but they were so far from learning just how cruel the world can be when it's deliberately set against you. I lost everything and for what? Exemplifying the very scientific principles I'd been told were the light against darkness. I found the truth, and I fought for it, and I wound up dragged through filth and muck and laughed out of every university until I finally slunk off and found other ways to live. Now I was being given a second chance to do it all differently, and nothing from heaven or hell was going to stop me.

"Gentlemen," I said to those assembled before me. "Let's go."

With that, I turned and made for the bulkhead. I gave no one, not even myself, any time to think or voice protests. That ship towered ahead like all my nightmares made real and I had to go inside. I had to know more. We had glimpsed something in that tent. We had pulled apart all the tangled knots, all the myths, all the legends, and cut right to the central truth of our long-forgotten origin. The clay. The gods. The ship. At night I was wracked with nightmares and in them the ship spoke to me in my own voice. My pursuit of the truth, it told me, had elevated me beyond science.

This was something divine.

And it was thinking of this that I passed through the tunnel with no more fear than a man going to the bathroom. I was even smiling for a while, and I gestured to the entrance like I was inviting the men to step onto an elevator. They looked at me like I was strange, especially after they climbed in and found the congealed and blood-spatters where Shauley had died. All that arterial spray had soaked the dusty floor into gooey pulp, and there were a few scattered pieces of rotting bone and flayed skin, but of the rest of the body, we found no sign.

Divine or not, I had no intention of losing my life on this little venture. I took control quickly and began to photograph the variety of tracks all around us. Most looked human, but quite a few were round ovals resembling an elephant's prints. Others were long and slithery, and others were completely unrecognisable.

"What exactly are we looking for?" the man beside me asked.

"A gallery or a workshop," I said. "This was all made by an artist. He'd have at least one of those."

I knew he had no idea what I meant, but I gestured for us to move on. We walked quickly past the very boxes Shauley and Whittle had, and I saw that atop a few there were empty spaces in the dust from where the men had taken a few tools while walking the same way. The effect was oddly unsettling, but I didn't have much time to think. We were soon at the first doorway where we found signs of a scuffle amongst all the white dust. This was where Whittle had been snatched. Close by, I could see where Shauley had walked off towards the second room he'd found, but the doorway was out of sight. The shadows in the ark felt like they ate light, and our beams lit little more than narrow disks that fell weakly upon the floor.

"Up?" one of them asked, pointing towards the stairs.

"Up," I replied.

The steps were ancient, but they held. I knew from analyses they were a kind of organic woven fibre harder than steel, but organic in origin. How that resulted in a ship this size floating, I don't know. But we climbed the first flight and found the steps to be as firm as steel. On the first platform we found another doorway, and I had us make a short excursion but there was nothing of particular interest. We returned to the stairs and continued climbing, briefly poking our heads through each doorway in the hope of finding something new. We never saw more than empty rooms with cages for a long, long time. But I knew there must be more and, with any luck, it'd be close to our point of entry.

From behind me, I could hear one of the men was counting steps. He was grinding marks into the back of his hand with his thumbnail, along with diagonal slashes to indicate left or right turns. He was preparing for a worst-case scenario, a desperate flight in total darkness to safety where he'd have to reverse each step one by one if he had any hope of making it home.

On the eight floor we stopped briefly. There was no railing on any of the platforms and I kept far away out of fear of heights. One of the men stepped right up to the edge and dropped a glowstick into the chasm below where it flew straight down, illuminating the gnarled ancient walls and steps in a neon green glow until at last it struck the floor and stopped shrinking in size. From so far up, it was just a speck.

"Jesus Christ!" the man cried, snatching his shotgun up before thinking better of firing. Somehow, the glow stick was moving. It bobbed side to side before disappearing into some unseen nook. "We're not alone!" he hissed.

"We knew that," I said. "Come on. A few more floors, at least."

We moved onwards, but from then on two men remained with guns drawn to their shoulders, constantly turning side to side to cover the space behind us. They, at least, managed the climb quite easily but I was starting to lag. Thankfully the twelfth floor we reached showed signs of human life. There was a thistle-broom nearby and a small table with pots and vases. Some of the doors had hieroglyphs around them, and the posts on this door were carved in fine and beautiful patterns. This was not a sterile empty space waiting to be filled with thousands of hand-made animals and I entered the hallway feeling giddy with excitement.

I pushed a few doors open and found old wooden beds next to small tables. There were small figurines carved out of wood on quite a few, along with small metal plates I think were used to hold candles. In total, we found twenty rooms with these simple and rustic signs of occupation. There were ancient blankets rolled up onto shelves, plates laid out for food. One room even had a few toys left out on the floor. They were crude but clearly meant to be horses, and I couldn't help but laugh as I held one up in the light.

"Oh, we were busy," I muttered.

But after that the rooms became strange. Signs of normal human life were replaced with something more manic, more frightening. It was in these rooms that the dust piled up highest, reaching up to our knees. The walls were scratched and gouged, and all-too-familiar faces were carved into the wood.

"Bowling balls?" one of the men snorted, pointing towards one.

I swallowed the acid in my throat and had us move on. Those pictures reminded me of crude cave paintings, and I had a strong instinct as to what had made them.

We kept going deeper into the structure. It was half-a-mile long, and I doubted we had any chance of thoroughly exploring any given floor, but I couldn't quite stop myself from trying just one more door. I should have been more careful, but I kept on going until we were well over half-way in the ship, and the scratchy low-hanging corridor we stood in stretched off in both directions, lost to darkness.

Suddenly, one of the men cried out in terror and brought his weapon to bear. He fired before anyone had a chance to speak, and the sound was so loud it practically floored me.

"Good God!" the man next to him roared. "It was a fucking rat! Ceasefire!"

The lone gunman lowered his weapon and started to laugh. His pale face glistened in the light of my torch. His eyes were bloodshot and wide, but you could see the relief clearly on his face.

"It was just a rat," he repeated. "I'm just... just a bit jumpy, is all."

"What room did it go in?" I asked.

"Two doors on the right," the leader answered.

I walked towards it, beckoning for them to join.

"What are we looking for?" one hissed. "It was only a rat."

"There aren't any rats on this ship," I said. "Not alive."

I pushed the door and a sea of dust that flowed out into the hallway like water, wedging the door stuck in a half-open position. I stepped back and waited for the hissing sound to stop and for the dust to settle. Once it was quiet I poked a light through and saw a small mousy face staring at us from the corner, resting on the dust at chest height. It was an albino thing, a lot like a rat but with webbed limbs and barbed tail.

"What the fuck?" one of the men muttered.

The creature lifted its arms and blew out the sails between its hands and legs. We all jumped back, but it made no more movements, instead staring at us intently and hissing. I noticed dark eye-like ovals on the skin it had stretched out, and I realised we were looking at a threat display.

"Nothing to be worried about," I said. "Just some kind of—"

Something fell from the ceiling and ate the rodent. It happened so quickly I had only flashing impressions of claws, teeth, and long spindly limbs extended to their furthest reach. One of the men turned his flashlight upward, and we saw what might be described as a praying mantis, if they reached two feet in length and had a centipede's body. Its clicking mandibles ground the vermin into dust that sprinkled down from above like salt from a shaker.

"It's eating it," someone hissed.

"Or at least," I said. "It thinks it is."

"What does that mean?"

"Don't worry," I answered.

The mantis left us alone, and we returned quickly to the stairway. For the next few hours, we continued to explore the prow of the ship floor by floor until we reached the top. On each one we encountered stranger and stranger forms of life, including a wasp's nest made by more of those small rat-like things. About a dozen broke from the larger horde and rushed us, but stamping on them made quick work of our attackers. Each one exploded in a welt of pale milky fluid, but their skin and organs flattened beneath our feet like wet soil. The effect was quite odd, and I even peeled one of the cleaner specimens off the floor and bagged it for later examination.

Further on, we stumbled across lone insects buzzing in a small cloud like snowflakes in mid-air. They were like wasps, but with fewer legs and two pairs of shimmering dragonfly wings. We shooed them away and found an arachnoid the size of a tv struggling on the floor. It was infested, rotting from the inside out. And we watched as small pustules along the surface of its crustacean shell popped and small larva came crawling out.

That wasn't all. We found fungal flowers that had torn through multiple rooms, their meaty pale caps glowing white in the dark. Small creatures with four needle-like legs, roaming the ceiling with sharp mouths that pecked randomly at the wood like birds snatching up seed. All in all, we saw a fair bit of the ship's life cycle on the upper floors and got to watch a lot of things eat, either nibbling away at the stalks of mushrooms or snatching small insects from the floor, and in every example we watched as they ground up their prey and left a sprinkling of dust. The only real clue we got as to how things worked was in the rat-hive, where I found a fat swollen queen surrounded by workers who were rolling up the matted dust and depositing it in small holes along the hive-wall. They were eggs made from the same base-clay dust that littered everything on this ship. I watched long enough to see some of the larger ones hatch into mewling cubs no bigger than my thumb.

At a guess, I'd say that a fair-sized lump of the ship was infested with these lifeforms. In just a few hours, I'd filled every pouch I'd brought, and we were all lugging at least one duffel bag filled with pots and jars that clinked with every movement. I decided to call this particular excursion done, and we all moved as a group back to the stairway, ready to begin the descent.

"Not the worst thing I've done," one of the men sighed as we checked our surroundings checked for signs of being followed. "They look scary, but they're just hiding away in the dark."

"Like a wax museum where everything moves," another said.

"Exactly," I replied, surprised at just how accurate that statement was. "They were harmless."

One of the men who'd been bitten quite badly by one of the rats grimaced as he checked the wound. It was already starting to fester and smell.

"Harmless my ass," he grumbled. "I hope whatever they're hiding finds and eats the fucking lot."

I stopped dead in my tracks.

"What did you just say?"

"All these fucking vermin," he growled, poking the leaking wound on his leg. "Something has to eat 'em. They're all sneaking around, silent as hell. Did you notice that? It's the dark," he said. "They don't worry about sight, they worry about sound."

"That's why they're all up here," another chimed in. "I thought you'd have figured that out by now, doc."

"Shit!" I cried. "We've been looking in the wrong place! We should have stayed on the lower floors. What we're looking for will be down there."

"Do you hear yourself?" one of the men asked. "I thought you wanted to be safe? Didn't you see that glowstick moving?"

"Exactly," I answered. "Let's go."

We descended the stairs and quickly returned to the entrance, rushing past one black doorway after another. The misty air of each hall was thick with floating moats of dust, and it reminded me of looking into the cabin of a sunken ship which, I suppose, we were. After a while I stopped looking, not liking the look of the shifting watery darkness. But the feeling of danger only sharpened by the need to go on. We'd come so far, I desperately had to know more.

Well, we found it. The bottom floor had strange tracks not unlike the oval ones we'd found by Shauley, recently made and slinking off into the dark further along the ship. Without wasting time, I had us follow them until the shaft opened up into a larger chamber. It was an aching groaning space towards the rear of the ship with the ceiling out of sight. If it wasn't for the cloying stillness, you could have thought you were outside. But there were clear tracks through the dust, so many they looked like paths in the snow. This was a busy space, quite possibly even some kind of meeting space.

"Guys?"

I turned around to see one of the men gazing at the opening in the rear wall where we'd just emerged. Something was glowing green far off in the distance, hovering where we'd been walking just minutes before.

"Is that...?"

We had made a critical mistake. All of us faced the one direction, and before either of us could say too much, one of the men near our rear was plucked screaming into the air. He had been lifted headfirst by a grotesque hand as large as my torso, the knuckles grotesque and the fingernails cracked and bloody. With a single squeeze it crunched, and the man's head was pulped into nothing, his limp body falling to the floor with a wet thud.

We started shooting, all of us, but the effect was pitiful. White clumps of soil flew off the monster's chest and face, and the shot sent wild shudders through its frame, but it weathered the strikes like a well-trained boxer. Once it was done shrugging them off it was left with a hundred small pock marks that bled thick milk down its skin, but that strange gaping face with three empty holes showed no signs of anger or pain. It simply reached and grabbed another man, and I soon realised our hopes of stopping it were close to nil. We should have retreated, run even. But a look behind us showed another strange thing emerging from the darkness, its head a gloriously abstract carving reminiscent of raindrop hitting a puddle.

Meanwhile, the ball-headed shape began to twist and pull at his captive with the detached curiosity of a child. It pinched his wrist like it was manipulating an action figure before pulling too hard and tearing the arm off whole, along with a thin strip of muscle that was left dangling from the torso.

"We were so close!" I screamed, barely aware of what I was saying. I couldn't countenance failing at this stage and without really thinking anything through, I decided my best chance was to strike out alone. I ran past the dying man and the golem who held him, narrowly avoiding a sweeping arm that reached to grab me. I could hear some of the other men screaming for me, but they had no chance to follow. I switched off my light and trusted myself to fate. From behind came the steady discharge of two shotguns that, after a few seconds, were reduced to a single desperate man shooting and yelling defiance into the dark.

***

Do not stop.
"I won't," I muttered, crawling through the dark.
Keep going.
"I will."
This is a gift.
"My gift."
My words were a hushed sob. I was speaking just to hear the comforting sound of my own voice. It had been at least a day. By sheer chance, I'd reached a small room all the way on the other end of the ship during my flight, and I'd hidden away in it while listening to the ever-so-quiet footfalls of the clay men that lived here. It had been so tempting to stay in the one place where I might avoid their groping hands. But it wasn't that simple. I had no food, only a small supply of water, and sleep was impossible. After a long time huddled in the dark, I finally pushed the door open and began to crawl my way along the righthand wall, desperate not to make a sound. All my equipment had been abandoned barring the light and gun; whatever I brought out of the ship would just have to fit in my head.
You're so close.
"I know," I hissed. The words sounded a little too loud for comfort, so I stopped and waited for signs of the slightest change in my surroundings. I had no idea where I was, but I could only assume danger wasn't far off. Thankfully, nothing moved, and I released a breath before continuing.
The others failed.
"They all did," I whispered, a little more carefully this time.
They never wanted the truth.

"No one wants the truth," I replied.

You won't have to share it with them.

"They never deserved it."

You are close to where he worked.

I stopped. I couldn't risk turning the light on, but I waited to see if I could feel anything, some possible change in air pressure, that might tell me if I was near a doorway. I must have stayed like that for a full minute, only to reach my hand out and nearly fall through a vacant spot in the wall. I was hardly a tunnel rat. I couldn't even tell that I'd been kneeling next to an open room. I might have laughed under other circumstances.

I crawled inside and pulled the door shut with aching care. Hoping for the best, I turned my light on and revealed a modestly sized space with rows and rows of desks. I was the only living thing there. It was a workspace with one corner filled with vases of clay and half-finished pieces lying haphazardly on the ground. Some had been smashed, beaten, stomped. Others were still standing, precious, beautiful.

He really was a good sculptor. Each one was a meticulous and beautiful rendering of a different bird. They didn't look like perfect replicas of the real things, but rather like the ideal of how they *should* look. There was a shelf filled with thousands of pairs of sparrows, crows, parrots, and hens, all inert but incredibly lifelike. I picked one up and noticed it felt different from the clay samples I had taken. I figured it for a practice run, a way to hone his skills before trying for the real thing.

"Not like the others," I muttered quietly.

He destroyed these works and many others. He did not understand the curse, did not understand why the real ones failed.

"How long was he on this ship thinking the fate of humanity depended on him?" I asked myself.

He never stopped trying.

"So why did he smash these ones? Rage? Frustration?"

He died of old age. Alone.

At the far end of this room was another doorway. I approached it, shaking, ready to enter the next chamber when the door I'd closed juddered forward with a terrible grind. It moved no more than an inch and I snapped around, fixing my light on it—wild shadows flying around the room like gargoyles on a cathedral's spires—but it was still. For a moment I thought I'd imagined the sound when, once again, the frame shivered, and the door moved forward another inch. A single white finger probed the gap and reached around the door, soon followed by two others.

Run.

I turned just as a round head peered at me, but I didn't wait to see what it was. I ran, passing into another room filled with dozens of sculptures of life-sized deer, each one hauntingly beautiful, a complete a far cry from the wretched misshapen thing that chased me. Others lay smashed on the floor, broken before they could ever be finished. These rooms were chained together in an open row of workshops where the ancient artist had practiced making all kinds of things. I ran straight through each one, trying my hardest to ignore the rising boom of footfalls behind me.

His talent wasn't enough, I thought.

You're getting close.

The rooms started to change, and I noticed that they were now filled with those familiar empty cages. It made me hope I was close to where we'd entered. Although close is a relative term when trapped in a nightmarish labyrinthian city of pitch-black wicker walls.

Left.

I burst out of the cage-room into yet another corridor and headed left without even thinking. Those footfalls continued, and as I sprinted, I found long white arms appearing out of doorways on either side. I ducked them as best I could, but at the very last moment, one grabbed my hood and lifted me from the ground. My heart was in my throat and my vision narrowed to a static-white tunnel—I think I pissed myself, I don't remember—but I quickly wriggled my way out of my jacket before the arm's twin snatched at the space where my head had been just moments before.

I hit the floor running and carried on, legs powering like pistons while my lungs burned with acid. I could hear more of them coming and there was just enough oxygen left in my brain for me to start wondering what the long-term plan really was.

Keep going.

They won't follow.

I ran for what felt like forever until, eventually, I looked back and saw more of those strange things lingering far off in the darkness. It was only a fleeting glimpse, but I felt as if they should have been closer than they were. I didn't want to think they were slowing. I didn't want to feel that sort of hope. But I found my feet moving faster nonetheless, as if whatever lay ahead really might just keep me safe.

You're here.

I stopped at last. Where I stood was a cross-roads of sorts, quite possibly in the same chamber we'd been attacked in the day before. Dozens of small footpaths had been carved in the dust by regular passage and they converged on some space far ahead. I followed to the centre where a small crater a few metres wide had been made in the snowy ash. As far as I could tell, I was alone, so I took the time to catch my breath. But after that? I had no idea.

So close.

"So close," I murmured.

The air in that place had a reverent stillness. My torch seemed to stretch farther than usual, lighting the space around me in a cool lunar glow. Endless flakes of dust fell around me and for a moment I thought of standing in a snow globe. I felt like I was at the heart of the cosmos, like the whole world was holding its breath.

He blamed himself. Blamed his mortality.

Something stirred, and I faced the darkness. Its footsteps were quiet like a deer's in the snow, but I could feel the vibrations in the sole of my feet.

He needed something better than he was.

It approached. I realised this was the truth I'd been looking for, the explanation for it all.

He needed a god.

"And he made one," I answered, my voice a quiver.

Where there had been a need for breath, the artist had made something to breathe in his place. In the darkness it had stayed for the last eighty millennia, crafting endless creatures and shapes to bring to life. Ersatz creations for an ersatz god; it had never stopped trying to fulfil its purpose.

It stepped into the light, and I saw the face of a weathered old man with a furrowed brow and a grey crown of hair, something inherited from one who'd given it life. He was born of racial characteristics that no longer exist and yet I recognised the face of a man who was intelligent, patient, and committed. It was the face of a priest or a teacher, an idealised representation of its creator that stood 12 feet tall. Time, or perhaps the curse, had worn it down into a haggard leper of a man, skinny and gaunt with lesion riddled skin. Even as it stood, parts of it fell to the floor in wet clumps that writhed and died. I decided it must be blind since it had no interest in me, not even passing. It strode past and reached down, grabbing some of the ever-present dust to compress and roll into slithers of skin it slapped onto its crumbling torso. It was re-fashioning its own body even as it rotted to pieces.

When one of its limbs came too close to me, I stood aside and let it wander ahead where I followed. Its feet carved wide paths in the ash, and I kept close as it wandered with purpose through the dark. After a while, it came to stop by some mounds of dust, and it lowered itself to the floor with a ground-shaking thud. Slowly it took some of the loose material and compressed it back into solid lumps of clay. Carefully it began to fashion something. I couldn't be sure what, but I found all fear gone. I could have stayed there for days. I still don't know how long it exactly was that I stayed there. The god never moved and nor did I. I couldn't. I was rooted to the spot by the sheer beauty of its work, and I watched with intense fascination as it rolled and shaped and twisted and pulled until at last it had the perfect image. Its enormous hands were deftly skilled, and the final product appeared whole before me, almost as if by magic.

It was me. My clothes, my hair, my face, even the coat I'd shaken loose just hours before. Every last detail was recreated with inhuman perfection.

The god looked toward me. Its stony blank eyes regarded me with no human emotion I recognised before rising from the floor. It turned back swiftly towards the darkness and exited the light. And just like that, I was alone once more in the dark.

Not alone. You have a gift.

I turned to the statue. It was perfectly still almost as if it was waiting.

Waiting for someone to breathe life into it.

"No," I whispered.

Yes.

"Why am I not surprised you're here?"

I opened my eyes. I was lying in the tunnel just behind the bulkhead with no memory of how I'd got there. Standing over me was a very grim looking older man. His name, as far as I knew, required a level of clearance that was somehow above even the president's head.

"Because you make a habit of shitting all over my dreams?" I grunted, pushing myself upright while wincing from the pain. I must have been out for hours, lying on the hard, frozen floor. Sheer luck had stopped me from suffering hypothermia. Thank God I had my jacket.

"You really shouldn't have gone in," he gestured to the ship. "There are a million different reasons to leave things like this buried and I would hope that over the years even just a few might have sunk in for you."

"There are no good reasons to ignore the truth," I replied before adding: "How did I get here? Do you know that at least? How I got out?"

The man shrugged.

"I was hoping you'd tell me, along with a few other details perhaps," he replied.

"Ah well," I said. "Funny thing is, my experiences within that ship are classified."

"Really?" He raised his eyebrows.

"I've come to the conclusion that the information I learned from my excursion is too dangerous to share with the public and, uh, none of you men-in-black pricks meet my steep criteria for security clearance. Why don't you have your people talk to my peo—"

"Very funny," he said. "I don't know why you do it. It doesn't change anything. No one will listen."

"They don't need to," I said, begrudgingly taking his hand as he pulled me up. "Now, are you assholes going to arrest me, or is this carnival finally over?"

"It's over," the man smiled. "The others are being evacuated now. Charges will be pressed against Dr Greaves for illegally taking donations from organisations associated with fracking lobbyists. He won't see prison time, but he'll never work legitimately again. As for you, we didn't feel it was worth our time to tarnish you any further. At this stage, you'd be lucky to get something out there on Reddit."

"The students?" I asked.

"Strongly encouraged to change their current avenue of study. You know how it goes. First the carrot, then the stick. We'll get them out of the field soon enough."

"I remember quite well," I replied. "What about the samples?"

"Some kind of fungal parasite that leeches genetic traits from whatever it finds in the atmosphere. Some quirk of temperature and humidity makes it best disposed to absorb breath, but nothing's technically stopping it from going all grey-goo in the back of a warm cupboard. When you factor in its potent ability to absorb memories, then, who knows? Maybe even you might understand why it needs to be kept under our strict control. We've had access to the samples for a few days while we waited for you to pop up. Its ability to absorb even the most complex of human memories makes it an apocalypse waiting to happen. We found your lead biologist dead in her lab while the thing she was experimenting on finished up her written report."

"That's a shame," I said. "She was a hard worker and very smart."

"Yes, it is," he replied, eyeing me with disdain. "Yet another avoidable death."

"Good thing you've got all the samples then, isn't it?" I said. "Locked away for all eternity, I imagine. God forbid we get to study it!"

The man laughed uproariously like I'd just made a very clever joke.

"Your words, not mine, doctor," he said before leaving like he'd won the argument (something he loved to do). But I didn't pursue, instead allowing myself to be taken away by a crew of paramedics to check for signs of injury. Far away, the man began marshalling several groups of people to work on sealing the ark away for all eternity. I watched as, once again, the world set itself towards the goal of destroying the truth I'd worked so hard to unearth. But this time, I didn't feel despair or dejection. I'd learned the full truth this time, and although my stomach hurt like hell and my head was full of holes, I smiled from ear-to-ear.

I knew the truth. The *whole* truth, or so I thought.

"Christ," one of the paramedics laughed, shaking a cloud of white clay loose from my jacket. "It's like you're made of the stuff."

Little-by-little, my smile began to fade.

158

HOARDER

"God, it must've been horrible lying down here for weeks."

I gave Jessie a withering look as he got up to change the water in his bucket. When he saw that both Mrs Janners and I were sharing an uncomfortable silence, he tried to act as if nothing had happened, but the effort was clumsy.

"I'd bought him a mobile phone," the older woman said, her voice mousy and tired. "He just wouldn't keep the damn thing on him. If he had perhaps..."

"No need to explain," I replied.

"It's just I tried to see him whenever I could, but he wasn't a nice..."

"You don't owe anyone an explanation," I said, trying my best to appear empathetic and non-judgemental. "We're here to just clean up and help out. Now, if there isn't anything else we need to know, I think it's time we got on with things on our end and you can carry on with your day."

"Oh," she said as I took her by the arm and started walking her out of the bedroom. "Oh, there is one more thing." She turned from me and walked towards a small cupboard door beneath the stairs. "There's a small basement down here where he's got a few more things boxed up. Look, the key's just in the lock ready so," she opened the door and gestured downwards. "It's awfully dark, so if you haven't brought any torches I can..."

"Oh, don't worry about that. We bring plenty of light in case something happens with the electrics," I said. "We'll make sure to clear the basement out. Is there anything in particular down there that you might want to keep?"

"If you find any photos, can you put them aside?"

"Of course." I smiled before taking her to the door and saying my goodbyes. After she left, I went back and looked down the tiny basement stairway and made a mental note of when and how it would be best to approach that part of the job.

I found Jessie in the downstairs bedroom where he was still on his hands and knees scrubbing away at the faintly human-shaped stain in the floor. We had already disposed of the rectangular section of carpet that Mr Rittle had lain upon, and now we faced the daunting task of trying to clear out any seepage that had soiled the underlying wood floor.

"Sorry about that," Jessie said when I came in. "It just slipped my mind, and I forgot she was standing there. I know it wasn't very professional, but it's just it's weird, y'know?"

"It's alright," I said, running my dusty hands through my hair. "Just be careful. If she hadn't already paid us a deposit, that could have cost us the gig."

"You're right," he replied. "I've done this job for long enough. I should know better."

"Yeah, but to be fair, this is..." Mr Rittle was unique to us in a few ways. Not only had he died a horrific and messy death, but he had a strange fixation of acquiring other people's garbage and his enormous 43-bedroom manor was filled with trash he'd bought and stolen from anyone he could find. There was no rhyme or reason to what he kept or why. All around me stood stacks of misshapen books and stolen bin bags interlaced with leaflets and old food wrappers. Looking to my left, I saw a bent and rusty nail framed with the Roman numerals CLXXIX engraved in the wood, while on my right was a small cluster of toenails arranged in descending of thickness. "This is something else," I said, finally finishing my sentence. "When are the others arriving?"

"Pinnie text me fifteen minutes ago to say they were on their way, but Jay's still on holiday," Jessie replied, standing up to change the bucket once again. Walking over, I took a long look at the stain, pausing briefly to kneel down and examine a slight pitting in the floor, almost as if someone jabbed the wooden boards with a knife over and over. Seeing me fixated on the floor, Jessie returned and said, "Yeah, it's slow progress."

"Aye," I agreed. "But still progress. Keep at it."

I unearthed the first painting behind a pile of laundry as tall as a man. The sodden mouldy clothes had rotted much of the canvas, spoiling the painting until it looked like a psychedelic nightmare. Despite the coverage, or perhaps because of it, the subject looked all the more haunting. It was a church, the outline dissolving into a shadow-black mould. Alone, standing unusually tall by the front door, was the figure of a barely visible man painted blacker than black, glistening through the canvas like liquid obsidian. The paint looked so fresh as to be wet, and I hesitated and stopped myself before I touched it out of mindless curiosity.

Holding it, I suddenly felt watched in the cramped confines of the towering filth. I turned to check the doorway behind me and for some reason I frightened myself by imagining the painted man standing in the corridor. It was a silly thing to daydream, but it bothered nonetheless and when I put the painting aside, I made sure to turn it facing towards the wall.

Over the next few days, another four paintings were found. The second was discovered by Pinnie, who brought it over with a disgruntled expression. While he was usually untalkative, something about his silence on this occasion struck me as sombre and depressed. When I asked if he'd looked at it, he answered, without stopping to talk to me as he made his way back upstairs:

"Blood hideous thing."

I took a quick peek myself and was startled by the faint impression of something juddering towards me through the frame. In fact, I was simply looking at a copy of the same painting I had found except the perspective had moved closer towards the church door, enlarging the subjects and creating, in my mind, the illusion of movement. A proper look revealed that the image was static (what else did I expect?) and while the figure and church door were shrouded in the usual darkness, the mould and filth had done unusual things to the spires of the church, lending them a subtle fleshy quality.

That same day, Jessie was found being sick next to the third and fourth paintings that were found as a pair. Quietly I moved the canvasses aside to avoid further damage and checked him out to make sure he was okay. He was insistent that it the intense smell coming from a jar of pickled-something he'd dropped, but when I looked at the two paintings he'd found I came to suspect otherwise. Much like the others, they were of the same subject, each one bringing the church and the painted man closer and closer to the viewer in a most unpleasant way. Slowly the pastor came into focus until the blackness was broken with tiny flecks of detail; a squarish bit of off-white for a face, two long needle-like stabs for hands, and the tiniest fleck of red beneath his feet.

As the man came closer with each new painting, so too did the church and mould merge to create an increasingly surreal architecture. By the final painting, its spires looked like tumorous growths of bone and meat, standing unnaturally tall against an alien sky of red and violet bruises that burst across the canvas. It reminded me of every piece of rotting flesh I'd ever seen, and I felt a visceral urge to look away.

After that, I sent Jessie home for the day, suspecting that the paintings had affected him quite severely. When he returned the next morning, he was quiet and baggy-eyed. Pinnie suggested to me that he'd been drinking, but I had a gut-feeling something else was playing on his mind. After all, I'd cleaned up that jar and seen the cabbage-headed foetus he'd been holding, and I knew the paintings were just one strange facet of this job. I started to wonder if it was sensible to leave each of us alone as we burrowed through this unnatural hoard.

"It's like we're journeying through someone else's madness," Jessie said one lunch and surprisingly, Pinnie gave a nod of agreement. "I found a piece of paper today that just read 'everything here has taken a life' and I can't stop wondering if it's true, or if he just thought it was true, or if it's a joke, or a prediction, or what?"

"How does a toenail take a life?" I asked.

"Infection?" Pinnie suggested gruffly. "My grandfather died because his belt loop caught a door handle and he went straight over, turning at the hip, and wacked his head on the floor. He was so scared of the drop he had a heart attack."

Jessie let out a tempered snicker but immediately covered it with his hand. A moment later and I let out a chuckle and then, not long after, so did Pinnie.

"He just went over like a windmill," Pinnie added after the laughter had died down before adding, as if it was some important reassurance, "Jay will be here tomorrow. We can get through this job even faster with him."

Something about the absurdity of that lunch had calmed me and I returned to work feeling a little more grounded, except bad luck would have it that barely an hour after our conversation, I found the fifth painting. At first, I tried not to look at it, but I couldn't help myself. I'd put it against the wall and continued working, but my every movement felt watched. I could feel it there, behind me. Every time I bent down to grab something off the floor, some instinctual alarm went off and I would snap up alert as if expecting something to…

I don't know. I felt like a kid taking a long walk home as the sun was setting on a winter afternoon, briskly moving between each streetlight, terrified that something would snatch me from the shadows in between. After I nearly dropped a whole box of milk bottles, I was forced to admit that I was letting my imagination get the better of me and I finally leaned the painting back to get a good look at it.

As I did, the light from above fell across it in one smooth movement, the shadow withdrawing like a pulled curtain and I swear that figure shuddered out of the background and right up to the very front of the painting, his whole face taking up the window of the canvas. I cried out, let go of the frame, and it fell backwards with the thud of a church bell. The pastor's face was leering up at me, a strange impression of a misshapen milky head framed by a sturdy-brimmed black hat, the face devoid of any real detail as if seen through a cataract. And yet it radiated hate, a pencil-thin mouth sneering at me through the incohesive brush strokes.

I was shaking when I pulled it back up, and much to my shame I later asked a passing Jessie to take it down to the others because I was too busy. I couldn't quite bring myself to touch it again, not after I noticed the wet paint against the wall where it had been leaning.

"I assumed he'd been painting them," Jay said, holding the canvas with both hands. When I'd heard he'd found one just a few hours into his first day at the house, I felt a lurch in my stomach but was relieved to find it wrapped top to bottom in brown wrapping paper, a thin piece of string tying it all together. In one corner was a label with Mr Rittle's address.

"Could be a different one," Jessie said.

"Should we look?" Jay asked. Before he'd begun working in the morning, Pinnie had taken him aside and shown him the paintings.

Jay had yet to speak about their effect on him, but I could clearly see a fear in his eyes as he'd asked whether we wanted to look at the sixth canvas.

"I think we have to," Jessie said. "We've seen the others."

"No," I replied with a shake of my head, and both Jay and Pinnie voiced their agreement, but Jessie piped up,

"It's probably not even the same one. For all we know, this was a Christmas gift. You guys can't be serious, can you? We really need to look at it."

For the life of me, I couldn't understand Jessie's angle, and I dismissed any argument and instead instructed Jay to take the painting down with the others while I kept Jessie busy on the upper floors. Personally, I felt immense relief to know the painting was hidden from us, for we were barely 8 rooms into the house, and I already felt emotionally drained in a way that begged to give up on the job. And something about Jessie wanting to open it unsettled me; he'd never had a ghoulish streak before. Did he not feel the same repulsion that the rest of us did?

When the day ended, he came to and asked once more if he could look, and I told him no. I ignored his complaints and told him he needed to keep his head focused on the task ahead, trying my best to emphasise the money we'd be paid for doing it. He nodded a faint agreement when I reminded him about his upcoming wedding, but as I watched him stagger to his car, I wondered if I'd made any impact on him at all.

When he didn't come in the following day, I initially thought he'd just taken the day off. Normally I would have been furious, but I believed he had good reason on this occasion. Having spoken to Pinnie and Jay, it was clear we were all finding this job unusually stressful, and I hoped that when Jessie returned, he might bring back enough good energy to raise all our spirits.

Except at the end of that day, as I was locking up, I went to check on the reception area where the paintings were kept and noticed that the latest one in its brown wrapping paper was stacked at a slight angle. I approached it and felt a knot in my throat when I saw a fold of torn paper stuffed between it and the canvas beside it. By the time I leaned it back, my stomach was in my throat, and I found no relief at what I found.

The paper had been torn open, revealing the painting within, except now there was just the church door rendered in peculiar child-like detail. Around the edges veins of corruption curled just out of sight, like bloody smoke, but there was no pastor, no grim-faced spectre standing guard. I reached out and touched the slimy paint and saw that it was still wet and wiped it away on a nearby desk. As I did so, I noticed something rather alarming on the floor.

With everything being moved around, it was hard to say if the scratches in the wood were new or old, but I left the darkening house as quickly as I could, looking up at it in my rear-view mirror only when I felt that I was far enough down the driveway to be safe. And yet I still nearly veered off the road at the sight of a black figure standing by the doors. Of course, by the time I straightened up the wheel and steadied the car, I checked, and nothing was standing there. I told myself it was just my imagination, but when the morning came, I was not surprised to find out Jessie had failed to turn up to work.

We found no more paintings after that, but Jay, Pinnie, and I continued to work under an increasingly anxious mood. Together, we had no problem avoiding the paintings, and I desperately hoped that would be the end of the weirdness. But I quickly realised how wrong I was, for nearly every room had a litany of bizarre and unsettling finds. There were scrapbooks filled with bloodied clothes, strange words carved into the walls, mirrors with delayed reflections, but they were the least of it.

The worst was the sex doll.

In all my years clearing out hoarder's homes, unpleasant sex stuff was incredibly common. When Jay first radioed in, telling everyone he'd found a homemade sex doll, I almost felt a kind of relief. It almost felt like something we'd expect in a normal place. But even a simple cursory look at the thing made of padded foam and old women's clothes, all covered with uncomfortable rust-brown stains, had me questioning Jay's conclusion. Before I could say anything, Pinnie spoke up.

"Where's its mouth?"

"Are you sure it's wise to be touching it?" I added.

"Gotta have a strong stomach for this job, you told me that on the first day," Jay said. "I mean, it's a sex doll, right? It has to be? He's an old man with urges and... and..."

It was an absurd facsimile of a woman, a misshapen lump of green, blue, and purple padded foam cut haphazardly into a misshapen hour-glass figure like an amateur mannequin. For a face it had a porcelain mask shaped like the image of a geisha, except instead of a demure thin-lipped smile there was a clownish, red-lipped snarl beneath lurid spherical eyes. They were carved with great anatomical detail, glaring at me with the wide-eyed excitement of a nightmarish gargoyle. Set above them was a molten brow that sagged into an exaggerated frown.

"There's no actual holes," Pinnie remarked, picking the thing up and turning it head over heels. "Fuck!" he cried out, startling Jay and I and dropping the doll where the mask thudded against the floor. "There's something sharp in it," he groaned before sucking on his wounded thumb.

Gently, jay and I picked it up. I briefly noted a small chip above the brow where it had fallen, and carefully turned it over and examined it until I identified a long sliver of metal embedded in the doll's thigh, resisting all efforts to remove it. The needle was pitted with rust, and at the tip was the slightest hint of a pearlescent shimmer that winked violet and crimson as I turned it over in the light.

"I can't get the damn thing out; we need to be careful handling this thing. And Pinslow," I added, "you need to look into getting a tetanus shot."

"Infected by a sex doll!" Jay cried out, his whinnying laugh like nails on chalk. "That'll raise some eyebrows!"

"It's not a fucking sex doll, you daft bastard!" Pinnie swore, still smarting from the wound. "It hasn't got any holes for... for, well, you know!"

"Well..." Jay muttered, holding the doll up once more so she stood amongst us, her inhuman face making uncomfortable eye contact with me. "What else is she?" he asked, and I realised his voice was not petulant, but pleading.

He genuinely wanted an answer.

I think we all did.

I was coming into work a little later than usual when I noticed something unusual. The sex doll had been pulled out of the skip and placed next to it, her eyes drinking in the barren garden that surrounded the home. For a moment, I paused and momentarily wondered if somehow the expression on the doll's face had changed to a grin. But then again, she looked different in full daylight, and I shook the thought from my head. Barely a second later and Pinnie strode out, his arms full with an old television that he threw into the skip with glee. Without speaking, I gestured to the doll.

"Reminds me of Maria Lewis," he said with a gruff laugh. "Same size, same shape, and just like Maria, she's got a nasty bite." He held up his thumb, and I grimaced at the open wound throbbing just beneath his nail.

"Christ," I scoffed at the joke. "Well, just like Maria, she's destined for the bin."

"She deserved better than that," Pinnie replied, going silent for a moment too long before appearing to remember that I was still there. "Maria, that is, the real one, not that uh... not that thing."

"Shall we put it in the skip now?" I asked.

"No, we should put the heavy stuff in first. I'll chuck her in later."

For a moment I was about to argue that the doll would hardly make a difference to the skip's weight distribution, but I decided to let the older Pinnie's judgement stay in effect. And yet a day later, when the skip was loaded out for a new one and driven past me, I couldn't help but notice the doll was not in it. She was standing beside the door once, her mouth cast in a downward expression of theatrical sorrow.

"Did you do this?" I asked Pinnie as he passed me by the doorway.

"Do what?"

"Changed her face?"

"No," he answered innocently. "How would I do that?"

"Just... just make sure she's in the next one."

"Sorry!" he cried with an affected wince. "I forgot about her. Still, she's hardly hurting anyone, is she?" Pinnie carried on walking casually as if it was an honest mistake, but briefly stopped to readjust the doll's unkempt wig without a second thought.

"Just make sure she's gone tomorrow," I shouted after him, to which he merely waved his hand in acknowledgement, as though there was nothing to worry about. I hoped that was true, but when lunchtime came, and we all gathered outside, I noticed the doll was missing.

"Some kids were eyeing her up," Pinnie said when asked before gesturing to an upper-story window. Now the doll leered down at us with a barely visible expression of joy. "Figured we can't let them get a hold of her, 'specially if we never got that dirty needle out."

"She's upstairs?" Jay asked.

"In her room. Her mum won't let me speak to her, though I don't know why. We'd left the disco holding hands and now..."

Pinnie trailed off into a heavy silence, and Jay and I gave each other a funny look. Unwilling to press the awkward silence any further, we ate the rest of our lunch without speaking. I later asked Jay to check Pinnie's van for the usual flask, but he came back empty-handed, and I was left wondering if something else was going on with the older man.

Sure enough, when the day was finally over, I went to check on Pinnie and found him sitting next to the doll, elbows on his knees and his head buried in his hands. I stood in the doorway for a moment, hesitating to speak.

"Are you okay?"

"Just tired is all," he answered, looking up at me with blood-shot eyes. "And this fucking hand of mine is killing."

The infection from his thumb had spread along his wrist and was making progress towards his forearm. The skin looked shiny and tight, close to bursting, and I told him he ought to take the following day off.

"Can't do that," he growled. "Got too much to do. Besides," he added with an almost drunken slur, slouching upwards to put his arm around the doll, "I've got to walk Maria home. You'd think I might have forgotten her until now, but no, she's been in my thoughts every single night since it happened. Didn't even go to her funeral, but I never forgot. She's in my thoughts more than anyone else's."

Quietly Pinnie burped and closed his eyes, a thick rope of drool making stalactites down his chest. Without waking him, I reached out and took the doll and carried it downstairs, leaving the poor man asleep on the box he was sitting on. Once outside, I threw the offending thing in with the rest of the rubbish, and just to add insult to injury, I grabbed some nearby bin bags and hurled them on top of the doll, feeling satisfied that the job was finally done.

I found Pinnie where I'd left him and went to shake him awake when he lashed out with terrible speed.

"It were different back then," he cried, his swollen hand snapping out to clutch my wrist with iron strength. I cried out and pulled back but he held on firm, that unbearably hot palm sending shivers up my spine. It looked like the hand of a bloated corpse, and I saw that his forehead was drenched in sweat and his eyes were burning with delirium.

"We didn't know much back then as boys, and we were always taught that girls would lead you on strange games before getting to the point. She never said no," he hissed, his expression pleading with me in desperation. "It took years for me to realise, to understand why she'd done it and the part I played. But what had happened weren't at all like I imagined, like what movies show you. I didn't know, didn't *think*. It weren't until I saw the way her ma looked at me that the first seeds of doubt settled in."

Suddenly the fire within him died, and he sat back on the box, falling asleep almost as if he was under a spell. Shaking, I pulled my hand free and turned to see Jay standing in the doorway with an ashen white face.

"Did you see that?" I asked incredulously, but he ignored me, saying instead:

"I think I found the others."

"Other what?" I asked.

"Come see."

I left Pinnie slouched over himself and followed Jay to a small room one story up from where I'd been. Slowly he opened a door to reveal a cluttered display room with a horse-shoe shaped arrangement of cabinets and boxes all draped in colourful bed sheets. One of the sheets had been pulled back to reveal a horrible sculpture; it was a porcelain mask with ten needle-tipped limbs sprouting from the centre, its face twisted into a drunken grin. It had the same features as the doll's, except with a very different expression.

"Looks like something a school shooter would make in metal shop," Jay grumbled. "Look, the legs are just welded bike chains and knitting needles filed down to a point."

I didn't reply. It was hard for me to repress my arachnophobia in the presence of those two-feet wide monstrosities. There was a busyness to the arrangement of their legs that worked its way right under my skin.

"Look, there are others," Jay said, pulling a second sheet away to reveal another mask nearly identical to the last, barring the expression. "They creep me out."

"You're telling me," I muttered before pulling away another sheet. "Huh," I grunted at the sight of the smashed glass and empty display.

"What's wrong?" When he saw what I saw, he added, "Do you think someone stole it?"

Silently we pulled away all the remaining sheets until all twelve display cases were revealed. Six of them had been smashed and three of the sculptures were gone, but in one of the open cases, I saw that a mask had been returned. Both Jay and I crowded around it and stared in silent disbelief.

"Is that blood?" Jay asked, pointing to one of the legs. It looked like a quill dipped in dried crimson ink. Slowly I raised my eyes to the face and took a sharp inward take of breath; there was a grossly familiar chip on the brow. "You don't think...?" Jay started to ask, but I walked away before he could finish. Silently, I went to the window, and he followed, leaning over my shoulder to look down at the skip in the driveway. Impossibly, the doll was sitting on top of a pile of bin bags.

With a terrible stuttering motion, it turned its head to look back at us.

"How's he doing?" Jay asked. I had just come from the hospital to check on Pinnie, where he'd said some worrying things during my time beside him.

"He's okay," I replied. "Just delirious from the fever."

"And no sign of that thing in the skip? Could it have been... could he have been the one...?"

"I don't know," I replied. "I just don't know."

"I saw it move," Jay said and for a moment, his words were left hanging in the air until I finally responded.

"Me too."

"I did something bad," Jay said, his voice almost mute. "Do you remember years back, my first few days with you. Do you remember finding all that copper in my van?"

"What did you take?" I asked, guessing where things were going.

Shaking, Jay reached down to the plastic bag at his feet. Instead of removing his lunch, like I expected, he pulled out a large clunky polaroid camera.

"I thought it was a joke, or it was broken, or I was just... I thought I might have been going mad, but after that thing we saw yesterday I'm starting... what if it's not? Pinnie had binned it," he said. "But that's not the point. It's what it... look," he grabbed a handful of polaroids from the same bag as the camera and handed them to me. One by one I shuffled through them like a pack of cards but saw nothing except slight variations of a barren desert floor, looking like something you'd expect a rover on Mars to send back.

"What of it?" I asked.

"I took those out here, facing the garden," he replied. "I thought it was busted but... well, look at this."

Holding the camera in both hands, Jay took a photo, and we waited as it printed. And yet the picture that came out was much the same as the others he held.

"I don't get…"

"Now look," he told me as he turned to face the house and took another picture. A few seconds later, he handed me the photo.

"What the fuck is this?"

"Honestly," Jay stammered, "it wasn't until I brought the camera back because, y'know, I felt bad, and I was putting it back in the skip when I must've dropped it and hit the button and it took a photo and… and…"

"You saw this?"

"Yes. It happened this morning. I've been holding onto it all day and I was going to tell you when you got back from visiting Pinnie, but I'm still not sure I can make heads or tails of what I'm seeing."

"It looks like the church out of those paintings," I said. "Or something like it, I think." The photo showed a bright white sky devoid of all features, with a towering building looming over the frame, too large for any sense of height to be gauged.

"That's not the worst of it," Jay grimaced. "Here, I took this earlier."

Jay took another white photo from his inside pocket and showed it to me. It was very similar to the last one, close to identical except for the clearly visible form of Jessie standing behind one of the second-story windows.

And he was not alone.

"He's gone," I said as I laid all four paintings out. Somehow, they had gotten worse, their frames and canvasses consumed by a throbbing mould that was a riotous explosion of colours. And yet despite the growth, the church was still visible in at least three of the images, and the doorway was plainly empty of the painted figure. From beside me came the sudden and loud flash of the camera, and I turned to see Jay shaking a polaroid while he waited for it to develop.

When it finally developed, we saw a rotten crumbling version of the same hallway we stood in, knife-like lances of desert sun blasting through open cracks in the walls and smashed windows. All the wood was sagging and in a rank state of decay, while most of the trash had turned to ashen dust. But most odd was the roll of fabric turned into a makeshift bed on the floor, a tally scratched into the wood that counted to thirteen, and a series of tin cans laid out with water in them.

Sharing a brief look, Jay and I agreed to go upstairs, where we slowly began mapping our way through the house. It was a peculiar and alien experience, marking out the broken floors and collapsed rooms, discombobulated to find that we were climbing stairs shown to be completely destroyed in the photographs.

But there were subtle signs of habitation, including recently disturbed footprints and barricaded doors. Carefully, we followed them until we reached the room where Jessie had been standing. However, when we took a photograph, we found only an empty window, piles of sharpened sticks lying beside it. It wasn't until I took a photo of the doorway, we'd just passed through that I saw Jessie standing alone, glaring down the hallway with terror etched on his face.

I felt a flare of urgency and ran out into the same hallway. I felt helpless, unsure of what to do until I did the only thing I could and took a photo of the corridor. The picture that printed was horrifying, showing a lonely stretch of hall that broke suddenly into open air. Standing there, leering through the open hole, was a grotesque face, hauntingly reminiscent of the masks we had found. Whatever wore that visage was a monstrous thing, for the features were rendered upon a towering giant.

When I took a photo of the space behind me, Jessie had gone, fleeing just out of sight. I turned and snapped another, and nearly jumped at the sight of that horrible face looming through the corridor, its hairy head and neck squeezed ineffectually into the small space, filling the corridor with shadow as it tried to force its way forward.

"What's it doing?" Jay asked.

I took another, saw that the thing had moved forward by a few inches, snapping wood and buckling the floors. Now, one of its hands was stretched outwards as if to grab something.

"I don't understand," he said. "Is it reaching for Jessie?"

"No," I muttered. "He's gone."

"What's it reaching for!?" Jay again, taking an uneasy step forward.

I took another photo and saw that the giant was now just a few feet from where I stood. Something about its eyes, those round hungry glistening orbs with small harsh pupils and no irises, terrified me, but it was nothing compared to what I felt when I realised that its face had been lit up by the flash of the camera.

"It's reaching for us," I said, my words immediately followed by the sound of Jay fleeing hysterically down the stairs.

"Jay!" I screamed, turning a corner to find the basement door beneath the stairs swinging open on its hinges. I ran up to it but hesitated at the first step. "Jay!" I cried again, hoping to God he'd reply to me from anywhere but down there. And yet, as soon as the last of my echoes rang out into the dark, Jay let out a terrible shriek from deep within the basement. I took a deep breath to steady my nerves and descended.

It was more normal than I might have expected. Rows and rows of shelves had been laid out and filled with the usual rubbish that Mr Rittle enjoyed so much. Jars of fermenting medical curiosities, boxes of stolen Christmas decorations, ornamental gnomes with mud still caked on their feet; there was nothing down there that, at first glance, might be responsible for Jay's disappearance.

But that earthen chamber was bigger than I first thought. The first room was typical in size, but in one corner was a jagged hole cut into the soil which led into another similarly sized room. And then there was another, and another, and another. Until then, I had believed the manor house to be an impenetrable nightmare, but it turned out to be just the tip of the iceberg. I soon found new stairs leading to lower floors haphazardly dug into the very peat itself.

Nothing was empty; there was no spare room, and it was on the third set of stairs that I realised the rooms were getting larger and I had taken such an unusual series of twists and turns that meant I couldn't be sure what the way back was. I started to wonder whether it would be okay to just leave, but I called out Jay's name one more time, just in case. No one replied and in a final effort I swung the camera around from my neck and took a photo of the basement.

Unlike before, it did not show me anything at all like the place I was standing in. In fact, this was a perfect replica of the very first painting I found in the manor. I had come to understand that the camera showed some alternate (or perhaps future) version of the place I stood, but if it did, then nothing about the last picture made any sense. I took another and grimaced to see that the painted figure had somehow appeared in the doorway of the church. Nothing about it corresponded to my location, and I came to realise that if the camera had any kind of logic or rules, it wasn't anything I could understand. Feeling all hope wane, I took one last photo and saw that the painted figure had lunged forward, moving closer to the camera's point of view.

I decided to take no more and let the photo fall to the floor. Hesitantly, I turned, getting ready to leave and call the police, when I faced the stairway with my torch and revealed a person standing at the top. Their face was obscured by something strange that glinted in my light, something metallic or ceramic, but the outfit clearly belonged clearly to Jay.

"Jay?"

I stepped forward, seeing how ragged and torn his clothes were, glimpsing his pallid torso coated in drying blood. "Jay, are you okay?" I asked, but he stood there, shaking jerkily with his head twisted up to face the ceiling. Something was hovering over his face and his neck was bulging and throbbing as if his Adam's apple had swollen and was roaming free.

When he lowered his head, it was with unnatural speed. What happened was so fast I barely had time to process it, pouring through the images in my mind as I later ran through the labyrinthine corridors of shelves while my chest burned in desperate need of air. No matter what, the sight had been enough to send me running away without any need of comprehension. It was only later that my thoughts coalesced, and I realised he had glared at me with the face of the masked sex doll.

His movements down the stairs were erratic and clumsy, and if he hadn't fallen, he may very well have caught me then and there. As he skidded face first down the lumpy steps, I saw a glistening mechanism of metallic legs and clicking gears bloodily jammed into his broken distended jaw. Blood gurgled from his swollen tongue and lips; something had been forced down his throat and I could see its roaming legs shift and move beneath his grossly expanded gullet.

Given the way that he was moving, it was elsewhere in his body, too. The mask wore an expression of a slavering hunter. Blood borrowed straight from Jay flowed freely down its mouth and lent it a spectral appearance. I didn't even wait for it to hit the floor before running, but when it finally caught up to me, I saw that it clanked across the floor like a four-legged spider.

I threw down shelf after shelf to slow it, but it skittered over any obstacle with the wretched speed of long-limbed arachnid. And yet I was quicker than it around corners, and I easily kept my distance until, finally, it disappeared from my tail and—while I was very much terrified that it might be hiding in any one of the numerous pitch-black nooks and crannies—I deliberately turned and started for the stairs.

It was waiting for me at the very top, screeching out as it raced forward. Something about its exertions had altered Jay's body. I noticed his arms and legs were swollen and bones visibly moved his skin. As it grappled with me, I understood why; to stop it reaching for my face, I had to grab Jay's arm by the wrist, desperately holding it back, except instead of holding it still, I saw that something unsheathed from the very flesh itself. Sliding out from between Jay's finger bones, pushing muscle and bone aside like tenderised meat, was one of the spidery legs belonging to the mask.

Horrified at the thought of it touching me, I threw the thing aside and let it tumble back down the stairs. By the time Jay's corpse had risen, more of the legs had pushed through the skin of his limbs and the cohesion of his body was giving way. The more this thing moved Jay around like a meat suit, the more it tore him apart. But at least I had a clear route to the exit, and I fled to the second set of stairs, desperately hoping this thing would be too slow. But somewhere along the way, I got lost again, and sure enough, the clicking sound of my chaser was never far behind.

I'm still not sure exactly what happened, but somewhere in that basement I passed a tunnel, or perhaps a kind of grotto. I was a few paces ahead of it before my brain registered the sight and my footfalls slowed to a stop, almost as if my brain acted without my conscious intervention. I came to a stumbling halt and glanced backwards to confirm I'd really seen what the flashing images in my mind suggested.

Mr Rittle was sat at a small workspace, smiling to himself as I ran past.

"Good evening," he said politely, when I stopped and faced him.

Upon his lap was a pile of lifeless metallic legs splayed outwards like a crab's. To his left he had placed a porcelain mask that had been delicately removed from one of the spiders. Without looking up from his work, he reached out and placed a small screw into alignment with a dozen others. Then, reaching into the machine's guts, he began to turn a large winding handle that clicked with each jerking twist of his wrist. Each rotation caused the legs to flicker with spasms of life.

He looked up only when the thing that chased me stumbled into view, stopping momentarily to glare at me and then at Mr Rittle.

"Psst psst," Mr Rittle chirped, as if luring a cat from some bushes. "Come here now. Give it up." Carefully he patted the space beside him, and the monstrosity scuttled over and sat down in an awkward hunch.

"Now," he said, turning to me. "Something you ought to know in your profession: sometimes it's not a 'hoarder's house', but rather it's a 'house that hoards'. Some buildings don't exist in just one time or place, and they are filled with things that come from all over creation. Do you understand? Dangerous things, fun things, all of the unique." Silently he gestured to Jay's twitching corpse. "Do you have any questions?" he asked.

"No," I said, before turning heel and running for my life.

"That is the first intelligent thing you've done since stepping inside this place!" the old man yelled after me, his voice breaking into a bellowing chuckle. "But you're not the only one who can leave!"

"Honey," she said as she rolled over in the bed, coiling the duvet around her feet. "Please come to bed."

Standing with my back to her, facing the silent garden, I lit the room up with another flash of the camera and waited a few seconds to see the developed photograph. I studied it for a few seconds afterwards and then dropped it to the floor along with a hundred others.

"No," I said, shaking my head. "I don't think I will."

He was out there, getting closer with each flash.

It has been a few weeks since I last saw Jay. Similarly, Pinnie has disappeared from hospital. There are mixed reports on that one. I found reports that doctors and nurses who worked on his ward suffered from a spate of suicides, and at least one mortician died under unusual circumstances. Speaking to an orderly, I heard that there were rumours something unusual had happened in the morgue in the early hours of the morning and while there was nothing concrete about what that was, he confirmed that the place had been sealed off for weeks and they were using a temporary morgue set up elsewhere.

But then again there were rumours of a half-naked man in hospital overalls running down a dual carriageway close to the house, and one doctor told me plainly that Pinnie had checked himself out and disappeared. Although when asked about the suicides, that same doctor had averted her gaze and said,

"It was hard on all of us."

I acted on a hunch and asked if she'd seen Pinnie during his stay. For a moment, she looked as if she might respond, but then she burst into tears and refused to answer any more questions.

As for me, well, I've had *visits*. He comes, most often at night, bearing strange things. My wife is getting irritated with the growing clutter and right now it's only just a few boxes and strange ornaments. I want to tell her I'll get rid of them. I want to tell her that the strange moods I've been experiencing will stop, that Pinnie and Jay will be okay, and that any day now I'll go back to work, and it'll all be normal again. But most of all, I want to tell her why any of this is happening. It's just... I don't know how?

I've tried throwing these things away again, but what does it even matter? Sometimes I still throw away the most dangerous or hard-to-explain things—a bloodied knife, a bag of medical waste, a large package of heroin with a pearlescent symbol—but he just brings more. All my wife sees is a plain box sitting on the doorstep, but the camera shows me that wretched figure standing expectantly over his offering. At first, I thought all he wanted was for me to keep these things, but amongst his most recent gifts was a canvas, some used and ancient brushes, and a set of unlabelled paints that stink when opened.

I know what he wants, but... I'm losing everything. It's only just started, but I know where it's going. Bit by bit, my home is filling with the strangest things and pretty soon there'll be room for nothing else.

THE FORTRESS

I first caught sight of the fortress from the back of the pickup truck, the convoy's engines growling behind me as the tarpaulin roof thundered in the wind. I leaned out over the side to get a better look and glimpsed the fort half-buried in a distant dune, like a child's toy left out in a sandstorm. For a few moments I forgot the heat and the sweat, and the God-awful way dust collected in every nook and cranny of my body and imagined the convoy as a row of little toy men in little toy cars, winding a path between mountainous dunes and swirling eddies of golden sand.

It took us another hour before we reached the fort, and several times it dipped out of sight only to reappear larger than before until, slowly, it lost all sense of miniature perspective. Individual windows became visible, and rising towers were revealed to be ramshackle things on the verge of collapse. By the time we could see the brickwork clearly, the truck started to slow, and the guides called for us to ready our climbing gear.

"You ready for this?" Liz asked as I put my feet on the searing desert floor, already having to use my hat to fan the sweat from my brow.

"Probably not," I replied. "I'm afraid of heights."

"It's not far," she chuckled. The rocky outcropping the fortress was built on had been swallowed centuries ago by a roaming sand dune that was hundreds of metres high. Now the desert had finally seen fit to release the plateau, buildings and all, like an ocean wave travelling at glacial speeds. "The foundation can't be more than ten metres from the ground. If you want, you can wait for the workers to build a ramp?"

Liz gave me a shit-eating grin before walking off with a coil of rope under arm.

"It's my find," I cried after her. "And you know damn well I'm not giving up first dibs."

"Maybe you should."

I turned to see Hakim gathering more tools from the back of his truck.

"Why did the French come out here?" he said to no one in particular. "And why are we here now?"

"Finding out why they were here *is* why we're here," I told him.

"And if they have to come dig us up in a hundred years, will they ask the same stupid questions?"

Something was clearly bothering our guide, so I silently went over to his side and began to pack my things while I waited for him to get to the point.

"I don't like this place," he said eventually, and I realised he was more nervous than angry. "I don't like the soil, the rocks, the wind... I just don't like it."

I tried to disagree with him, but I looked at the fort and sensed a flicker of motion behind aching black windows. Deep down, I realised I didn't like the place either, and so I said nothing while I helped him pack. To be fair to Hakim, despite his reservations, he still scaled the short rock face with no complaints, stopping every few metres to hammer anchors into solid stone so our own ascent wouldn't be so risky. Liz waited impatiently beside me, her feet pacing circles in the dust. We ascended together just a half hour later, Liz scaling the cliff using a few safety lines and her own power while I was hoisted up by three men who remained on the ground. It wasn't an issue of weight or even athleticism, but I began to panic just a few feet off the floor and simply couldn't be trusted to get myself up there on my own.

I treated it like a rollercoaster, shutting my eyes and doing my best to forget where I was and what was happening until, at last, Hakim cried out and I looked up to see him reaching over to hoist me up. Feet firmly on ground, I immediately stumbled away from the ledge and over to the fort. The dune had exposed a corner section, and I faced the southern wall. Looking around, I saw a narrow rocky ledge that led to an open doorway set some distance away into the East-facing wall. Sand was still pouring out of it like water from a bottle, presumably emptying the interior and doing part of our job for us. The effect was remarkable, since I could approach the nearest window and, leaning in, see the southern corridor standing empty, as it must have done over a hundred years before. The fortress breathed a cold gust of tomb-like air that pulled at my hair, and I thought of ancient ruins and cursed pharaohs from the books I read as a child.

I caught movement in the corner of my eye and turned to peer into the shadows. For a moment I thought I'd seen nothing, but then a gentle current in the darkness stirred and I felt a tantalising thrill of fear as a slither of black fabric flourished at the very edge of visibility. It looked like the hem of a dress, ragged and beautiful, like I'd just caught sight of a ghostly Cinderella fleeing the ball.

I jumped when Liz appeared at my side and shone her torch in that direction. We both saw nothing but a sandbank just a few metres away. No dress. No Cinderella. Not even a place for her to run to.

"God, what *were* they doing out here?" Liz asked.

"Let's find out," I replied.

"Graham!"

Watson descended from the helicopter with wide arms and a cheery face. He grabbed me as soon as he could and pulled me in for a hug. "Jesus! What a thing you've found out here!"

I turned back to face the looming fortress. Wooden walkways zig-zagged up the cliff face and continued to sprawl across the exposed structure. Men had worked tirelessly each night for a week to clear as much as they could, but from where I stood on the ground, it looked like we'd achieved remarkably little.

"Most of our luck has been in the bailey and some of the walls' interiors," I said. "The cliff has made clearing the sand easier than we could have hoped. Wherever there's a break in the East-facing wall, most of it starts to flow out over the sheer drop. Of course, that only counts for so much of it. The real work will begin when we need to excavate the parts of the building still under the dune."

"You've hardly been idle," he scoffed, slapping me on the shoulder. "Come on! Show me what you've found."

I took him up the walkway, trying my best not to look down through the creaky wooden slats. I told myself it was better than the alternative. I'd had to watch the workers inch their way across the narrow ledge with nothing to keep them safe and by the time they'd finally secured the first safety line, I'd sweated right through my shirt. At least I had a floor to stand on now, and in a few seconds both of us passed into the rear gatehouse, where I called for Liz to come and meet our most generous sponsor.

"There she is," I said, spotting her moving down one of the unlit corridors.

"Silly of her to be running around in the dark," Watson grumbled as we both made our way down there. He wasn't wrong, either. A little sunlight filtered in from somewhere so that the corridor wasn't pitch black—I could clearly see her outline in the dark—but it was hardly safe. We'd already had one collapse on the western wall.

"Liz, are you okay?" I cried out, concerned she might be in some trouble. She turned to face me with a whip-sharp turn of the head, and the gesture caused the breath to catch in my throat. "A-are you hurt?" I stuttered.

I felt a terrible dread settle in my bones, and if Watson spoke at all, I didn't hear him. We both picked up our pace, my torchlight bobbing wildly over the crumbling, stony walls.

"What are you doing!?"

I jumped at the sound of her voice coming from behind, her words crystal clear in the straight and narrow corridor. She was stood in the room we'd just come from, her confused face lit up by the blazing sun.

Watson burst out laughing.

"Poor Graham seems to be suffering in the heat," he cried. "He thought you were wandering around in the dark."

"Didn't you see her too?" I cried.

"No no no," he said, shaking his jowls like Churchill. Something that I was convinced was an affectation. "I was just following your lead. You looked concerned and ran off, so I ran with you. Good to know you take safety so seriously, Graham."

He clapped me on the shoulder once more and trotted off to meet Liz. I knew I should join them and smooth over any introductions, but a lingering curiosity had me take one last look towards the darkness. I saw a billowing wisp of black fabric with a cobweb white hem slink into the darkness. It could have been my imagination, or maybe even just the cries of workers distorted by the rocks, but I seemed to hear a peal of feminine laughter. The sound was grossly out of place in that dusty old building, and it disturbed me deeply.

"Come on."

Liz was suddenly next to me, her hand pulling my sleeve as she looked at me oddly.

"There's nothing down here, remember?"

"I hope so," I mumbled, finally allowing myself to be led away.

"There's something quite alarming about it, isn't there?" Watson said, puffing away at his pipe. He loomed over me and for a moment I thought I saw the twinkling of cosmic dust in the darkness of his shadow. I wiped the sweat from my face and blinked the glare out of my eyes. When I reopened them, the floor had reappeared, along with the six or seven yellowing bones we had uncovered during the dig. Just looking at them made my chest tighten and skin prickle with sweat.

That was nothing compared to how the machine made me feel.

"Could it have been a punishment?" Hakim asked. "Something like the stocks?"

"Usually, military forces don't want to... maim, kill... permanently disable their soldiers or workers," I replied. "Humiliate and shame, maybe even hurt. But if you really couldn't keep someone in line, you'd just shoot them."

"Sometimes cruelty is both the means and the end," he replied.

We had unearthed a contraption quite unlike any other I'd seen, something the original occupants must have adapted from one of their wagons. However, it was constructed, the end result was a pair of large wheels about 6 feet apart with rusted iron manacles that would have clamped firmly around a person's wrists and ankles. The engineering was complicated, most of the metal and gears and teeth mangled beyond recognition, but out of curiosity I applied weight to the largest winch and found that the two wheels rotated slowly in opposite directions.

Watson sucked air through his teeth but didn't speak. He didn't need to. It was obvious how the machine would work. Put someone in the centre, suspended over the ground, legs and arms pulled as far apart as you could, and then turn the winch to wring their whole body like a wet towel.

"How many do you think there are down here?"

It was Liz who spoke. She was knelt beside me, pawing at the ground, having just unearthed another jagged femur. I had a feeling we would find a lot more over the next few days. Something about the rust-red gears and richly stained wood made me think the machine had been put to long and agonising use. I couldn't help but picture someone strained between the two wheels, sobbing in the desert sun as some twisted bastard turned the winch at a snail's pace, grinding bones and popping sockets while tendons snapped like guitar strings.

"Well, something happened to the people who came here," I said. "We knew it wouldn't be a tea party. I guess this is our first bit of insight into what actually happened."

"You can't seriously be suggesting they were all put through that, that... *thing?*" Watson chuffed.

"No but, I mean... at least a few of them were, right Liz?"

"I won't know for sure, but this has to be the seventh victim so far," she answered, holding up yet another rib.

"Some kind of mutiny?" Hakim asked.

"It *was* out in the sun," I said. "Left out and tied up in the heat like that, one crank a day, a sixth of a rotation each time... day after day. You could have kept someone out here for weeks if you knew what you were doing. Right where everyone would see 'em as they went about their business. Maybe it was about sending a message? And if there was a fight, it makes you wonder who ended up winning?"

<hr>

"Where do you think she went?"

I was looking out over the edge of the tower, my stomach churning at such a height. Behind me, Liz unfurled the dress, the sight of which made me deeply uncomfortable. "Bit plain," she added, dusting it off with her hand. "White hem... black cotton, wool, maybe. I can see why she ditched it. It would have been a bad mix with the weather."

"Looks like a mourning dress," I said.

"That explains the veil then, doesn't it?" she replied. "Not much else, though. Don't understand why she was up here."

"She burned her only way down for warmth," I said, gesturing to a small spot of stone that was charred in a circular pattern. Beside it were a few broken lengths of wood that I guessed were the rungs of a ladder. "No food. No water. Just about the only thing she had to stay warm at night. If I had to guess, she was escaping from whatever was going on down in the bailey with all those torture machines."

"Still no personnel logs? No idea who she might be?" Liz asked, and I shook my head.

"Isn't too much of a stretch to think she was the only woman here," I said. "Wife of an officer, maybe. He probably died early on in the journey, maybe before they even reached this place. Either way, that would explain the dress. Not to mention why she had to go to such drastic lengths to stay safe. Whoever started killing who first, it wouldn't have been safe for her alone."

"So," Liz said, "once again... where is she?"

The tower, like all the others, was hollow, with the top floor accessible only via a long climb. Either via rope, like Liz and I used, or a ladder like the old soldiers did. Either way, we had found just about every clue as to this woman's final moments except for her bones.

"Maybe she jumped," I said, returning to the nearby ledge. Such heights made me nauseous, but it was preferable to the sight of that all-too-familiar black dress with a white cobweb hem. "Desperate beyond measure... starving, dying of thirst... and everything going on in that courtyard. Do you think she could see it? Could hear it, even? Day in, day out, no stopping, just... just screams. Maybe she couldn't take it anymore and took the only escape she had."

"In that case," Liz replied, "her body is lost forever. Jesus... imagine what she went through in her final few days? Awful... just awful. It's like this place is fucking cursed." She laughed, perhaps not aware of how seriously she should consider that final statement.

———

I could see the tower from the window in my tent. Even if I pulled the flap shut and zipped it tight, I felt its presence there like a burning candle on my skin. Sleep didn't come easy to me in that place, and without realising it, I'd find myself rolling up that window and looking out towards the tower over and over. With no noise pollution, the night sky was so beautiful and there that thing was jutting up into it like a thumbtack in the roof of your mouth. It made me think of shadow puppets, all black with no detail. Looking at it was uncomfortable, but I didn't stop myself because it was a little like tonguing a loose tooth. Even if it hurt, I just couldn't leave it alone.

Didn't help I could see someone moving about up there. I tried not to focus on them, but the mind doesn't really work that way. First time I saw them I zipped the window shut and went back to bed, pulling the covers up and over my head like a scared child. Wasn't even forty minutes before I was back there, squinting to see if I'd just imagined it all. Sure enough, there they were again, bustling back and forth. Sometimes they'd stop whatever it was they were doing, and I'd drop down out of sight, scared somehow that they could see me in the dark. No way they'd be able to, of course. I had no lights on inside my tent, but the hiding wasn't done out of reason. It was done because something about that place scared me shitless and my imagination already told me who was up there.

It's that woman, I thought, *she's upset we moved her things.*

I would've left it, I think, if I hadn't seen a light on the outer wall and realised one of the workers was making a beeline to it.

They might have seen what I saw, some person up top, and decided to do something about it. Or maybe something else made them go towards it. Either way, I remembered that we'd left our own little rope ladder hanging down, and I had panicked thoughts of some idiot trying to go up there on his own and falling to his death. Part of me wanted to just pretend I'd seen nothing, but even as I watched, I saw their light enter the tower and suddenly disappear. The feeling that someone's life was in danger became too powerful to ignore.

I had to stop whoever it was from going up there, so I geared up, taking a torch, a knife, and a good length of rope. I kept thinking about that woman stuck up there, all that time... The last thing I wanted was to spend the night up there if anything went wrong, so I made sure I had enough to get back down if all went wrong.

By the time I reached the tower, any sign of the worker was gone. There was no light either above or below, and when I held my breath to listen, I heard the aquatic sound of footsteps on the floorboards above.

"Hello?" I cried, and immediately whoever was walking around up there stopped for a moment before picking up once again, this time faster and more desperate. It almost sounded like a struggle. "Who's up there!?" I cried, this time even louder. Now the footsteps died down for good, and I was left stood in the dark with my torch pointed upwards—where it didn't even reach the ceiling—in the hope that somehow, this might all turn out okay.

Something whipped past my head and struck the floor with a terrible crash. Terrified, I turned my torch on it and saw the broken bulb of an electric lantern. This was the irrefutable proof I'd been dreading. Someone was up there, someone from our team, and they were in trouble, stuck way up high and without any light.

"Oh, you've got to be fucking kidding me," I moaned, hoping the sound of my own voice would make me feel less terrified. I grabbed the first rung, lifted myself up a foot, felt the cloying fingers of panic start to pull at my consciousness, and immediately stepped back down.

"No no no no no," I muttered over and over. It was time to turn around and go get Hakim, I decided. He could go up there, but not me.

I looked just in time to see the door slam shut and it was like the whole world disappeared. No distant wind or rustling tents. Even my footsteps lost their echo, but the sound of my breathing just kept getting louder. Panicked, I flicked my light from side-to-side but all I saw was the odd lump of rock or broken wood. Somehow, I knew I wasn't alone. Something was in there, just out of sight. Above or below me, or maybe all around me, but it was in there and it was waiting.

I heard a creaking, the sound of hinges that hadn't seen fresh air in over two centuries, and bringing the torch up, I saw that the door had been pushed open by a few inches. A deliberate act if I'd ever seen one. Something designed to unnerve... to toy.

I watched as four gnarled fingers curled their way around the door, waiting like the legs of a funnel-web spider. Before I had time to think of who or what it was, I found that I had already climbed the first three rungs of the rope ladder.

It was no easy feat getting up, but any fear of falling had been overridden by the sight of that hand waiting for me. One. Two. Three. I barrelled up each new rung, ignoring the way the rope bucked and swayed beneath my feet. I was ready to climb all the way to the top of Everest if it meant putting as much distance between me and that thing.

I was about half-way when the ladder started moving independently. I never looked down, but God, I knew that something was coming, and my imagination kept painting pictures of who or what that might be. By the time something brushed my ankle, it turned my mind to paste. I think I'd been operating on a kind of childlike logic up until that point, and so on some deep level, I kept expecting the dream to burst. I don't know... it was like the feel of that hand cupping my shoe, it switched my brain from child-mode to monkey-mode, and something else took over the climb upwards. My arms were steady, my feet were certain. I was sobbing and begging for help, but it was like my body was doing its own thing to keep me alive and it was doing the job a hell of a lot better than I had on my own. Within moments my head was through the trapdoor and my arms were pulling me up and over the edge so that I was safe, up on the roof.

I looked over and saw the worker, wide-eyed with a small plank of wood held in a tight grip, like he'd been only seconds away from smashing my brains in. Without waiting another second, I rolled over onto my hands and knees and grabbed a knife from my belt. Even as my mind told me it was insane, I began to cut the rope ladder.

"Help me!" I cried, gesturing to the trapdoor. Whether he spoke English or not, he understood. He grabbed a piece of broken glass, gripped it so hard it drew blood from his palm, and began to clumsily saw through his side of the ladder. Together, we severed the rope and sent it tumbling away into the dark. I would have given anything to hear the thud of flesh against stone, to know that we'd hurt our pursuer in some way, but the rope ladder disappeared down into that abyss without a single noise.

Exhausted, I tried to catch my breath, but the man beside me wouldn't relent. He was crying out in French and pointing to a corner of the tower. There was the same black dress that Liz and I had found, somehow having escaped its crate to return home. Already I could tell what the man was trying to say, even if the specific words were lost on me.

We're not safe here. She can come back.

Thankfully his mind, less frayed than my own, picked up on the spools of rope and climbing gear I had stowed on my back. Moving with tremendous urgency, he snatched them away and anchored two lines to the parapet, sturdy lumps of immovable stone that would easily hold our weight. It took him only a few minutes to get them ready and just like that, I was stood with my back to an enormous vertical drop while he spoke words to me that I had no hope of understanding. Liz had talked me through some of the mechanisms on the rope and its latch before. I just had to hope it would carry me through.

Going over the parapet was absolutely dizzying, and more than once I felt my hands and legs panic and begin to flail of their own accord. To be fair to the worker, he actually stopped to help me get started, if only for a minute or two. I probably should have waited for him to join me, but as soon as his head disappeared back over the ledge, I assumed he would be coming down beside me any second.

In a sense, he did just that.

I was about fifteen feet off the ground when he passed me. The force of him falling, the air that he displaced and the eerily silent passage of his body hurtling past at terminal speed, it felt like a punch to my gut. I never saw him hit the ground, but I heard it. A sad and pathetic *whump* as a soft body hit soft sand with enough force to send a plume of dust up into the air. I might have taken the time to stop and look down, to satisfy that morbid curiosity we all know we have, only I couldn't take my eyes off the face glaring down at me.

She was old. Older than I would have thought it possible for any one person to be. She looked like the kind of thing you'd see in a medieval wood cutting, like some medieval peasant would stumble across her, tearing at a coffin lid with crazed hunger. I wouldn't have even recognised her as a woman if it wasn't for the white sailor's collar around her neck. It was stupid, but I couldn't quite get rid of the thought that she looked exactly like someone who had spent two centuries drying out under a sand dune, impossible as that might be.

She disappeared out of sight just a few seconds later and it was then my rope was seized by something from above, and slowly I could feel my body being hauled back upwards. Wasting no time, and paying no attention to the God-awful chorus of whispered fears that filled my mind, I took out my knife and severed the rope, falling the final bit of distance freely. The last thing I could remember was thinking to myself,

I must run as soon as I hit the ground, no matter what is broken or what is hurt, I must move!

But it was all moot. Whatever happened, I hit my head hard enough to lose consciousness, and by the time I opened my eyes, the sun was beginning to rise and I could hear the panicked voices of people crying out for a missing friend. Looking beside me, I could see that the worker's body was gone.

Hakim was dealing with his crew, some of whom sat solemnly in the shade of one wall, some of whom raged as he tried to instil some sense of order. It was one of those odd moments where I felt the need to call the police, or an ambulance, or just some authority figure who could come and make it all go away. It was a stark reminder that we were on our own out there in the desert. No one could come, even if they wanted to.

"I thought Hakim vouched for these fellows?" Watson asked, leaning in so as to not be heard. Liz, who saw us speaking, stepped over to listen.

"He did," I replied.

"Not well enough!" Watson hissed. "One of these men is clearly a killer, and a twisted one at that!"

Watson had chosen a poor choice of words given the scene before us. That machine—the first of many we'd unearthed—had been put to use in the middle of the night and no longer did we have to use our imaginations to picture what that meant for bones and tendon and muscle. Nor did I have to wonder what the fate of the missing worker was...

The man in front of us had been twisted in half and broken apart like tissue, with only some straining ligaments and bits of vertebrae still connecting the two halves of his body. The rest of his abdominal cavity had broken free, and now lay in the baking sun, covered in sand and already attracting the first of many flies.

"They're *his* people, aren't they?" Watson grumbled. "How in the hell did he let a monster into this place with us?"

"He was born in Bristol," I snapped. "He speaks the language and has a few friends and family in the area. He's hardly the fucking president of Algeria."

"Security was his responsibility!"

"To look for thieves or potential leakers," I replied. "Not... not Hannibal Lecter!"

When Liz finally spoke, it was quietly.

"Why didn't we hear him?" she asked, and I could see the question troubled Watson as much as it troubled me. "Why didn't we hear him scream? He was injured but alive when they put him here. He must have been, the blood is still fresh."

"Maybe he didn't scream," I said, stepping closer to get a good look at the man's face. It was a far cry from the terrified man I'd known briefly the night before. Now he looked at peace, as if he had endured his torture the same way he might have endured a good massage.

To my relief, the three of us were given an excuse to leave the broken body when we heard the first of many cries from the gatehouse. This time it was no longer anger at poor Hakim we heard, but terror and desperation as the men glimpsed something on the horizon.

"Oh no," Hakim said as he stepped up and saw what was coming. One by one, Watson, Liz, and I joined him and echoed that same sentiment.

In the distance, a monstrous sandstorm approached, a roiling inferno of sand that choked the sky and uprooted the earth. I had never glimpsed anything so large in my entire life. It stretched from one end of the horizon to the other like a curtain pulled across creation. The sight of it was enough to feel like the rules of perspective had broken, like the dizzying laws of gravity were on the verge of collapsing and we would find ourselves falling into it to be torn apart by elemental forces.

"Hakim," I said, "We need to get everything out of the camp and up here."

The expression on his face could only be described as desperate. For a moment, I thought he might protest as he glanced back at the broken body that lay suspended and dripping over the floor, and then back at the approaching storm.

"The workers... they won't stay here. Not with... not with *that*," he stuttered.

"This isn't a multiple-choice exam," I told him. "There's no other way. We have to bunker down here."

It was night, and the storm was finally upon us. Outside, the sky was little more than a sickly haze and visibility was reduced to less than a metre, even with a strong torch. Without one, it was absolutely haunting. Alone, in the small supply store I'd claimed for my room, I waited as it felt like the sky collapsed all around us. Watson wasn't happy, neither was Liz, but Hakim and I had called in a chopper to get us out of there the second the weather allowed. They saw that as bailing. Not that it mattered. The workers had already fled, setting out in the convoy in desperate hopes of outrunning the storm. I would have gone with, but they left without warning, ignoring my cries to wait as I ran after them.

I wouldn't have looked back either.

There was nothing to be done, not really, except wait. Something I would have found a hell of a lot easier if I could sleep for longer than a few minutes at a time. The storm raged relentlessly, and I could hear a dozen boarded windows straining under the assault and at least one shutter banging furiously in the wind. Just above my head my own barricade rattled with each dreadful gust, and I finally gave up on sleeping when something broke and a thin trickle of sand started to pour down onto my head.

I figured it was best to maybe wait this night out with the others. Torch in hand, I left and walked down the corridor. I knew it was no more than a few hundred metres in length but at night those walls seemed to stretch elastically so that you couldn't be sure of where you stood or how far you had to go. You had only the fetid gloom of a few feet in front of you to let you know you were moving anywhere at all. I tried not to let it bother me as I kept walking until, at last, I came to a turn in the wall's interior. Around the corner, the wind was suddenly louder, and I soon discovered why. One of the doors had been opened, the wooden bar nailed across the frame pried loose and tossed aside. Hakim was stood leaning against the jamb with a glazed look in his eyes. Already, the sand was beginning to pile around his feet and ankles.

"You need to shut that thing now!" I cried, but my voice faltered when he turned to look at me. His eyes were wide and his skin paler than the stone he leant against. He stuttered something, a half-whispered croak of pure terror, and pointed at the darkness. My eyes followed, taking in the scene outside. It was like something from another world, like a glimpse at the surface of Venus or Mars. I could see no sign of any of the interior buildings or walls, only a haze so thick it obscured even the floor.

I reached out to pull the door shut and even in just a few short seconds the wind burned my skin raw.

"Jesus Christ, help me!" I cried, giving Hakim a little shove. I felt like I was fighting a hurricane one-on-one and my loss was only inevitable. Instead of helping, though, he reached past me, shoved the door open even wider, and pointed at the storm.

"It took them!" he cried. "Liz and Watson! We have to hurry!"

Before I could stop him, he ran out into the courtyard and was gone without a trace after just a few steps. It was like the storm had eaten him alive. God, I might have gone right back to my room if it wasn't for the sight of a black dress when I turned to look down that corridor. Just a fleeting glimpse, but that was all it took to remind me that staying alone wasn't an option.

A few steps out into the storm and I had to cover my face with my sleeve and squint through the wind. I made the mistake of opening my mouth to cry for help, only to get it filled with sand before I could utter a sound. After spitting it back out, I kept my lips firmly closed and began to stumble through those dreadful winds. I don't know how long I wandered for, but it seemed to take impossibly long before I finally stumbled across the west-facing wall. It offered a mild reprieve from the wind, and conditions were slightly clearer. Already I could see the tarpaulin-wrapped body of the man we'd found torn apart at the midsection, the man I'd helped in the tower. Something about the way it flapped in the wind unsettled me, and I crawled over to get a better look.

The pegs binding it to the rocky ground were still there, but the rope had been cut loose. It was hard not to draw conclusions about the sticky red handprints and slug-like trail of rusty blood smeared across the sand. I decided it was time to turn back, but one glance the way I came, and I saw the outline of someone standing just on the edge of visibility. The bell-shaped outline of their clothes made my stomach drop like a stone and, without much further thought, I continued to fumble through the wind. Without even paying it much attention, I found that my feet followed the trail of gore. There were simply no other landmarks, nothing but a swirling, featureless void of white sand that seemed to smother the very torch in my hand.

Somewhere along the line, I realised with some certainty that I was being led and corralled. That something about this place, from the very beginning, had been pulling me along by the nose and this was just another part of some strange clockwork mechanism I'd woken that very first day when I poked my head through the window. Perhaps that's why I wasn't surprised when the trail led to one of those strange machines, the blood coming to a stop at the base of what looked like an old wrack.

Like a curtain pulled aside, the storm simply stopped. For a few brief seconds, the silence was overridden by the sound of thousands of tonnes of sand falling to the ground for miles and miles in every direction. It felt unreal, like a glimpse of another world, like an entire layer of the desert had been lifted and dropped back down by some childish god. It was every bit as frightening as the stifled cries of Hakim. He had been fastened to a plinth of wood with a central hinge. Slowly, levers were being worked to snap him backwards at the waist. The hinge had barely moved further than ten or fifteen degrees, but already his ribs bulged outwards and the muscles on his legs strained to the point of snapping.

Beside him were several other machines, all of them turning and grinding with the kind of creaky mechanisms you'd expect to lower a portcullis on a medieval castle. Chains as thick as my arm clunked through gears, wooden beams as wide as my torso strained and turned...

None of them were empty. Watson lay on one, partly bisected, but only partly. Liz lay on another, resembling a doll caught in a bear trap. She looked at me with broken eyes while my brain tried to understand how her feet could be pressed against her ears and pointed in the same direction as her nose. Neither were dead, but they didn't appear completely alive. They merely shook, like frightened dogs in a kennel.

A scream began to rise in my throat, but it was caught when I finally saw the torturers step out in front of their work. It was that *her*, that creature in the black dress whose mere presence radiated a special kind of malignant hatred and pitch-black despair. The way she looked at me made me feel like the very flesh around my head would bubble and melt away. More than anything, it was the fact her face was alive. Warped, wrinkled, weathered and discoloured... but *alive*. Not faked. Not rubber. Not prosthetic. A lifetime of horror movies hadn't come close to preparing me for what it was like to see something so warped and alien. The way her features twitched as she appraised me kneeling on the floor left my mind a writhing hiss of white noise and terror.

It would only be later that I remembered the other torturer. How he stood, I do not know, but his face was every bit as slack and lifeless as it had been when I'd seen him splayed across that first machine. Somehow, his broken and twisted spine supported a torso that balanced upon it precariously like a spinning top. Dislocated shoulders popped and clicked as they tugged at levers, but his eyes never moved. With no wind to whip the sand into a frenzy, I saw him all too clearly, standing there like a badly controlled puppet. It was the worker, the one from the tower. And behind came others. Soldiers and officers and labourers and ancient travellers, their clothes speaking of dusty old centuries long-forgotten in the modern world. They were such grotesquely mutilated things, snapped and bent and twisted and cracked open and spun inside out. The variety of it all was daunting...

The woman stepped forward, her hand stretched out towards me, and without waiting another moment, I ran. I pulled myself up and sprinted in the opposite direction with only hysterical terror to occupy my mind. In those few moments, my vision narrowed to a tunnel and my mind turned to jackrabbit fear and it didn't stop until I barrelled through an open door, and everything went black. It wouldn't be until someone else found me, twenty-two hours later, hiding in a wardrobe, that any semblance of lucidity would return.

The fort, according to satellite photos, simply no longer exists. The sandstorm has reburied it and I suspect it won't re-emerge for some time. At least, that's my hope, anyway. Watson was too wealthy a man to simply go missing, and I spent a considerable amount of time after my rescue being hounded by his lawyers and family. At the very least, the fact that Watson and I hadn't exactly gone after the fort legally meant no one went to the papers. Money like that can stop these sorts of things getting out and Watson's family treasures their reputation highly, so that is at least one silver lining.

It hasn't stopped me digging, however. I'm not sure I'll ever get any real answers. The closest I've gotten is a letter from a wealthy member of the Third Republic around the time of the original colonial expedition might. After the loss of the Rosetta stone to the British, this man implored the French government to act on rumours and myths from West Africa that spoke of a civilisation even older than the Egyptians. He mentioned an ancient fort that was founded not so much on any principle of strategic value, but instead on protecting a site of supposedly buried treasure. He argued if the government would not act on it, then it might come down to a few wealthy men having to sponsor a military regiment.

Given the fort's location—and the complete lack of anything nearby to guard—I can't help but think it fits the man's letter. There were civilisations in the Sahara, once upon a time. Old ones too, older than we could possibly imagine.

They say that, in the right places, even death can die. Perhaps that's what I saw? The lingering echo of that place's most recent trauma. No. Not an echo at all... All those people being tortured, all of them still breathed. And that woman... she was not a spectre. Not when I saw her. She was as real as you or I, only old and withered beyond all human experience.

And she's still down there.

BOUNDARIES

I sit down in my chair and flick to a new sheet on the clipboard. These days, most therapists use tablets. Sometimes I think I do things just to be contrarian, I'm not sure. The clients don't mind. They don't even notice. In fact, it's *exactly* what they expect to see, and I wonder if that's why I do it. The current guy doesn't seem to notice, nor did the last one. I forget his name. It begins with a K. I had to spend the last forty-five minutes carefully wording any questions to avoid bringing it up. It was awkward, distracted me from his problems. He's a flasher, or at least *was*.

He's terrified of women. I can see it in the way he looks at me. If I laughed at him too harshly, I think there's a very serious risk he'd kill me. Good thing he isn't very funny. But where did *this* guy come from? The current one? I don't remember booking him, but Tracy wouldn't let any random in. Was it that guy with addiction problems? Oh Christ, it's like the name all over again. I'll have to tread carefully.

"Why don't we start with a little introduction," I say, fiddling with my pen. "Start off by telling me a little bit about yourself."

I always assume I'm the only one who daydreams during long silences. This guy looks like he's been thinking too. Would he have just stayed silent the whole session? That's a strange thought, but he's looking at me quite happily. I don't normally see people with a peaceful glint in their eyes.

"Is everything okay?" I ask. "Do you feel comfortable?"

"I'm very comfortable," he answers. God, he doesn't sound anything like I thought he would. That voice could be on radio, or more likely on some government tape ready to broadcast on BBC for when the world finally ends. Yes. That seems like a better fit. That's a voice I could imagine professionally explaining to me to keep calm and drown the children to spare them the horror.

It's detached. He sounds like an alien, looks like one too. If I've ever seen someone wearing a human-skin suit, it's this guy.

Oh shit, he's talking.

"...move has been difficult for me. I think you would call it a culture clash."

"You feel alienated?" I ask.

"I feel lonely," he answers and makes eye contact—probably not autism. In fact, for someone meeting a stranger, he's almost so relaxed he's stoned. Probably not social anxiety then either.

"It's common to feel lonely after a recent move. Where did you come from?"

"I used to live at the bottom of the ocean." He smiles. Oh good, he's a nut.

"Care to elaborate?" I ask.

"No," he shakes his head. "Does it really matter where I come from? You are all so obsessed with knowing things."

"When you say 'you', are you referring to women?"

"No." He shakes his head and I suppress an eye-roll. "Humans," he replies. "All of you are obsessed with questions and answers. It's like, imagine a cockroach interrogating you over your mortgage? It's just like..." he shrugs and laughs, and so do I. It's the image. It's just stupid enough to work its magic even as another part of my mind mutters an aside.

Narcissist.

"You feel like you need to explain yourself?"

"No," he laughs again and this time I don't join him.

"You feel like people *ask* you to explain yourself?"

"I feel bored," he says before sitting upright and I instinctively move backwards. My heart flutters, I nearly laugh at my own fear. Why did I back away? Did I think he was going to lunge? Jesus, I feel like I'm at a zoo and all the bars have disappeared.

"Very bored and very lonely," he adds.

"Do you…" he hasn't given me much to work with, has he? And I'm pretty good at spinning nothing into something. "Why do you think seeing a therapist might help?"

"Oh, I didn't want to see a therapist."

"Well," I say, and gesture with my arms at the room around me. Am I getting irritated? Is it showing? I hate these kinds of games. "You're seeing one right now." I tell him. "Why come here otherwise?"

"I didn't want to see a therapist," he repeats himself. "I wanted to see *you*."

Oh.

Okay. I try to think of something funny to say, almost as a reflex. But I don't think this is a good time to start laughing, nervously or otherwise.

"Why?" I ask, finding it the only word willing to leave my mouth.

"Because I'm bored and lonely," he says, like it's the most natural conclusion possible.

"You wanted a therapist to kill time?"

"No," he shakes his head. He isn't *just* odd looking, is he? No. I missed it somehow. He's actually quite unpleasant. That skin of his looks fake, uncanny almost. Something about him seems entirely off. He reminds me of a puppet or a mannequin. "No," he repeats, "I was bored and lonely and I saw you in the street and I followed you here. That girl outside didn't want me to come in, she said you had a patient. So I thought I'd be polite and wait. Then one man left the room, and I tried to enter. That's when the girl told me I needed an appointment, and another man beside me told me I had to wait my turn. He grabbed my arm. After that, things suddenly became less boring.

"See," he says, smiling like he's proven a point. "I was right, wasn't I? I followed you and I hadn't even spoken to you yet, but in less than a few hours, I found two people."

"Found them for what?" I ask. My heart is in my chest. I shouldn't have been so jokey. Had I missed something? Some noise? God, I hope Tracy's okay. There's a panic button under her desk and I hope to hell she's hit it.

"Found two friends!" His smile is so wide now it's starting to redden at the edges. Is the skin going to break? I think he might actually be... "I'm not bored or lonely anymore. Both the man and the girl were exhilarating, but especially the girl. She was a *delight!*"

Did he just pat his stomach? *Why did he do that?*

"I need you to leave," I stutter. I'm not laughing now, am I? I'm waiting and watching him like a sparrow facing down a tomcat. He purses his lips, his whole face snapping back to normal like a rubber band, and then considers my question. Did he just tilt his head? I think he did. Jesus, he moves like a fucking animal.

"Okay," he nods. "I don't normally do this. But what the hell! You only live once."

The way he said that. He emphasised the *you*. I don't like that. My head feels light, but I can't let go of all sense now. I have to stay here stony faced and watch him leave. I have to because otherwise something might happen. I don't know what, but I have this terrible feeling deep in my stomach that I'm alone with this man. There is no next patient out there, nor is there Tracy. They're gone. Dead, perhaps? I don't know. But if I screamed right now, the only one who would come barrelling towards me is *him*.

"Please don't return." I manage to muster the words just as he leaves. I immediately regret it because he looks back and smirks and for a split second, I really do think he's going to come at me.

Why did he pat his stomach!?

But he just opens the door and leaves. He doesn't even shut it and for a moment I'm telling myself to stand and call out to Tracy, but instead I open my mouth and feel the tears come. I sob. I sob so hard my whole body is shaking and I curl my knees up to my chest. I'm not quiet. I desperately want someone to come in. I think I hear the elevator ding. *Has he left? Please come in, Tracy. Please. Don't leave me alone.* The longer I sit there while nothing happens, the more I start to accept the nightmarish feeling deep in my stomach. Something *is* wrong. Tracy isn't coming. And that's when I hear the flies. There are only one or two, but their buzzing is as clear as day.

Fresh meat.

The words pop into my mind like a neon sign in total darkness. It's those flies—those big fat blue-bottle flies whose meaty buzzing reverberates through my head like microphone feedback. They're attracted to something. They *want* something. I can't take it anymore. I need to go look. I take a moment to catch my breath. I don't want to leave my chair, but I make myself get up, anyway.

I approach the door with a tentative greeting, hoping to hell that Tracy will answer. But she doesn't, and I step into the reception area and finally see that what's left of my receptionist still at her desk, hands calmly on the keyboard. I recognise the acrylic nails painted red. The colour matches the gory stubs of her wrists. I can't help but wonder where the rest of her has gone, and why the only sign of my next patient is a greasy stain on the carpet and something hanging from a lightbulb.

I've spent all day answering questions. Normally, I'm the one asking. Is that ironic? I always thought I had a good command of irony, but right now, my mind is dust. I think the policeman driving me home has tried speaking to me once or twice. I can't bring myself to reply. I don't like being this close to a stranger. I can smell the dampness of his clothes and hair, and I only ride in other people's cars when something is wrong.

He drives a different route to reach my house and when we arrive, it takes me a moment to recognise the building from such a different angle. My car isn't in the driveway. This is the house my neighbours must glimpse during the day, the building I leave behind each morning. Are the walls always that high? It looks so big now. And there's something else, something different about it. This isn't the same exact same house I return to each night.

My bedroom light is on.

"Anyone home?" the policeman asks. He tries to sound calm, but I can detect an undercurrent of tension in his voice. He's noticed the lights as well.

"There shouldn't be," I say. "Can you take a look?"

"Of course," he answers with a smile. That crooked English nose of his makes me think of a postman. I don't know why. It just does. "I'll be back in a second."

He's trying to seem calm, but just before he steps onto the welcome mat, he checks his shoelaces, briefly adjusts his helmet, and his hand falls to the baton and radio on his belt in one smooth sweep. *Am I being paranoid?* When he knocks on the door, I decide that, yes, I am. I hastily undo my seatbelt and leave the car. When I start to run, I know he hears my footfalls because he looks back, and for the briefest moment, he's afraid. But then the fear slips away, and he's pleased to see me. I realise that I'm holding my keys out to him. How else was he meant to go inside?

He takes them and quickly unlocks the door. He goes first and I follow soon after. My house looks oddly empty. I'm not sure how to explain it except that it feels as if the rain is trying and failing to keep the silence at bay. *Just a storm,* I tell myself. To help the sullen mood, I turn the lights on while the policeman checks around. Before I reach the last switch, he's already in the kitchen, and then the living room, and then he comes back. I say nothing when he looks at the staircase and neither does he. We just smile at each other before he sets off while I linger patiently by the foot of the stairs. The sun hasn't set yet but God, it's dark in here. The top of the stairs is barely visible. It looks like a hole.

I'm safe, I tell myself.

There's a muffled bang and I jump. *Probably just something falling over,* I think. Time stretches on. When I look back towards my living room, I see that the sun has continued to set and now my opaque windows are catching the shadows of nearby trees. The way they lie across the film-coated glass makes them look like strange hands clamouring to get in. He was so quick moving through the ground floor. Why is he taking so long? I hate this fear and anxiety. It physically hurts. This is why people go into scary murder basements and call out to the dark. In the real world, it's always a toppled wheelie bin or a winged bird that's making those strange sounds. It's only in the movies that Michael Myers slips out of the shadows.

It really has been too long now. I want to cry out and ask if he's okay. Shouldn't I at least hear him shuffle about? There are only three rooms up there. It doesn't make sense. I should go up there. I should take the first step because in real life there is no murder basement filled with monsters. And right here, right now, that's just my upstairs floor. It's just a place. It's where I'm going to sleep tonight, where I'll drink wine and watch Netflix and maybe half-heartedly browse Tinder.

There's a sound, something from the kitchen. It's a gentle rumble, like the pipes when I run the tap. Except that can't be the case, although sometimes I hear that sound if I run the bath and pop downstairs to grab a bottle of wine. That must be what it is.

Someone's running a bath.

I should leave. I've done the maths. Something is wrong. But for some reason, now is the moment my legs decide to work. I climb the first step and I feel something welling up inside me. It's anger at being afraid. Whatever's up there, I need to prove it doesn't exist.

This afternoon was a one off. A kook. A nut. Nothing to worry about, but deep down I hear a voice screaming over and over:

Leave. The numbers don't add up.

I reach the top of the stairs. I can hear water running clearly now. Someone is running me a bath. Wait, why would I think that? Why would I think someone is running *me* a bath?

I push the bedroom door open and am greeted with the prone form of the policeman. He's lying completely still, naked and pale like a chicken in the supermarket. He's looks almost peaceful, arms by his side, and next to him are his clothes all neatly folded. At the back of the room, I can hear someone in the bathroom. They're humming, and the cadence of their voice is sickeningly familiar. I have to leave now. There's still time. There's a door, slightly ajar, but I don't think I've been spotted.

The door swings open. I freeze. I try to scream, but all that comes out is a brittle hiss. Even my throat has seized up.

It's him. He's come back for me.

"I've run you a bath," he says, gesturing to the room behind him. For some reason I respond,

"Okay."

I think I nod, but I might just be shaking from terror. I want to mention the policeman, but I can't acknowledge it because what if that's what sends the madness all crashing down?

"Come here," he says, and I obey. Holy shit, why? He seems polite. Doesn't he seem polite? I don't know what he wants, do I? All that matters right now is surviving, because each time I look at the man on the floor, the more his death registers in my mind. There's a fucking dead man on my floor. Half-hour ago he was a real live human being, but now he's just cold cuts in waiting. Now he's just a *thing*.

I don't want to die.

I reach the man, and he doesn't touch me. He just gives the door a little push, and it swings open all the way, revealing the tub still running.

"Go on," he says.

He wants me to get in.

I step forward and dip my fingers in the water, just to see if it's real. It's not only real, it's scalding, and I cry out involuntarily. Oh shit. The sound of my own voice makes me feel like I've dropped a stack of plates right next to a hibernating bear, but he just tilts his head like a dog. It takes a second for me to realise he wants an explanation.

"It's too hot," I say and from the sound of my own voice I must be crying. He shrugs as if to say, 'how am I meant to know?' then reaches into the tub to undo the plug while turning on the cold tap. He stays there staring at the water, his back turned towards me. Is this the moment I should run? Is it even an option?

"I think that's okay now," he says and my heart breaks at the missed opportunity. If only I wasn't so fucking paralysed with terror, I might just have a chance of fleeing. But there's that voice again:

Don't turn your back to him.

He wants me to check the water. It means getting closer to him. Oh God no, please no. I don't want to. He looks wrong. His eyes and face and mouth look all wrong. It'd be better if it really was Michael Myers. Underneath that mask was just a man. An actor. But underneath that face is something completely different.

I try not to look at him when I touch the water. It's cooler now, not ideal but good enough I suppose for...

He wants to me get in. The thought sweeps over me like a panic. *Oh God, he wants me to climb in. I'm here and I'm all alone and he wants me to have a fucking bath! Why? Why would he want that? He's staring at me and waiting. Is this preparation? Preparation for what!? What... what am I meant to do?*

He doesn't speak again, but he does gesture to the tub with the faintest hit of irritation, and I find it terrifying to behold. He's not human. He's an animal, a thing. What will he do if I make him angry? Tracy made him angry, and all that was left were two disembodied hands and a stain. I can't let that happen. I have to...

I start to unbutton my blouse. He does not look at me hungrily, but with great curiosity. This is wrong. This is all wrong. Even as I strip away my tights and hesitate before pulling down my underwear, I realise this isn't what I think it is. Something's missing and somehow that scares me even more than if he was drooling at the sight of my naked body.

There they go, dropping to the floor past my ankles. I step out of them and use the momentum of my feet to keep going. If I stop, I may pass out and never return. I take extra care when getting in the bath. I don't want to slip, or struggle, or even pause. I don't want to give him an excuse to touch me. This whole time he's just looked. He hasn't savoured, I think. He's just looked at me like a dog watching traffic.

"Good," he says once I'm settled in. I'm breathing so heavily the water ripples with each exhalation. It's a fight to keep the sobs bottled up. "While you have a bath," he adds, "I'm going to eat. After that, you can join me. Does that make sense?"

I nod.

He nods too. Then he steps out of the room, turning the lights off as he goes. I'm left in the dark, only the grey light of my bedroom filtering through a slight gap in the door while I curl my knees up towards my chest and watch tears run into the water. For a moment I consider actually washing myself, but then I hear it.

It sounds like wood splintering, followed by a wet, pulsing gurgle. Oh Jesus, that sound. Oh fuck, I know what that sound is. It's awful. I can hear what he's doing, and I think I'm going insane. *That's why he patted his stomach.* He's groaning while he eats. He's groaning and this time it really is like a sexual release. He's cracking and snapping and tearing and gagging at the rate of his own consumption. Stretching, pulling, breaking. There's no escaping this. I can't see anything, but I know he's eating the policeman and I'm stuck in this bath while that thing gorges itself just outside my door and when he's done, he's going to come in and gorge himself on me and oh God...

Oh God, please let me die first.

It feels like an eternity and when the slobbering and snapping finally stops, the water has gone cold. There are a few seconds of silence and then he enters, and I see that he is completely clean. He should be covered in gore. *Perhaps he didn't...* but then I glimpse the stain on my floor just before he shuts it. There's no carpet for that mess to sink into. It's just a puddle formerly known as a man. Is that a joke? Oh shit, I really am going insane. But still, that's the truth of it, isn't it? Moments ago, there was 250 pounds of crooked nose policeman walking around but now he's just calorific content. Was he eaten whole? Was his body collapsed, crunched, compressed, and forced into the man's gullet?

I look at him standing there. His head is turned. He's watching me again. Should I start washing myself? Is that what he wants? He looks so normal, and I find that most upsetting. There's no bulging gut or sagging waist. I don't understand. I don't understand any of it. Where has the policeman gone?

The man sees me staring and gives me a quick smile before patting his stomach.

It's too much.

I pass out.

When I awake, I'm on my sofa. I'm lying down and I'm dry and dressed. They're the same clothes I wore earlier, and my hair is still wet; I feel violated at the thought of him touching me. Somewhere behind me he is moving, but I'm afraid to turn and look in case it draws his attention. I hear the sound of plates and I think he must be in the kitchen, who cares? My door is just a few metres away. I think I can make it, so I begin to move my leg. There might just be a chance I'll be able to slip out without him noticing.

"Come eat," he says, and I freeze before one foot is even on the ground. I twist my head around in fear and he's staring at me, head tilted as if he's listening to the sound of my racing heart. His face is so neutral he looks stupid, and I wonder if there's even a brain in that head, or whether it's hiding just out of view. I can almost imagine puppet strings rising into the rafters.

"Come," he repeats himself and somehow he laces the words with a kind of poison that curdles my stomach and causes acid to rise up in my throat.

Without really knowing why, I stand up and enter the kitchen. The table has been laid out for a single person and he beckons for me to sit at my place. I comply, pulling the chair in while he sits across from me.

"I like you," he says, and I'm struck once more by just how cold and disinterested his tone is. He doesn't say it as a consolation, or as a point of pride. But rather it's just a novelty, like he's observed an unusual sign on the side of the road. "You will eat."

Eat what? I wonder. There's nothing on my plate. I expect him to explain, to say something, but he stares at me for long seconds in complete silence. When he finally opens his mouth, no sound ever comes out. Instead, it keeps growing like a rubber prosthetic until something bulges against his lips. I'm so terrified I shut my eyes without thinking, wrenching them open only when I hear a loud tear and something large explodes from his mouth and onto the table in a clattering of gore and acid. It comes to a stop on my plate and by the time I look up from the dismembered torso sizzling on my tablecloth, I see that the man's face has returned to normal.

"Eat," he says.

"I can't," I mutter hopelessly.

"You can't fly or regrow lost limbs or walk on the sun," he says. "But you can eat." He waits a beat while I look down at the dimpled lesion-riddled torso, bones and organs visible through tissue-thin skin. "Don't make me demonstrate this fact to you," he adds. "You *can* eat."

I want to dissociate right now. I want to have another out-of-body experience and imagine someone else doing these things. I don't want to know what I'm capable of. I don't want to have to do this, not step by step. I want to hide, to retreat deep within my subconscious. Even as he reaches outwards and sinks his fingers into the soft belly to pull free a strip of flesh, I keep waiting for my mind to go somewhere else.

Anywhere else.

"Eat," he says, perfectly calm, giving the slither of flesh a flick to catch my eye. "You're boring me."

When I look, I see something move behind him and I realise it's his shadow, except it looks nothing like him at all. The mere outline suggests a kind of dimming madness. The firing neurons of a dying brain as all colour drains, time stops, and one by one the lights turn off. He reaches out and grabs my wrist, and his skin is like soft coral. He puts something in my fist and then lets go before sitting back. I know what he wants me to do, I'm just not sure I actually can. I open my hand and stare at it. It doesn't even look human. It looks rotting offal and smells like it too, like something cut open from the belly of a predator.

"Eat," he repeats himself and I realise it's for the last time.

I don't want to die.

I open my mouth. I throw the scrap of skin and muscle in and swallow it whole, only for it to immediately come back up and slither across my tongue. It tastes like battery acid with a rotting flourish, and it hits the cloth without a noise, quickly followed by a stringy river of bile. When it finally ends, I bring my teary eyes up to focus on his face.

He looks sad, almost disappointed.

"I'm bored."

Something snaps. The knife he's placed beside me is long and serrated, and it's in my hand before I even realise I've made the decision. *Now* I've finally dissociated. Now I'm watching someone else step into my shoes and take over. And this woman, she takes the blade and drags it against his wrist with such savage strength I could almost cheer.

"Fuck you!" she screams... I scream. "How's this for fucking boring!"

I'm sobbing as I say the words, but the sound of defiance in my voice pleases me. And it doesn't stop there. I'm up and running before I see the outcome. I've never felt as fast as I do right now. I've never felt my heart beat like this, or felt my muscles burn with such savage purpose. I hope to God my body understands what's at stake right now, because I can't afford to hold anything back. I'm only a few steps from the front door now. I've put all my hopes on this one gamble—the door needs to be open.

The room darkens. Something has cast a shadow across the doorway, and I already know that I'm going to die. I feel like time is slowing, like any second...

There's a loud knocking and I slam into the door with a thump, surprised that I've made it.

"Hello?" someone says from the other side and the shadow flitters away, letting light fall across my back. I'm hyperventilating, my skin ice cold and my entire scalp so tight it feels like a rubber band ready to *pop* right off.

"Are you there? Please let me in. I heard about what happened at work today and I don't think you should be alone. Are you okay? I can see you up against the door."

I throw the door open as fast I can and fall forward into my sister's arms, into safety.

Or at least I hope it's safe.

⸻

Once outside, I find myself saying that it'll be okay now, that everything is safe and well. Her cardigan is pressed into my face and I'm holding my sister so tightly it hurts. I never want to open my eyes again, but I know better than that, so I pull away and start hobbling down the garden path while she's still asking a thousand questions. My mind is sluggish, and it takes time to realise she won't stop asking until I reply.

"We have to leave," I say.

"What's wrong?" she asks. "Oh my God, what happened!? Is everything okay?"

I grab her wrist and start pulling, but manage to walk only a few metres before I skid to a stop and my sister runs right into the back of me. I steady her by gripping her elbows so hard my knuckles turn white, but she doesn't cry out. We are both silent in the face of such all-consuming darkness. My garden and the path that leads from it are never as pitch black as they are right now. The only light comes from my house, and it fades quickly in the face of such a malignant shadow. What little wind there is reeks of meat and fills my nose with the coppery stench of blood, hot and damp against my shivering skin.

"What the fuck," my sister whispers, her voice a papery scrawl. There is something at the end of the gate and it is eating light like a black hole. And yet I feel like I recognise it. I feel like the sun has swivelled around to reveal a great big eye that's bearing down on me with scornful contempt. The weight of it is enough to crush my soul.

My sister feels it too. Her face is like a startled rabbit's, devoid of any rationality, an empty vessel slowly filling with the ancient impulse to freeze or flee. She chooses the latter without any warning, and I'm screaming after her as she bolts into the night. For a few seconds there is only the sound of footsteps, followed by a startled yelp. I can't see her. I can't see her anywhere. It's like the sky opened up and ate her.

But now the way is clear, and I take it. Sprinting as hard as I can for the gate, I am soon out onto the main road, suddenly aware that no one's out in this weather. The streetlamps are trying to fight back the darkness but failing. They can only make lonely little islands I dart between in panic. I keep thinking of something lurking in ambush in the spaces between each light and without realising it, I'm holding my breath and closing my eyes. I'm barefoot and I think my soles are bleeding. I can't be sure. They're so cold I can't feel a thing and it's too dark to see. There is only pain, and it's too much to bear. Not just my feet, all of it. It's too much and I have to stop. Up comes a wall and I practically fall against it in exhaustion.

Where am I? I vaguely recognise the street, but it looks different in the dark. Maybe he's gone? Surely he would have reached me by now? Maybe he doesn't know where I am. Maybe I've gone too far. I dare myself to turn around, to look behind me, and I do, seeing only an empty road. My own house is nowhere in sight, and I've never been so happy to be lost. There's nothing but a dozen streetlights lined up like ever-diminishing soldiers.

And then the furthest of them goes out.

It's accompanied by a loud pop and the sound of shattering glass. Another bursts, and then another. One by one, the islands of light disappear, and I feel him coming closer. It's not just something that slithers through my mind, it is a raw physical sensation that pulls at my skin and turns my muscles to jelly. It is enough to motivate me to move, and I look towards the nearest house and hobble towards the door, grateful for the sight of bright lights in the windows and... is that a woman?

I hit the door so hard my fists sting, but I don't stop until the door opens and I nearly plant one right on the old man's face. His wife is behind him, terrified, and I barge forward sobbing. The man looks threatened, I think he's still in survival mode. Is that a bat? But the woman has locked eyes on the state of me and there's a softening in her eyes. I'm babbling and they're listening. They lock the door at my suggestion and immediately take me to the living room while the woman runs into the kitchen to phone the police. I want to take in my surroundings, but all I notice are the back and front doors, thinking that if he comes through one, I can flee the other. But what then?

I can't just keep running.

"Drink this." The old woman arrives with a glass of water, and I take it, surprised to find I actually want it when I gulp it down it in one go. I must have been thirsty. The woman speaks again, and I jump. I look at her blankly and she repeats herself: "The police are on their way. What did you say happened? A man attacked you? Killed your sister?"

Has the old man got a bat? No. It's a cane, he's just holding it like a bat. It makes me uncomfortable to think of what will happen if he has to try and use it. God, they don't really know, do they? No one does. And they'll never believe me. I answer them as best as I can, anyway, struggling to meet their eyes when I do. I don't want to deal with this feeling. It's like shame, like if anything were to happen, it'd be my fault. But it would, wouldn't it? In a sense, at least. That makes me feel like dirt.

Outside, something shatters and I'm up in an instant, running towards the backdoor while the old couple call after me. They're terrified too, but right now I don't care. I have my hand on the backdoor but my body freezes when a knock comes from the door. It's loud, the thumps spaced a little too far apart. An ersatz knock for an ersatz man.

"Hello? Police. Let me enter."

It works. The old man shouts something to me and turns towards the door. He told me it'll be alright, I think. I don't know. I'm too busy trying the handle and coping with the realisation it's locked.

"Where's the key!?" I howl, my voice like a banshee's. I think the old woman answers, but it's just a platitude. Right now, her husbands at the door and pulling the chain. I don't have time to find the key, but the stairs are between me and the entrance, so I sprint towards them and flee into the unlit upper floor. My feet greet the last step and I'm out of view just in time to hear the door open. I stop running now and start tiptoeing my way to a nearby door. From downstairs, I hear the old man's greeting cut short.

After that, there are no other sounds and I hurry to the nearest bedroom, looking for places to hide.

I don't think this is the master room – there's a small table with a sewing machine, old exercise equipment covered in white sheets, and a double bed filled to the brim with tiny cushions. I'm reminded of the couple downstairs. I almost feel sick at the thought of the old man swinging his cane as that thing descends on him and his wife, but I make for a large treadmill folded up in the corner of the room anyway, hoping to hide. It's big enough to hide me and I slide under the sheet without making much noticeable difference.

I think.

I hold my breath and will myself into total stillness, my chest close to bursting. Once again, I think that I can't keep doing this. Sooner or later, I'll have to give in. He won't stop following me. Even now I can hear footsteps rising on the stairs. My body vibrates with a tension I don't think I can contain for much longer, but I do not make a noise, not even when the door glides open. I can feel him looking at me right through the cover at my back and I feel utterly pathetic, like a child. Who am I fooling?

I'm so close to throwing the sheet up and giving in when I hear him leave. I know I didn't imagine it. The door really did swing shut, but I hold my breath and keep still. How much longer should I wait? It feels too long. What if he left the house, and I just didn't hear him? The sound of my heartbeat is like a thunderous drumming, I could easily have missed it. I decide to leave my hiding spot and look outside the nearby window. I move as silently as I can, shuffling along on all fours, my way lit only by moonlight. The worst thing that could happen now is a loose floorboard, but I don't dwell on that.

A quick peek out the window shows a man walking past the house. I wonder if it's him, but I can't be sure. There hasn't been a peep out of the ground floor for a long time, but I do pick up the faintest hint of a draft. Chances are, the front door is still open. Oh God, I hope the old couple are okay, but I know they're probably not. That was probably him I spotted after he'd left, finally full after tearing his way through my life and eating every poor bastard along the way. I can't even bring myself to think of my sister, but for a moment the grief mingles with terror, and I slide back down to the floor, all relief tempered by the memory of the price I paid for a few measly hours of life.

I can't stay here. I decide that if I'll leave, I'll do it so quickly that even if he is lingering in the darkness, there's a chance I'll be able to sprint past and escape. If he has finally left, then there's nothing to it. I can just keep running until I find another house, another safe place.

I prepare myself, moving towards the door and making sure to take deep breaths so my lungs are ready for the exertion. Before any doubt sets in, I crawl out quietly and approach the stairs. I can't hear anything, but I can't see anything either. All I have to do is get down the stairs and out the front door. It's not too far at all.

I explode into action like a runner at the tracks, throwing myself down the steps two, three, at a time. I feel the energy rise up inside me and for a few fleeting moments, the door looms ahead like the gates of heaven. But to my right, in the darkness, something shuffles and catches my eye. There are only five or six steps left. I'm already half-way, but I turn my head and lose my balance. One ankle twists, the other misses its mark and slides down the remaining steps heel first. By the time I reach the bottom, I have deflated, unable to rise or respond.

I can't move my eyes.

He is standing there, his jaw dislocated and his eyes hollow, looking more like a rubber suit than ever before. The woman is trapped between his leech-like jaws, folded painfully between thick sheets of muscle that drip yellow fluid down her face. Her skin bleeds upon contact, a thousand pin-prick stars of blood blooming from her pores. Her ankles are by her neck, her soles are facing in opposite directions. I don't understand how, but she's still alive and I'm reminded once again of a dying animal caught in the thralls of shock. She can't even look at me. She just stares into empty space while the man's body heaves, and powerful muscles compress her whole body with audible cracks. There is a shudder of movement, and she is pulled further inwards, his lips curling around her head like a hood with the string drawn. She's trying to wiggle her feet now, her eyes fluttering side to side while her mouth gapes open in terror.

When it is over, she slips into his abdomen with a final gasp of air, and I let out a terrible sob. He stands there for a few seconds more, shivering with excitement, until his eyes finally roll back into their sockets from some impossible space in his head. I have given up trying to understand him, but I'm beginning to suspect he's bigger on the inside than the outside, and that there's room enough in there for me and others to spare. He offers a thin-lipped smile before turning to the open door. He is thoughtful.

"This is a very strange place," he says, possibly to me but maybe to no one in particular. "No one will eat with me. But you eat with each other. I see it. But no one will eat with me."

He sounds almost sad.

"Have it your way, then. I will continue to eat alone. I will leave."

He walks towards the door but stops and I realise I feel nothing. No relief or excitement or dawning terror. I can't quite bring myself to believe this night will end in anything other than abject horror.

"Oh, yes," he adds like an afterthought while turning to face me. *Here it comes,* I think. *My death.*

"You can have your sister back."

It takes them three days to stabilise her, and I am there the whole time. Sometimes I wonder if he returned the right person. I imagine it likely he can't tell us apart, or if he can, he doesn't care. But then

I sometimes catch a light of reflection in her eyes that convinces me this is my sister, even if her skeleton has been reduced to two-thirds its original height, every hair singed off, and her skin thinned to a translucent sheet.

She hasn't spoken. The police have questions, but I have no answers. At least they let me visit her. I love her, even if I never liked her. Besides, no one has ever deserved a fate like this. They say they will be able to graft most of her lost skin, but they are baffled as to the full extent of what happened. So am I, I tell them. She is diminished in every sense of the word, and as far as the neurologists can tell, her brain is riddled with lesions the size of almonds. You can tell when she looks at you there's nothing but a patchwork web of thoughts and memories, trying but failing to fire. I have worked with dementia patients who share the exact same look, but nothing quite compares to the sight of her bones sagging in her flesh. They had a word for it, but I don't remember. All it really means is that her skeleton is as soft as cardboard, seemingly dissolved from within and leeched of all calcium. If you lift her elbow, the forearm bends like a plastic ruler.

She should be dead, they say. And I agree, often dreaming of working up the courage to walk in here and finish the job. When she looks at me, I think that's what she is asking for, but I can't say for sure because sometimes all I see is a broken and battered doll with a misshapen and swollen head, like something you'd find at the bottom of a dumpster. I can't read that sort of face. She's crossed some threshold I hope to stay far away from. But I still visit. Guilt is a powerful thing, and it's one of the few genuine emotions I can feel. That and exhaustion. When I manage to sleep, I dream of the ocean and he's always there, somehow aware of me from an incalculable distance.

I don't think I'll ever feel safe again.

IT'S LOUD IN THE DARK

You wanna know what's funny? People have the ability to project their thoughts as invisible waves through space, and they have special little organs that let them receive these invisible waves... and it's called *talking* and *listening*. People take it for granted. You only hear what people want you to for a reason. Skipping that isn't a superpower. It's not nice to see the link between everything you do, and the instantaneous emotional response it sets off in people around you. You don't need to see the flush of blue-wave disappointment that rolls through your father's mind when you show him the A minus you got on a test. You don't need to see how a lover feels when they see you in discoloured boxers and woollen socks. It's good enough that they lie. You should be happy with those lies because a person is not just the sum of their thoughts. That momentary flicker of revulsion a partner feels when they walk in on you spewing your guts up into the toilet after eating some dodgy takeout. That's not who they are. The fact they push that disgust aside and still help you up, *that's* who they really are.

I hate seeing these things. I hate *feeling* other people's intrusive thoughts, the parts they can't filter, the parts they choose to ignore or lock up. Sometimes I get words, but I have to focus real hard. Most things look like colours that wash up all around me, although I guess that's really just a metaphor I use for your benefit. There's an element of taste, smell, touch, and even sound too, all rolled up in there. Envy is sharp and bitter. Love is like the twang of a guitar that blends the world around it into a peaceful harmony. Hatred looks like the after-effects of a nasty burn – the pitted flesh, the glistening blisters, the gut-wrenching pain. Sexual thoughts are almost percussive, but it depends on the person. Some people have a pneumatic drill thumping away in their head, for others it's more like the crashing of waves on the beach.

It would be better if I knew I could help people, but I'm no superman. I get a lot just walking down a busy street. Someone's always getting hit, or coerced, or abused, or beaten or kicked or stabbed or...

Jesus, it's always something.

Once, on a long road somewhere on the outskirts of Manchester, I heard a cry for help. It was more of a prayer, really. It's so rare to get a clear broadcast, like something you pick up on the car radio. This wasn't a mishmash of sensations. There were words, a litany screamed into the void in the desperate hope that God was listening. I spent weeks driving up and down those roads. I stayed in a hotel nearby, pausing my journey, my life, everything, in the hope I could find this poor person. I climbed fences and scoped out gardens. I broke into houses when people left for work. I got arrested, twice. But the police wouldn't listen.

Please let me die. Please let me die before he comes back. I'm so hungry. He feeds me so little. Please let me die.

I never heard them again. Never found where they were, or what might be happening. The closest I came to figuring it out was a whisper of despair left floating on the air just outside an old brick building deep in the woods. It was small, a shed really, but with thick walls. And inside were all these thick iron pipes coming outta the ground and then going back into it. It might have been something to do with sewage. There were *Keep Out* signs all over the place. Something about the stains on the floor gave me a bad feeling. And it was probably just my imagination playing up, but looking at those pipes I couldn't help but picture someone handcuffed to them.

In the end, I gave up. Whoever they were, they stopped praying. I never heard them again.

I've had to stop trying to help people in general. A lot of doctors have recommended I be locked up for my own safety. A few judges too. I think luck, and not a whole lot else, has kept me free on the streets. This power of mine isn't radar. It doesn't point me to the damsels in distress so I can bust down the door and save them. That'd be like pointing at a wave and tracing it back to its origin. Most of the time, all I can do is listen and move on.

And even listening can be dangerous. Not everyone wants to be heard. The funny thing about psychopaths is that, despite being utterly self-obsessed, they aren't involved in their own little world like everyone else. That's because they can't possibly imagine that they might need to share it. The world is theirs to enjoy. A great big complex challenging toy-puzzle, and people are the pieces they move around for fun. They're sensitive to everything around them. And they are always, *always*, on the lookout. Sometimes for victims, sometimes to learn more about the lumps of meat they call other people, and sometimes because they're afraid of getting caught.

It was an intake of breath that nearly killed me. A single slip up that forever taught me to be careful about how I react to other people's thoughts. I was on the tube and people-watching, as I often did when I was a kid. A young guy had been on the carriage with me for about half-an-hour by that point. He looked a lot older to me back then, but thinking about it, he was probably only nineteen. He had a baseball cap down over his eyes, but I knew he was projecting his mind into the whole damn train, drinking the world in. The grimy chairs, the rattling windows, the murky speckled floor – he was observing it the same way a cat watches the street. He was only pretending to fixate on the floor, pretending to be disinterested in the other people.

I was too young to recognise the signs. I just thought he was another flavour of person. His thoughts tasted dull, devoid of recognisable emotion but filled with an astonishing detail. He was as lost in the process of appearing harmless as I was in drinking in his thoughts. It was only when the train slowed down and the doors opened that his thoughts changed. No one else could've seen it of course. A young woman stepped onto the carriage and this guy's mind just freaking exploded. There was recognition, anticipation, fear, excitement, arousal, and something I would later learn was a special kind of rage. It was like this guy had been sitting and waiting, seeing the world in grey. But now he was seeing it in colour. Some input had been fed into that robotic brain and it came alive with malignant intent.

It wasn't just what he wanted to do to this woman that made him come alive. It was the fact that he'd *planned* it, and he was now waiting for the perfect moment to execute.

I gasped, overwhelmed by the madness spewing out of his head. And he never moved a muscle. Not once the whole time. But he heard. He knew. The consequences of my actions rippled through his mind as a single pulse of acknowledgement. He didn't ask questions or wonder how it could be possible. He simply knew that I'd seen into his head. He knew it the same way he knew that the train would start up soon and I'd be stuck there with him. His certainty in the situation was terrifying. He wasn't plagued by a single gram of self-doubt. I lurched up, leapt towards the doors, and in less than half-a-second he was following me. That I had somehow seen directly into his mind was no more interesting to him than the birthmark on my leg. A small detail that he might remark upon as he rolled my naked body into the sewer.

Cruelty looks like blood. It spills out of other people's minds and into mine like red wine out of the bottle and into the glass. This guy made me feel like I was drowning. The worst part was knowing I couldn't go home. I was close, but I couldn't do that. This guy was an apex predator, and he would've sat outside for days if he had to, waiting till my mum or my dad came stumbling out early in the morning. He would have watched. He would have waited. I couldn't read his exact intent, but it tasted of copper and was warm to the touch. It made me think of licking a box-cutter. I knew leading home would be a bad idea.

I couldn't hide, so I had to run. I had to lose him. I tracked a long circuitous route through the city—through parks and alleys and markets with sizzling meat and open produce—until at last it felt as if my legs were going to turn to chalk and crumble. I had to lose this guy; I knew it. So, at some point, I doubled back and started heading towards the same platform I'd fled. I can sense large groups of people moving around, and I timed the journey carefully so that I was stumbling down the escalator just as the last passenger climbed aboard a departing train. I reached the carriage seconds before the doors closed, confident I'd given the guy the slip. When I turned back, he was standing there with a blank expression. He'd never relented during the whole chase, not once. He was barely even tired. If those doors hadn't closed just then, if my timing had been slightly off, he would have been aboard that train with me. And I probably wouldn't be here writing this.

True psychopaths are exceptionally rare, thank God. They're actually the least of my worries now. Dead people are a bigger deal to me. They're far harder to avoid. Cemeteries are a firm no-go. But at least the long-time dead have the decency of keeping it quiet. Their thoughts are like wisps of smoke. Recent deaths are a little more visceral. I drove past a car crash once and just blacked out. The police gave me a breathalyser cause they thought I was drunk. Thankfully I convinced them I just had a weak stomach and the blood-spattered windscreen had upset me. They bought that. How could I have possibly explained to them that the psychic shock of death had knocked me senseless? I had heard a man's death cry. I could feel the scream he never finished as if it was trapped in my own throat. But that wasn't the whole picture... the worst part was that the guy was still screaming. They couldn't hear it. But I could.

He'd caught a glimpse of himself in the mirror as his corpse was hauled out. And he'd started screaming, not with his voice but with his mind, with his soul. By the time I started my car up, he'd been at it for over an hour. When the ambulance drove his crumpled body away, he was still screaming. He would still be screaming in the morgue, and he'd still be screaming when his family buried him. And after that he'd scream for months, maybe years, until eventually the dark and the quiet and the total absence of sensory input would liquefy his mind and that scream would wither until it was nothing more than... well, a wisp of smoke.

I highly recommend cremation, by the way. The journey is the same, but at least it's quicker. Whatever energy the universe gives to us has to go back. You have to be dismantled. Dust to dust, right? That doesn't just mean the body. It means the very soul itself. Better to go quickly because if the sound coming out of a recently buried casket is anything to go by, it's fucking terrifying.

Everything is dying. It's all going back one way or another. Something about a human mind makes it resistant to that decay. I figure that process must vary a bit person-to-person. Some places can even carry stains from things that happened a long time ago. You're familiar with this idea, I'm sure. The notion that a really horrific death leaves a kind of spectre behind that haunts the area. It's not uncommon. The freakiest thing for me is that the thoughts are indistinguishable from a living person's. The only difference is they're not "live" thoughts, they're recordings. Sometimes that means climbing a normal-looking hill and catching whiffs of an ancient Neolithic ritual, their cries uttered in a long-dead language. Sometimes it means hearing the Germanic bark of Old English as you cross a random street in London. In Scotland, there's even a place where you catch flickers of ancient Roman battle cries. That's pretty cool.

What's less cool is that sometimes you pick up on a stain that doesn't belong to a human. You know what I mean. You do. Everybody has a little bit of what I have. Did you ever just randomly hate something as a kid? Usually, it'd be someplace like maybe the cupboard under the stairs, or the attic, or a well, or an old outhouse, or a spot in your garden where the patio floor has chipped away, and you can see down into the crawlspace under your house. That's not an overactive imagination. There are places where sunlight hasn't reached for a very, very long time. Old houses abandoned in the middle of the woods. Deep pits carved into the Earth. The hearts of ancient forests, the boughs of trees so thick and old that nothing can grow in the stony soil because it is forever night on the woodland floor. You know the places. You don't need me to tell you about them. Every one of us has intruded, at some point, on a part of the world that just feels indecent, even a little bit hostile.

I used to hate the space under the stairs in my first house. It was the way it *descended* into nothing, the way the ceiling got lower and lower, but the floor didn't go anywhere. And of course, it was dark, so dark you never saw the back of it. Even when I was a teenager and helped my dad move out, I never took the time to see right toward the back. I just hauled stuff out best I could, reaching my fingers into the blackness hoping to hell nothing reached out towards me. When all bar one box was clear, it occurred to me to maybe shine my light all the way in. I was tempted to push back against my childish fear and see the little nook all laid bare. I wanted to take that black, lifeless pit and expose it to the light and see just how mediocre and boring it truly was.

Because, after all, it was just an overactive imagination, right? That was always what my father had told me when I came to him bawling my eyes out over nightmares of being dragged under there by grasping angry hands. When I thought something had moved under there—a box that was rearranged leaving drag marks in the dust, a coat that was neatly folded now thrown across the floor, a toy I hadn't seen for years suddenly presented right at the very front of the pile of junk—it was just my imagination telling me something had moved when it hadn't. There was always a mundane explanation... right?

But when I finally had the chance to pull that pile of crap apart and tease the darkness away, I discovered that shadows aren't always silent. I stood there for a moment, and thought to myself,

Time to take the darkness apart, while clutching onto the torch.

Unbelievably, the darkness spoke back.

You're welcome to try, it said.

The solidity of those thoughts still haunts me. It was the way it felt like squeezing a diamond in my fist. Like the words were made out of the hardest stuff on Earth and would cut through my mind like a knife through butter if it so felt like it. I'd never had something *speak* to me before. I'd caught the occasional word or phrase from other people, but those were clear thoughts. They weren't *communications* sent out with postage stamps and return addresses. They were more like graffiti in a public toilet. But those words were sent right at me, laser-guided and dispatched straight into my skull. I couldn't begin to imagine what kind of mind had sent them. If there was an image or a sensation that accompanied those words, it was the taste of cobwebs and nothing else. God, it scared the hell out of me. I didn't raise my hand and challenge the shadows. Instead, I dragged the final box out and made sure to never lift my eyes.

I was too afraid of what I might see.

It's funny, but on the drive home my old man told me that he was proud of me for clearing the stairs out. He told me that, now he was finally leaving, he could admit that even as an adult, that space beneath the stairs made him a little uncomfortable too. Lots of people are like that. They get little vibes that they attribute to nothing. I once went out with a bunch of film students to help them shoot a final year project. The gear was heavy, and I had a car, so that's how I tagged along. Anyway, the director (well, the dude in charge, I guess. He was hardly a professional) had spotted an old half-burned house out in the woods a few years back and wanted a few shots of it. We got lost out there looking for that house. The guy was obsessed with it and yet after walking for three hours to find this place, when we finally got there, no one bothered to go inside.

I always think that's quite remarkable. First time I laid eyes on that place, I figured I was going to have to pull some theatrics to stop anyone going in. There was something in that house. Something smart, something old… something hungry. I don't know how a house can *look* evil, but it just did. I didn't want to be near it. What amazed me was that no one else did either. The director took one look, and I could feel his artistic obsession melt away. He took a few photos, awkwardly asked one of the actresses to stand by the front door, and after a while he just mumbled something about the light being all wrong and we left. No one chided him about it. We were all just thankful to put some distance between us and that house.

If I have any moral or lesson to impart, it's this: go with your instincts. That guy was a hardcore atheist. But he didn't try to prove to himself that the fear he felt in the house's vicinity was rubbish. He had nothing to gain by entering the house, and some part of him told him he had plenty to lose. So he didn't go in. How many lives were saved because of that one decision?

If only it was always that simple.

A few years back, I helped out with a missing persons case. I don't mean that the cops came to me and I held some scraps of old clothing to sense the victim out. I mean that I saw a poster, called up the number, and asked how to help. There was a volunteer search party going on and I wanted to be there. Even if my powers aren't that useful, I really felt like I needed to be part of that search team. Maybe it was the fact it was a little girl's face on the poster, about nine or ten years old, and she looked like an old childhood friend. Maybe it was because I got a feeling in my gut when I looked at her eyes that was like being submerged in ice water, and I'd never felt that way from a picture. But I really wanted to help.

Police figured the girl had gone missing in this large patch of dunes by the sea. It was about twenty square miles of grass-riddled sand that went up and down and up and down and... well, you get it. It was a massive patch of hills and as soon as someone went over the lip of a dune they disappeared from sight. Dogs went missing there all the time and there'd been times when kids had been found shivering under some bush because they'd lost sight of their parents while playing at the beach.

It made it an absolute bitch to search. The terrain was awkward, a deliberately over-grown patch of wilderness under strict environmental protection. Flash-floods happened a lot, erasing well-worn paths in a single night and replacing them with small ponds or simply flat-expanses of nothing. And new paths would spring up where the water cut through earth like it was butter. And of course, the dunes themselves were never still. They were waves in the sand, moving too slowly for the human eye but always moving, nonetheless. And sometimes that meant they'd reveal things that had been buried for years, decades even.

Like, say, an old military listening post that had been set up in World War II and quickly forgotten about. I didn't know that's what it was when I found it, of course. What I saw as I stumbled around in the dark, crying for this poor girl while hoping I didn't get lost myself, was a door in the middle of a hill. There's no other way to describe it, and it was every bit as surreal as you might expect. Because there I was in the middle of total wilderness when I swung my light and I saw an old doorway embedded in the rising sand.

The handle... God, how I can put it? It looked warm? Like it had been touched recently. That's how my mind picked it up. I just knew the second I looked at it that someone had curiously tugged at the metal until the latch gave way and the door swung open with a loud, eerie creek. Didn't need a detective to put two and two together.

Looking in, I saw a stairway going down two or three steps before it disappeared into sand that had filled the tunnel like rising water. It was a dead end that I desperately wanted to ignore. Except something told me not to, and when I glanced down, I noticed footprints in the sand. They were clear as day. Little ones, smaller than my hand, scuffing an awkward gait. That made me look closer, even though I sure as hell didn't want to. This place was wafting malintent towards me, practically blowing itself up like a puffer fish, scaring away predators. I didn't want to test it or push it. I wanted to leave it the hell alone.

But those footprints…

I got down on my hands and knees and saw that the sand didn't quite reach the ceiling. The stairway descended for maybe a metre and must've levelled off because in one place I could shine my light through right to the other side. The sand filled the stairway like water in a u-bend, and where the steps rose up again, there was an open space. The crawl there would have been gruelling with six feet of sand beneath you, and solid concrete right above. But if you kicked and wriggled, you could dig your way through. And for a kid, that'd be even easier.

But why the hell would the girl do that?

I wanted to ignore it. I really did. But why was I out there? It wasn't for fun. That was for sure. I wanted to help, to make a difference. Maybe on some level I'd felt that place all the way in the café where I'd first seen the girl's missing poster. Maybe that was why I'd come. I reckon other searchers had walked past that door and seen it and just walked away. They never consciously chose to ignore it. It just had an effect on you. Something that if you weren't used to, you wouldn't understand. Maybe I was the only person who would've ever spotted it. Destiny sounds real nice sometimes, but even back then, I was suspicious as hell.

Still, I knew I had to go in. I tried calling for the others, but the sea was less than half a kilometre away and the wind coming off it was something fierce. My voice was snatched away from me by the howling gale, and no one came to help. I could glimpse the odd light here or there, but I didn't know if they were just over the next hill or too far away to help.

I took a deep breath and got down on my hands and knees. For a moment, I nearly backed out. It was right when my head entered the tunnel, and I realised it was way too damn small for me. I had this sudden flare up of claustrophobia and it was as if my whole body screamed,

You want me to go in there? Are you fucking mad!?

But I had a shovel, didn't I? We all had them. I used it to clear out as much space as I could, going as long as I could before sweat stained my top and soaked my hair. Once it was as big as I figured I could get it on my own, I went flat onto my stomach and began to wriggle forward. I barely had enough room for my hands to help, so it was up to my legs to push me along. Every inch was a struggle, and each time I stopped to collect myself, strange thoughts entered my head. I imagined of the door swinging shut while I was stuck in a claustrophobic nightmare, pinched between unstoppable concrete and a cloying wall of sand and dirt. I saw my feet kicking frantically, my hands unable to find purchase as the whole tunnel pinched down on my midriff like a curious child crushing a bug. These were not the ramblings of an overactive mind, either. Something was putting those thoughts inside my head, and it was relishing the effect they had on me. It would have kept me there if it could, pinned between the sand and the concrete. The search party would have never found the door, they would have never heard my cries. It would have kept me in the darkness, and it would have relished my torturous death.

I could only hope it was bluffing. *Something* was alive down there, but I had to assume if it could force the door shut or re-arrange soil and earth to crush me, it would have done so already. I just had to calm myself and catch my breath, and when I did, I found myself able to wriggle free to the other side. There I found an open room. It was derelict, with only a few holes in the wall with trailing electrical wires to say where equipment had once stood. There were bits of old wood and metal on the floor, too rusted to recognise. But it was empty of anything meaningful. Whoever had cleared it out decades before had probably been the last person to ever disturb that room. Well... except for one person...

The sand in this place was scarce, but enough scattered the floor that I could see where disturbances had been made. The girl had entered, sure enough, and as I tracked her path, I saw clearly that she had passed through this room and through another doorway, opposite to where I stood. This tunnel made an unequivocal descent, knifing through the Earth and straight into inky darkness. Standing over the stairs, I could hear the faint drips of distant water and rustling echoes of every breath and movement I made. The sound of my own blood in my ears was deafening.

Death lived down there, plain and simple. You could smell it in the musty air. Hell, there weren't even any cobwebs or signs of rats. Anyone could have stood there and felt something reaching into their minds, beckoning them down into the depths. I felt like an ant who'd just looked up and spotted an enormous eye, framed by a magnifying glass, bearing down on it. Something was looking at me. Something was looking right at me, just on the other side of those shadows. If I lifted my light, I knew I'd see something terrible staring back at me.

I gripped my torch with a shaking hand, and went to challenge the dark.

You're welcome to try, it laughed.

I let out a cry as I realised I had met this thing before. All of a sudden, I was a kid again, staring into that empty space. It took everything in me not to panic and flee. Minutes must have passed before I managed to finally rally my thoughts, to remember that I was still standing, even down there so far from safety. Whatever that voice belonged to, it wasn't omnipotent or all powerful. If anything, I imagined it must be weak. Or else why not just take me there and then? Why not snatch me when I was a kid?

Deep breath. I raised the torch at last and saw that the stairs weren't empty. There was a shoe, a little one. A brightly coloured sneaker.

Fuck you, I thought. *I'm not letting you win this.*

I took the steps one at a time until I reached the bottom. These walls weren't as clean cut. Maybe water had run down and coated them in layer after layer of organic-looking limestone. Whatever it was, it leant the tunnel a slightly warped appearance, as if the ground itself twisted along like a corkscrew. It made my eyes hurt, but I stared anyway, making sure the tunnel was empty before I dared look down and inspect the shoe. There wasn't so much as a scratch on it. Even the shoelaces were still tied. I touched it and for a brief moment I willed myself into the object's past, seeing what emotions still lingered close to its history. Nothing about the process is reliable, but it was my best hope. And that was when the strangest image came to me.

The last time that shoe had been with the girl was on the beach. She was with her father, running and giggling. He told her he had a secret and whipped her up into his arms. She felt happy in that moment. Safe. She hadn't seen the man in so long. He promised her a vacation. But she mustn't tell Mummy. They were going to France, he said.

I dropped the shoe and stood baffled. I had no way of processing this particular clue. I knew this was *good* news, of course. I could go tell the police where to look. But then why the hell was the shoe down there? And how had it even gotten there?

This whole case had felt like the world reaching out to me. Surely the solution couldn't be so mundane?

Perplexed and unsure, I stepped backwards to gather my thoughts.

The tunnel snapped shut barely a few inches from my feet.

Hot, fetid air washed over me. Something like mucus sprayed my face. All the blood rushed to my head. The world spun. I felt lighter than air, and yet I didn't move an inch. When the tunnel reopened, it was the fluid motion of a puckering sphincter, revealing a muscular mouth like something that belongs to an arctic lamprey.

So close, it whispered.

The words prompted me to drop the torch. The sound of it hitting the ground brought me back to reality, and I snatched it up with fumbled urgency. Only when I turned it back on, the mouth was gone. I was faced with perfectly square man-made corridor.

Lucky boy, the darkness said. *Lucky once in your house, standing by the stairs. Lucky twice in the woods, saved by a friend. Now lucky thrice so deep in the dark. Just how lucky can you be?* It asked. *If you keep poking around in places you don't belong, your luck will run out.*

"Fuck you!" I cried. Whatever it was, it had made its point clear. It had set a trap, a clever one too. The girl wasn't on the beach. She was with her damn father, somewhere in France. Parental kidnapping. Oh so common. But from where it lay on the beach, the shoe had been taken by something else and put to use as bait for me.

And I still wasn't safe. I'd crawled right into the belly of the beast like a God damn idiot. I hurried back up the stairs, trying to ignore the rising waves of emotion that were crashing through the bunker. It felt like I was escaping a flash-flood of oil. I could feel that thing, whatever or wherever it was, flexing its muscles just out of sight. It could come and go as it pleased, I knew that much. What was it getting ready for? What did it want?

My light fell upon the way out and all the breath left my body like I'd been punched in the gut. For a brief second, a fractional moment of time too small to quantify, the tunnel I'd dug in the sand wasn't there. Instead, there was a mouth, just like the one down below, embedded in a wall of muscle that expanded infinitely out of view. But then the torch caught up with my eyes and the light revealed a plain mound of sand with a small crawlspace between it and the ceiling. There were no calcified spikes that threatened to skewer me. No bubbling ribbed oesophagus, slick with digestive fluids, waiting to swallow me whole. I suddenly realised I'd been a fucking idiot, and I'd left my shovel on the other side of the sand. There'd be no digging; I had to crawl back through the way I came.

You're welcome to try, the darkness said, sensing my thoughts.

I could feel it closing in on me as a kind of psychic pressure. I'm not sure I'd describe this thing as angry, so much as just cold and alone. It was everywhere and nowhere, something that wasn't human, that had *never* been human.

It lived in the dark, and only the dark.

It was only my torch that kept me safe. Wherever the light roamed, I saw dusty concrete and not much else. But wherever the darkness encroached, I could feel those ominous thoughts—that taste of dry cobweb—seeping back in like water through my fingers. I readied myself to leave, to keep the light fixed dead ahead, when I felt a waft of hot air blow past my shoulders. By this point, the distinction between thoughts and real sensation was weakening. The things it suggested to me were starting to feel as real as the ground beneath my feet. I don't know if I would have faced a psychic death or a physical one, but that thing was after me all the same.

Before I could let my nerves get the better of me, I began crawling, and then wriggling. The torch was effective in such a small space, lighting it up as plain as daytime. But behind me was another story. I could feel warm appendages caress my legs, could feel the damp creeping through my trousers where it pressed moistly against my bare skin. There was a hint of suction, maybe, as if something was getting ready to clean me out whole, like I was a chicken drumstick at a family BBQ.

My head emerged from the tunnel just as something snagged my foot. I lost all sense and reason, and in hysterics, I tried to kick and scream my way free. It felt so stupid that some sand was between me and freedom. My arms were pinned close to my side (had the tunnel been so narrow on my way in? I wondered), but there it was! Freedom was so close and all I had to do was loosen some damn Earth!

But panic only made it worse. I hurt my shoulder as I struggled, hurt it bad, and tears welled up in my eye. Frustration was starting to overwhelm me. I tried everything to calm myself, but it wasn't enough. Something had me, something had me in its jaws real good. My foot wasn't just caught, it was being pulled, slowly, inexorably back into a waiting gullet.

Luck runs out, the darkness said.

I screamed so loud that I was coughing up blood for days after. It was rough. In that moment, I felt all hope extinguish, all joy disappear. This thing's mind was flooding into mine, kicking off its shoes and rifling through my memories like a rude guest. It showed me what it had in store for me. It showed me that I wouldn't even be alone. There were others. So many others trapped down in the dark. At least I finally found out why I've never encountered anyone else like me. We were beacons to the predators that lurk behind every shadow. I had once called that psychopath on the train an apex predator, but *no,* this thing was the real deal. It had been stalking me for a long, long time.

Thank God someone out on the beach heard my screaming. They said it just came to them as clear as day, and I reckon I might have been lucky enough to broadcast my thoughts into another's mind. Someone not as sensitive as me, but sensitive enough to pick up on the need for help. Whatever the reason, they came to my rescue just in time. A hand, cold and clammy but so God damned welcome in the moment, grabbed my wrist and yanked me out. I didn't even care that it was my bad shoulder they tugged on. By the time I slithered out of that place, I was sobbing.

The darkness had done a real number on my head.

I don't remember much else. They got me somewhere safe, and I got a mention in the paper for going the extra mile. Story was that I got stuck crawling through and freaked out, that was all. A severe panic attack. Of course, an anonymous phone call put the real abduction case to bed. Easily solved and, frankly, not my problem after everything I'd been through.

I was lucky I escaped at all, although the experience left me with a crippling fear of the dark. People often think I'm overreacting, that I'm being a coward or superstitious just cause I won't go down into a basement, or take a lonely walk to an outhouse. I'd like to tell them the truth. Maybe even show it to them. But I couldn't do that. Seeing this thing, noticing it, I think that's what pisses it off. Anyone else could've gone into that place and had no trouble. It showed itself to me because I'd spotted it years before. And who knows? Maybe it's not the only thing like it. Like I said, we all have those gut feelings, don't we? Everyone, no matter where or when they live, has had those kinds of feelings. There are always places that will give us the creeps.

We should trust those feelings more often.

PLAY PRETEND

It was my wife who suggested roleplay, despite what she may say elsewhere. You'll just have to decide who you think is being honest. When she first suggested acting out roles, I was hoping for pigtails and pleated skirts, but I should have figured it wouldn't be like that. If I'm honest, there isn't much that I wouldn't have agreed to at that point in our relationship. Things weren't bad but... well, they weren't good either. One morning I woke up to a packed lunch and an orange juice on the breakfast table, and when I tried to make myself a cup of coffee she told me that growing boys shouldn't drink things like that. I typically skipped breakfast and headed right out the door each morning, but the way she sat there looking at me made me feel like I was missing something. It took me a minute to realise that this right here was the start of our little pretend play, so I sat down and ate the cereal and drank the juice.

The whole scene made me pretty uncomfortable. I guess I just felt on the spot. Sounds weird, but I've always had a bit of a *thing* about people cooking for me. My mum died when I was eight and my dad didn't really pay me much attention. I had to cook and clean and iron my uniform every night before school, and no one ever did my homework for me. Later on, my dad married some poor waitress half his age and treated her like a servant and I realised that must have been exactly how he had treated my mother. I'm not saying that this taught me to be the perfect man or anything (far from it).

I just didn't like things that made me feel like I was becoming my dad.

But there was my wife, making me cereal for breakfast and then handing me a neat little lunchbox with cartoons on it that I'd watched as a kid (*Goku... that was a throwback)*, and I'd be lying if I said I didn't like some part of it. Driving to work that day, I decided that this roleplay was probably just some kinda therapy and that it was best to go along with it, even after I got home that night to find that she'd run me a bath. Not only did she want me to be a "clean little boy", she'd even laid out some brand-new pyjamas. It was deeply uncomfortable... She perched on the toilet lid while I was sat upright in the tepid water not sure what to do with myself. A grown man with a beer belly hunched over in grey water... I felt so stupid.

"Do you need help washing yourself?" she cooed.

"Uh, sure," I replied, and she came over and pulled out a fish-shaped bottle of no tears shampoo. She washed my hair, using a small plastic cup to rinse my scalp. I had to lean back for her to get it all, and she held my head in her hands. I hated it. My eyes wouldn't stay shut, her hands were too cold, the water too warm, the porcelain of the tub too hard... And every time the water flowed over my head I would reflexively lurch forward and try to sit up, which of course meant I got suds in my eyes.

"Shhhh," she kept saying. "Just lie back. It won't hurt. I won't let it."

So I laid back and controlled my breathing and told myself that it was for her sake, not mine. One of my last memories of my mother was her reading a book while I sat in the bath, and I guess I didn't like how I felt in my wife's arms at that moment. But she just kept talking to me in that soothing voice, and somewhere along the lines I let go of conscious thought and focused on the sensation of the warm water rolling down my scalp.

"You can let go," she said, wiping some water from my face, and when I looked up at her, I realised that I was shaking and my heart was pounding. All of a sudden it all just came out, all the tension, all the anxiety, the constant state of near panic that I'd suppressed for my entire life... You're meant to say that this kind of stuff feels cathartic but I fucking hated it. It made me feel physically sick, even a little ashamed. She held me in her arms while I sobbed like a baby in the tub and when it was finally over all I could think was, "Thank God I can breathe again."

I let her dry me as I stood dripping wet on the tiles. And then I let her dress me in the cool dry pyjamas she'd laid out ready, the silky fabric raising goosebumps on my skin. By the time I curled up into bed, her arms cradling my head like it was a precious jewel, I was exhausted like I'd just gone for a quick thirty-mile run. The last thing I remember was the theme tune to Ed Edd and Eddy, and the flood of nostalgia combined with the feel of fresh bed linen put me to sleep hard and fast.

The next day at work I felt dirty. And I didn't much enjoy the thought of going home. I knew what was waiting for me and, sure enough, she was there with Spongebob pyjamas (brand new) in one hand and a plate of food in another. At first I told her I wasn't up for it that night, but she just told me to stop being silly and sit down to eat. And well... the food did look good. And, stupid as this is, I told myself it was me doing her a favour, you know? Like if I just agreed to have her do all this stuff for me it would be okay, so long as I agreed begrudgingly. So I ate the food and wore the clothes and I tried not to cringe when she called me her baby boy.

As much as I hated it, she was being really nice to me. I just wanted her to like me. She hadn't liked me in so long and this whole messed up business meant that she was being genuinely affection-ate to me. For years she'd always kinda looked at me like I was a dick. I don't know when, but somewhere along the line I stopped being her husband and just became *a* husband, just another emotionally stunted guy with a receding hairline. I could have been more attentive, I know that. But nobody told me how exhausting mediocrity is, and by the time I got through barely surviving work each day, I'd find very little energy left to give to her.

I felt lonely *all the time*, and something about being in her arms made me feel a little less alone. I secretly hoped that this roleplay was about dismantling the walls we'd both put up. It wasn't on my terms (I would've picked literally anything else), but hey, when is life ever fully on anyone's terms? Being in love really means being held hostage. And yeah, things were bad, but man, I fucking *loved* her with everything I had. So I had to work with what I had, and what I had was this weird roleplay.

I figured that it makes some sense that some women didn't want a *daddy*. That instead some women actually wanted to be a *mommy*. You see it online all the time, right? Daddy this, daddy that. You can't throw a stone online without finding some pornographic image of a woman being infantilized. So why couldn't it go the other way around? So long as it wasn't sexual, I figured I could do it. I'd wear the pyjamas, watch cartoons, and ask for help colouring in the lines. In the end, I didn't just go along with it for a few nights. I went along with it every single day that followed, and I found that every day there was a little more of it to go along with. The packed lunches became more elaborate. The food I ate grew simplified until it was practically the kinda stuff you'd feed a toddler. And one Friday when I finally told her I wanted a break, she just told me to stop being silly.

She used that phrase a lot during the roleplay, and this is going to sound fucking stupid, but she made me feel *silly* when she said it. Her voice immediately made me feel small and ashamed just like I had in the bath, and before I even realised I was doing it, I was sliding the pyjamas on and booting up my Xbox while she messed around in the kitchen. I'd actually planned on talking to her that night about going to couple's therapy, but she spoke to me like a little boy and I just couldn't stop myself reacting like one. It was like I'd been trained. That weekend I listened to her tell me stories as I sat on the counter kicking my legs, and I think I felt something die inside me.

On some level I have to take some responsibility. I ate the food I wanted to eat and when she asked if there was anything I wanted, I always had something to say. I watched the TV I wanted to and wore the clothes she put out for me and pretty soon I got used to not thinking about those things. Pretty soon every single day was spent with her. Some nights were movie nights, and we'd watch her favourite films while she told me all about the memories she had of first watching them. Some nights were Mommy nights where she'd sit and drink wine and watch her own shows while I played games. We made forts out of cushions, camped in the backyard, played cowboy and Indian using Nerf guns, and chased each other round the house for hours at a time doing hide and seek or some homebrew version of tag. If I had to describe this time, it was like being in a waiting room only I didn't have a number or a clock or any way of knowing how much time has passed. The only way I could even tell that time *was* passing was that I lost weight.

In fact, I lost a *lot* of weight. My wedding ring slipped right off my finger one day and where it went after that, I'll never know. I still don't understand this part of it, but I remember that I just kept getting thinner. For about three weeks I fell ill with some stomach bug, and I spent my days in bed watching telly while she checked my temperature and fed me chicken soup. And by the time I came out of it I was wearing a child's large set of pyjamas. I mean... how does that even work, right? I started the year weighing 120kg. In the end I got down to 45. Not only that, but my hair started getting thin and downy and I couldn't even remember when I'd last needed a shave. I asked her about this one day and she played it dumb, like she didn't know what was happening to me. But out of the two of us, she must've known because it was literally right in front of her eyes.

I was changing.

She recommended that I stay home until I felt 100% myself again, which of course meant that I never went back to work because I never *ever* felt like myself again. Looking back, it wouldn't surprise me if she forged a resignation letter of mine or did something similar to keep me at home. Either way, by the time the stomach bug passed I was trapped in that house. The outer gate that had once barely reached my chest now towered over my head, and I could barely get my fingers around the bars. It wasn't a new gate, or at least I didn't think it was. It was just somehow taller than me all-of-a-sudden.

Things stopped making sense around this time and, looking back, it's hard to disentangle certain memories and ideas.

I don't even remember the crib arriving. It was just... it was just *there* one day, along with a whole new room in the house that physically shouldn't have been there. I checked one late night when I felt lucid and, sure enough, the bathroom and master bedroom hadn't magically shrunk by 50%. But somehow a whole *new* room had just sprung up between them painted in baby blue. The walls were covered in paintings of airplanes and if I stared at them too long I'd feel real sleepy and my head would get heavy and boom. Next thing I remember, it'd be morning and I'd be staring at a bowl of cereal.

Whole chunks of time were purged from my head. And not just the recent stuff either. I was an accountant who suddenly couldn't do long division and struggled with his multiplication tables. Normally my brain was like a cacophony of fireworks that took every ounce of my willpower to keep under control. Stray thoughts just pinged off all the time and it was like... it was chaotic, but it was *me*. But with my wife, and with everything going on, it had turned into something more like a cobweb with holes poked in it.

You know when you listen to someone and their voice just turns into a drone and you realise that you stopped listening after a few words? It was like that but with my own thoughts. As soon as I got any momentum going I lost interest and time faded and I'd come to a few hours later bouncing up and down on my wife's knee. I could practically feel bits of my mind sloughing away like candle wax, leaving big patches of nothing behind and it hurt so bad. It hurt worse than anything physical that ever happened during that fucked up time. Something was cutting my mind up like a scrapbooker going at old magazines and I could feel it happening in real-time.

There were times when she'd take something off me like the remote and put it on the counter and it'd just hang there over my head and that... that just doesn't make sense to me. And the harder I concentrate to try and figure that out, the more it feels like staring right at the sun. And it wasn't just me. There were a couple of moments when she'd look at me and I wouldn't see my wife. Actually that's not right. She was my wife. Absolutely 100% my wife. She just had an extra two pairs of limbs and...

It hurts even now to try and remember too clearly. What I do know was that as time went on I felt less like precious cargo and more like a leaden weight she had to lug from place to place. Some nights I'd wake up and spot her stood in my doorway looking at me and the expression on her face... holy shit it was *murderous*. I'd have to lie there and pretend for hours that I was snoring gently because on some level I just knew it'd be bad news. The time we spent together started to change, and more often than not I'd try to stay out in the garden and play with toys. Only I wasn't really playing. I was just pretending, hoping that if my performance was good then she wouldn't get any more irritated with me.

Without knowing when, why, or how, rules were introduced. I'd go to do something like make myself a drink and stop, hand frozen half-way to an empty glass, and remember that I wasn't allowed to get glasses out of the cupboard by myself. I didn't know how I knew that. I just knew it. I wasn't allowed to play games past seven. I wasn't allowed to get my own snacks. I wasn't allowed in the garden without telling her where I was going. And if I broke these rules?

One time I threw a ball and broke a window and she exploded outta that screen door like a fucking bull. It felt so wrong to feel scared of her. She was meant to be looking after me. Those were the roles we were *meant* to be playing. But she grabbed my arm and pulled it so hard it popped right out the socket and I begged for the game to stop but nothing I said could snap us out of these fucked up roles we'd made. She dragged me into the house and I passed out around about the time my head bounced off the third step on our porch. When I woke up I was sat in a high-chair and strapped in real good.

Something hurt but I ignored it. All I wanted was for this pissed off woman to love me again. I was so terrified I would've done anything she asked. She was the only thing I had to keep me safe in the world and my head was full of all the amazing stuff she did for me. The food. The gifts. The movies. The clothes. The bathing. I could see how tired she was. It was *me* making her that tired. So I cried and I sobbed and I said sorry so often my throat got sticky and dry and I started to heave. When her terrible frown finally broke, she ran towards me with her arms wide open and pulled me outta that chair.

She told me to never make her hurt me again, saying it over and over again as she sat me down on the sofa and rolled up my pyjamas to show me my chubby legs. Something was jutting out of the skin and before I could figure out what it was, she pinched it with her finger and thumb and drew it out in one long motion. It was a needle, a little sewing needle that had been slid painfully into the thick fatty muscle of my thigh.

"There have to be rules," she said. "And there have to be consequences. But don't worry, I want you to know it hurts me just as much as it hurts you. We both suffer when you break the rules. I want you to know that you don't just hurt yourself, you hurt me."

I watched as she placed the bloody needle on her tongue and swallowed it.

When the doorbell rang I was looking at the diapers around my waist. I didn't know when or how they had gotten there, and weirdly I remembered thinking the exact same thing that morning, and the morning before that. The longer I thought about it, the harder it was for me to remember when I'd last actually used a toilet. The realisation horrified me. Some of the memories flashing into my head, it was like I was experiencing them for the first time all over. The timid woman I'd married was somehow suddenly so strong, able to not only overpower me, but able to actually lift me off the ground! To pick me up and lay me down on a small table and hoist my legs up and...

Jesus Christ, she changed me! I thought. And my whole body flushed with unspeakable humiliation. I think it was that feeling that let me keep my head together when the deliveryman came, like I had this little bit of defiance that stopped me trying to hide from the stranger.

This is my chance! I thought. *Wait no I'm not allowed to open the door, not for strangers. But I can speak to him. Maybe he can help? Someone has to help! But if she comes and finds me then I'm in trouble! I don't want to be in trouble...*

It was like being drunk, or like having my thoughts handcuffed to a maniac. I had to fight every step of the way to stay a *man* and not a child, and I pulled at the handle eager to get some perspective on what was happening to me. Only I never got to even see the guy because that was when the bathroom door slammed shut.

She's coming! And I knew that if she found me then I'd get one hell of a punishment. My legs and arms already hurt so bad. I wasn't a very good boy, I knew. I broke a *lot* of rules and it didn't help that new ones were popping up all the time.

I fled towards the kitchen, turning the corner just in time for the door to swing open and for this delivery guy to get a good look at me. I briefly turned to face him and the way he reacted to the sight of me... I expected to feel embarrassed, but I just felt scared. Something was happening to me and the fact that this guy could see it made it horrifyingly real. My body had changed and no matter what my wife wanted I wasn't a child. I was changing into something but it wasn't a normal kid. This wasn't Benjamin Button. Whatever happens when you cram a chubby middle aged guy into a three-foot package, the result isn't a cute little kid.

It's a nightmare.

I ran crying from the look in his eye and got as far as the garden when I heard my wife thunder into he living room.

"Who let you in!?" she cried. "I have children in this house! Who are you and why are you in my home?"

Poor guy was dumbstruck. I could hear him stammering away as I ran under the porch steps and waited. I'd learned this was one of the few places where she couldn't physically fit. The few times I'd hidden under there she'd had to calm herself down and that made things a little easier on me, at least in the short term. Now I hoped it'd keep me safe long enough that I could maybe even make a break for it when the guy left the gate. She'd childproofed it with some infuriating mechanism that my fat fingers couldn't work, but it sure did take a long time for that gate to swing open and closed and that right there was the best chance I was ever gonna get.

"Get out of my house!" she screamed at him as he flew down the steps. She followed, hot on his heels. "Who's your manager!? Who do you work for? I want to put in a complaint! I want you to know exactly how God damned badly you've messed up."

This guy was stuttering and mumbling and fumbling, unsure of whether to run away or turn and give this woman a decent account of himself. I hoped he would leave. I was hidden so well and if he opened that gate then I would finally have a chance to get the hell away from this living nightmare. This guy was still trying to answer when my wife stepped down onto the path and turned to me slyly, raising one eyebrow right in my direction where I thought I was hidden. Jesus Christ the terror I felt… I pissed myself. I thought I'd got one over on her but she knew the whole time and she had something planned.

"Look at this!" she said. "Look at this step! This wasn't damaged until you came along."

The guy looked confused as hell and I couldn't blame him. He'd been bombarded with conflicting complaints it was like he was grasping at air to understand everything he'd seen. It wasn't just my wife going off at him. It was the memory of what he'd seen. It was the memory of *me*.

He bent down to take a look and my wife encouraged him to get closer. I wondered why she was making him get so close to my hiding spot. Did she want to humiliate me? Did she want to parade the little freak around? I thought she must've known how much my body upset me and she was going to use that fact to torture me a little bit.

But it was nothing that tame.

Without warning his face slammed into the middle step, his head bouncing off like a coconut. Only she was there ready to catch it and before either one of us could figure it out, she had shoved his head right back against the wooden step. He started to swear, then shout, then cry, and then finally he screamed.

And screamed.

And screamed.

It lasted so long. She never stopped pushing and somehow, impossibly, *he* started to give away. The sides of his skull started to crumple, his eyes bulged, his teeth popped out and fell to the floor like coins from a slot machine. I had to pull my legs up just to keep them from landing on my bare feet. I had front-row seats to the worst fucking horror show I could ever think of, watching that guy get scalped in slow motion. Only it didn't stop at his head. She kept pushing until his shoulders started to pop and crack. Arms bent backwards, bone snapped, muscle and skin were peeled off with a sound like Velcro.

In the end he poured out of that little six inch gap and fell onto the floor in a quivering pile of skin and flesh. The only thing left on the other side was my wife's face staring at me through the gore-coated wood.

"Come on," she grinned. "Put your new toy away. I'll make you some lunch."

I was sitting outside pretending to watch the clouds go by, aware that she was behind the kitchen window and pretending to wash dishes. She was looking right at me, even if I couldn't see her. I'd watched her clean that guy up, watched her dump him in an old compost pile round back. He wasn't the only one down there. I saw all my old clothes, my laptop, my phone, my keys, my mail... everything that *used* to be me, and I'm not just talking about things. I'd never really thought of it much but I'd shrunk and changed and I guess all that meat and bone and fat had to go somewhere. I just hadn't realised that she'd tied it up in dripping bedsheets and plopped it at the farthest point in our yard. I don't know how to explain it... I just knew it was me down there. Bits of me I'd never get back because it had been sunbaked into leathery offal.

Couldn't even begin to tell you how it feels to grieve your own body like that. Whatever defiance I had was gone, especially after seeing what she did to that delivery guy. Coming to terms with who... or rather *what* I was, meant that I lost all desire to escape. I would've tried to overdose if it wasn't against the rules for me to go anywhere near the medicine cabinet.

I ran a thumb across the purple and yellow flesh of my thigh, the skin riddled with a thousand infected puncture marks.

Can't break the rules, I thought.

When a frisbee floated freely over the hedge I stared at it for a moment like I was a disinterested cat. My eyes tracked it but nobody was home upstairs if you get what I mean. Only when it landed gently on the grass and I heard the gate clang open did it dawn on me that I wasn't alone out there. It was a little girl and her reaction wasn't all that different to the delivery man's. She stopped dead in her tracks and started to cry a loud distressed wail. I wanted to ask her for help but I didn't want to face the way she looked at me, so I quietly scuttled off towards the bushes to hide.

Or at least I started to… that was when I heard the screen door bang and my wife came down the steps with a big smile on her face.

"It's okay," she cooed, reaching out to hold the girl. Only our visitor couldn't see the kitchen knife my wife clutched behind her. "I won't let anyone ever hurt you."

When she started walking towards our kitchen door something broke. I felt a special kind of hatred burn inside me. It wasn't a defiance so much as pure spite. The kind of feeling that'd make you scream "I hate you" over and over at your parents just to see them hurt. It sounds stupid but as much as part of me wanted to keep that little girl safe another part of me was just plain old jealous. After everything my wife had done to me, I couldn't bear the thought of her bringing another child into the house.

I started to run towards the two of them and my wife, spotting me, hoisted the girl up into her arms. Only that slowed her down so much that I reached them both before she'd even got up the first step. I tried to grab the girl's coat when I jumped but wound up grabbing a fistful of hair. Everything that happened next was a jumble but my wife slashed my arm and wrist with that big knife of hers, and I pulled so hard on the poor girl's head that a load of her hair came free in my arm. In the end though I think it helped because this girl started screaming like hell and when she got a good look at me, that was when the fear really kicked in and she started wriggling and kicking and punching. And my wife, who really wasn't ready for just how hard it can be to keep a hold of a pissed off kid, ended up dropping the little girl. Once her feet were on the ground that kid just zipped right out of there and I did everything I could to keep my wife away from her. It wasn't a whole lot, but I think it helped. I think between the way my messed up appearance got the girl running, and the way I managed to hold onto my wife's legs for long enough to trip her up a little, I think I saved that kid. Looking back on everything that my wife cost me... I guess that was one of the few little victories I ever had.

As soon as the gate clanged shut all that feeling of triumph dribbled away. I crawled back towards the porch steps as quick as I could and the best way to describe it is that even though I wasn't looking at her, when my wife's eyes found me I could *feel* them. Her rage, it must be what it's like to stand next to radioactive waste. I swear my shadow got darker and the ground got a little hotter. And the noises I heard... they didn't sound like they came from an upset woman. Not sure what they sounded like really, except maybe a strange kinda clicking. When I finally got under the house and turned I saw that she looked big enough to crush a man like a bug. I don't know how to describe it except it was a little like looking at something with 3D glasses, or the way your eyes feel funny just before a big migraine. I guess... for just a second I saw her as something that wasn't human but the part that really hurts my head is that she never changed. It was the same entity I'd married on the alter only now I got the same feeling I did looking at dead spiders or leathery roadkill.

She'd neve really been human, had she? And with my memory shot to shit, I wasn't even willing to bet that I'd even married this thing. You read about those parasites that lay eggs in their hosts. Looking at her as she scuttled towards me... Yeah I got the sense that's what she was. Some kinda parasite.

She stopped just a few inches from the steps, her face peering at me through the gaps. She blinked with a third set of eyelids and smiled so wide her skin started to lose its colour and break.

"I will drown you in my womb," she said, as calmly as she would ask if I wanted cut up hot dogs in my spaghetti.

I believed her.

———

I didn't come out of those stairs for the rest of that day, not even when my wife stood out on the porch and called me for dinner. I didn't fancy my chances with whatever was shambling around up there and pretending to be a wife, or a mother, or whatever else it felt like. I didn't want anything she'd prepared, and as time wore on I found that the hunger in my stomach sharpened my mind so that I didn't mind it too much. Besides, I could hazard a guess that she wasn't being honest about what was in my food and I didn't want anything she prepared.

Whatever this was between us, it wasn't a really a game now. The stakes were too high. And for me, tucked away under those steps with my stomach growling and my mind growing more lucid with every passing second, I really started to hate her. I hated that she'd hurt me when she was supposed to protect me. I hated that she'd lied every second of every day until this sick little plan of hers had come to fruition. But more than anything I hated her for what she'd done to me. I wasn't a man but I sure as hell wasn't a child. I was more like a monster and a joke and I just knew that somehow she'd been the one stripping meat and fat off my bones until my frame withered to this pitiable size.

I had to leave. I had to. She'd since locked the gate and I needed the key and if she stopped me well... I guess I needed a knife, didn't I? I needed something to keep me safe.

I waited until sunset and crawled out from under the house, making sure to stick to the shadows. Peaking through the kitchen window, I saw her stood there with a plate in one hand and a blank expression on her face. She looked a little broken, like she didn't quite know what to do now that I wouldn't listen to her cries of dinnertime. She just stood there and shivered until some flicker of movement caught her eye and she pivoted around to track it like a bird of prey. I had to drop out of sight more than once because of how sensitive she was to changes in the light, although I think I managed to avoid her line of sight because when I finally snuck into the house via the backdoor she was in the exact same spot, staring into the darkness like a blind man.

For a moment I thought I was safe in the shadows, but whatever this thing was, it didn't seem so committed to playing human. As soon as I got near the stairs her eyes fixed on me like a hound's and she came barrelling forward on every limb she had. What little of her was visible in the moonlight looked almost fish-like, like she'd been pulled out of the bottom of a lake. She still had the general shape of a person, I guess. Only it was like something wearing a human-suit, one that was falling apart. Her joints slipped up and down her bones like they were on a pulley, and they bent backwards and forwards and sideways...

As she got closer I smelled her and it was like rotten milk and dog shit left in a hot car. It hit me hard enough to water my eyes and make climbing the stairs difficult. Of course I didn't get very far... Between my short legs and the sight of her coming at me, I didn't have a chance. I got maybe four steps up before she grabbed my ankle with one hand and hauled me downstairs. She mounted me, legs on either side, and slowly undid part of her sundress.

I didn't know what the hell was going on, nor did I have strength to fight it. The last thing I remember was the sight of her ribs pressing against her skin like fingers trying to poke through a rubber sheet, like they were alive inside of her and wanted out.

"Baby need a feed?" she asked before grabbing my head and slamming it backwards into the step behind me.

I awoke with a foul taste in my mouth. I'd been strapped into the highchair and I looked around groggily until I laid eyes on a baby bottle. The congealed contents were the colour of a smoker's fingers with visible lumps of pink matter lurking towards the bottom like syrup in a milkshake.

"Straight from the source," my wife said, her misshapen fingers stroking my hairless head.

I realised that my legs were in agony and I saw that there must have been a dozen needles poking out of my skin and right through the pyjamas she'd dressed me in. She pressed a finger against one and for a second the pain became so white hot that I nearly passed out all over again. I fought hard to stay awake, desperate to avoid another feeding. Although a part of me wondered if I wanted to endure the second one while awake…

But when it all came down to it, it was just her in my way wasn't it? And that hatred inside me burned up like a pyre and I realised that I wouldn't mind dying all that much. I'd secretly hoped for so long that I could maybe fix this somehow, maybe even get back to normal and get my body back. I didn't know how but I'd let myself think that it could be possible. Sitting there, looking at her loom over me… I decided that living like this wasn't really an option anymore.

My hands were free. Who could blame her for leaving them like that? I couldn't hit her or kick her. I didn't have the reach or the strength. But I did have something sharp, so I reached down and tore a needle free and before she could try and get it out of my hand I shoved it through her palm. It went right through like she'd been made of nothing more substantial than some thick wool. It didn't even make a noise, although the stench she emitted became unbearably strong.

She looked angry. *Good* I thought, and I reached down and grabbed another and this time she tried to be quicker but it just meant her face got closer. So close that the moonlight hit it and for a moment I hesitated because I finally saw just how fucking God awful she really was. You could see where all that skin was just slipping away and hanging loose like a badly made mask and whatever was underneath... it looked a little like a spider. Not a spider's face mind you. No, like she had a spider *for* a face, only it was a spider with too many legs that were all curled up like it'd been stamped on a few times. Like her whole skull was a ball made out of furry rubber bands.

But she still had eyes... And they looked mostly human. And like I said she'd gotten in so close I could see those hairs twitch and wriggle and that meant I could lunge forward and jam that needle right into her eye, pushing so hard that by the end it was as embedded in the palm of my hand as it was in her skull (or whatever she had). I don't know what exactly was in there but it must've hurt because she let out a scream that drew blood from my ears and she ran off into the dark desperate to get far, far away from whatever had caused her pain.

I didn't have much time. I slipped loose from the chair and ran from the house, stopping only long enough to catch a glimpse of a shadow passing over the house as if something had flown over. It's hard for me to say what, exactly, but I had a vague notion that some of the lampposts in the nearby street were moving, and that they reached way *way* too high into the sky.

I felt her leave. Jesus fucking Christ I felt her leave and it was like the popping of a cyst. It hurt bad. It hurt like nothing I'd ever, ever felt. It wasn't a protracted injury, just more like being shot, I imagine. I don't know. It just... I reached the gate and saw somehow that my hand dwarfed the lock and by the time I'd fumbled it open I was already hurtling towards the ground like a falling tree. When I woke up the house was blazing and I felt like I'd just eaten 150 pounds of raw meat.

But at least I was the right size again.

———

I wound up having to take a trip to the hospital that same day so they could get the remaining needles out of my leg. I was laughing so damn hard that they wound up keeping me for my own safety which, well... I guess I can't blame them for. Between the needles and the children's clothes and the way I screamed with joy at the sight of my own hands and my hairy arms, I guess I must have really looked like a real loon. I didn't feel too bad being stuck in that place though, and they didn't keep me for long. They said something about spores in the lungs, I don't know. I don't even fucking care. I did tell them what happened of course but they just told me it was all the product of my mind.

They say my head is fucked. I mean, they say it a little more politely than that but that's the gist. It's fucked. They showed me a scan of my brain and it looked like an apple after it had spent three weeks on the ground in mid-August. I guess I'm not an accountant anymore. Most days I'm lucky if I can work a remote.

I don't really care though.

For a long, long time she kept leaving me a packed lunch on the doorstep of my new apartment. Fucking nuts but... I almost ate one or two of them. It was that strong of a habit, you know? But instead I always made a big show of throwing the food right in the bin. The last box was full of divorce paperwork although it didn't look official. More like a bad joke, but that was the whole marriage, wasn't it?

Just a bad joke.

I signed them in crayon and left them outside.

MORE CHILLS FROM VELOX BOOKS

MORE CHILLS FROM VELOX BOOKS

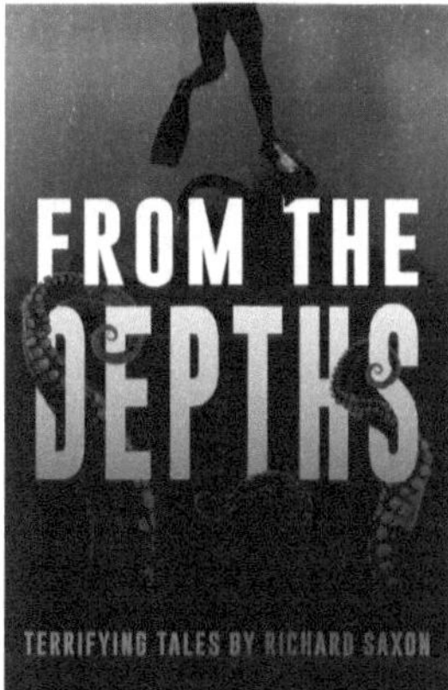

MORE CHILLS FROM VELOX BOOKS

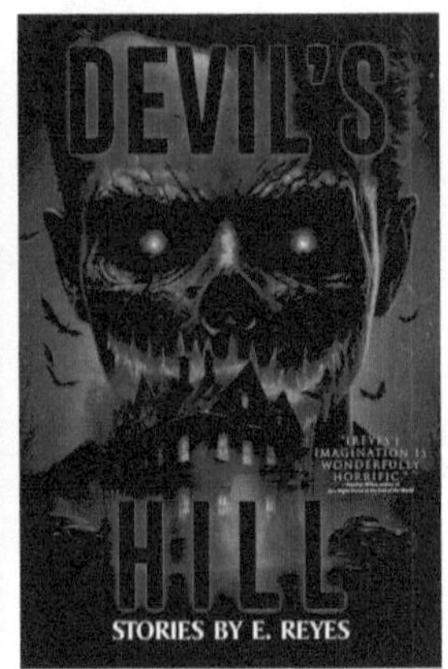

www.ingramcontent.com/pod-product-compliance
Lightning Source LLC
Chambersburg PA
CBHW061344310726
48974CB00001B/194